'For Anne-Marie

who loved books

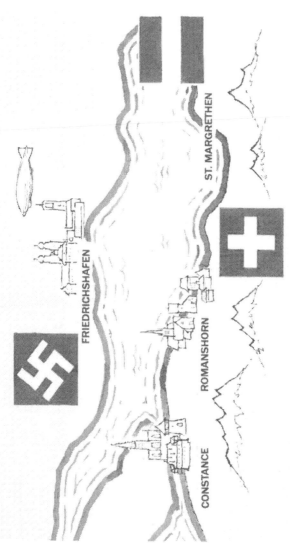

LAKE CONSTANCE

FRIEDRICHSHAFEN

CONSTANCE

ROMANSHORN

ST. MARGRETHEN

ST. GALLEN

The Legend of the Lake

'Tell me the story ... The one about the man who rode his horse across the lake.'

She sat on his shoulders, kicking her feet against his chest, spurring him on. The night was cold. Fresh snow lay on the ground.

'But you've heard it so many times, Lili ...'

'Please, Papa! I like it. Tell me it again!'

He knew the story cut short the distance and helped her forget the ice and dark. He listened hard to his feet crunching into the snow, suggesting to him the rhythm of the ancient tale.

'Once upon a time a rider from a far away land ...'

'Where?'

He was used to these early interruptions; she wanted a part in the story-telling.

'Far, far away.'

'Show me!'

He pointed, beyond the shore she had always known, stretching his arm, hand and finger towards the lights hinting at another shoreline, another country.

'Can I see?'

'No, it's further … beyond what you can see.'

The answer satisfied for the time being.

'A rider from a far away land is galloping through a valley. He sweats as he races through the fallen snow, under a pale winter sun. He wants to reach the other side of the lake before nightfall.'

'How, Papa? How is he going to cross the lake?'

'He'll take the ferry.'

'Like our ferry?'

'No, Lili. Long ago a ferryman rowed a small boat across the lake.'

'Like your boat?'

'Yes … a bit …'

'That takes a long time.'

'Yes. The way is hard, over stones and through thick thorns –'

'Did they scratch him?'

He hadn't thought of that.

'Yes, they scratched his face.'

'Mm.'

The way is hard, over stones and through thick thorns. He goads on his horse. He can see the snow stretching like a desert from the distant mountain peaks. He leaves town and village far behind. Not a house, not a tree, not a rock, as far as the eye can see. His horse flies along for mile after mile.'

Now we're flying too, the story-teller thinks.

'He hears only the cry of the snow-goose and the flapping of the moorhen's wings. There is no-one to ask the way, so he pushes on through snow as soft as velvet. When will he see the

lake and the ferryman's lantern? ... When will he hear the sound of water lapping at the shore?'

All is quiet. Tiny clouds of warmth drift past his face; but he knows she is not asleep.

'Evening comes early – or so it seems. In the distance he spies a light; trees and hills come out from the mist. His horse gallops on. Soon he feels the stony path beneath him and thorns once more across his face...'

He pauses a moment, pleased with the improvisation which has, as far as he can tell, gone unnoticed.

'The rider digs in his heels. Dogs are barking. In the village he sees the light of a fire. A window opens.

"Good eve, fair maiden! Tell me, how far is the ride to the lake and the ferryman?"

The maiden stares at the rider, looks behind him at his path, and smiles.

"Good sir, both lake and ferry are whence you came. Truly, you and your horse would both be drenched through and through, were the lake not sealed with ice."'

'Hmm.'

The hint of doubt in the sound she makes stops him in his tracks. He can tell she is puzzled.

'What is it, Lili?'

'So, the girl doesn't believe him?'

'No ... At first perhaps she thinks he's teasing her. She can't believe he's come the way he said. The ice is too thin.'

'How thin?'

'Oh, I'm not sure, Lili ... perhaps a foot or so.'

He wondered how thick ice would have to be to hold a rider and his horse.

He felt the warmth of her cheek against his ear.

'What happens next?' she whispered.

'The stranger shudders and is short of breath.

"I tell you, I have ridden across that plain."

The maiden throws up her hands in horror to the skies.

"Then in God's name you have indeed ridden across the lake. Did you not hear your horse's hooves knocking on a watery tomb? Did you not hear the waters churning beneath you? Did the ice not crack as you passed, inviting you to be the fare of the hungry pike and its fearsome brood?"'

She shivered at the mention of the pike.

'The maiden calls the villagers from all around – mothers, old men and children gather around the rider.

"Oh, lucky man! Come on in. Come to our steaming table and break with us our bread and eat our fish."

The rider stares at his horse; he only hears the first few words. His hair stands on end; his heart beats wildly. Behind him he sees danger grinning at him through the gloom. In his mind's eye he sees the dreadful depths of the lake, and his spirit descends into that black abyss.'

Her hands clasp tightly around his forehead; a dark sigh tells him she has felt the meaning of the unknown word.

'Thundering in his ear the ice cracks; waves of cold sweat wrap around him as he sinks from his horse … and dies.'

Silence.

'Lili, are you asleep?

1933

On the Swiss shore of Lake Constance

I

'There's a window left open. You can crawl through it, Lili. You're small enough.'

'But how do you know he's away?'

The two girls had endured the morning's lessons. They were walking back from school, socks around their ankles, along the track winding through orchards down to the lake.

'He always goes away at this time of year. The house is empty. Mama knows the lady who cleans for him. She says he won't be back for weeks.'

The farmer, at work in the fields, gave a friendly wave.

'Lili Vogelsang, are you coming to help with the milking later?' he called over.

'I'll be there, Herr Ursprung … Can Eva come too?'

'Sure.'

Lili stopped and turned to face her friend.

'But what if someone sees us?'

'It'll be the middle of the night. They'll all be in bed. Wait till everyone's fast asleep, jump out of your window and meet me at the corner. Don't forget your torch.'

Lili always had to be home by seven. She winced at the thought of the sharp slap across the back of her legs she got from her mother for being just a few minutes late … To be out after midnight …

'Are you sure?'

'Come on. It'll be fun.'

*   *   *

That night Lili waited in her bed fully-dressed, building up her courage.

She heard steps.

The clock on the mantelpiece struck ten.

Her mother was tidying up before going to bed. A door opened and closed; that'd be her father back from his game of cards at the Bellevue. Lili heard last movements in the living room, running water, creaking floorboards and tired words.

Horses neighed in a distant stable. An intoxicating scent of lilac drifted through her half-open window tempting her into the safety of sleep.

The clock struck eleven.

Lili lay under her sheets not daring to move. Her ears pricked up as bats left their upside-down perches in the barn, frogs croaked in the ditches and hedgehogs shuffled through the plants in the garden outside her window.

She gripped the torch in her hand. Keep it switched off till we get in the house, Eva had told her.

Everything fell silent but for the sound of blood rushing in her ears.

The clock struck twelve.

Lili got out of her bed. Her heart was thumping; her legs had turned to jelly.

'What am I doing?' she said to herself as she steadied herself to make the leap from her window into the garden. With the torch switched off, it was hard to see the path. She cursed Eva, not for the first time.

The moon peeked inquisitively through bluish-grey clouds. Slowly her eyes began to make out the silhouettes of trees and buildings.

She gritted her teeth.

A hand grabbed her shoulder. Lili's heart leaped pounding into her throat.

'Ha! Did I frighten you?'

It was Eva.

'Let's go.'

'Are you sure it'll be alright?'

A flicker of hesitation crossed Eva's eyes.

''Course ... Come on.'

The day's breeze had given way to stillness. A sliver of moon once more illuminated the familiar street, though bathed in an unfamiliar light. They edged their way towards the lake. The water lapping against the shore sounded to Lili like the monster catfish licking its lips before gobbling up its prey. She shuddered.

An owl screeched. The two girls grabbed each other's arms in fright, giggling nervously.

They arrived at the house.

Its ghostly walls reflected pale moonlight between two poplars, as tall as Swiss Guards, whose sombre heads disappeared into the dark sky.

All the children in the village were fascinated by the stranger who lived in the house by the lake. His frequent absences stoked their imaginations. Was he away visiting his mad wife in her asylum? During the winter months most of the rooms remained in darkness. Only one lamp burned through a downstairs window late into the night, and the writer could be seen through the leafless trees working at his desk or taking a book off a shelf. The return of light-filled days brought a steady stream of guests. At times he must have tired of their company:

No visitors please. Maximilian Meyer.

The gate groaned its disapproval as they ignored his polite request.

Blindly they felt their way along a wall.

'Go on! The coast is clear,' Eva urged.

All the windows of the house were hidden in shuttered sleep; all but one. It was just as Eva had said. The opening was tiny. Lili licked her parched lips. But before she had time to think, Eva was giving her a leg-up.

'Keep going and don't turn back.'

Not that she could once her head and shoulders were through the impossibly narrow window frame. Her fears vanished as she turned and twisted.

Lili was the nimblest of all the children when it came to climbing tall trees and shinning over walls. Even the older boys watched in admiration. When the cherries ripened she was first up the ladder and, with a basket strapped to her shoulders, would swiftly disappear into the highest branches.

She landed on the floor of a cramped storeroom. Brooms and brushes stood on moustachioed watch.

Once she'd fumbled her way to the door and opened it for Eva, the two intruders switched on their torches. Their criss-crossing beams scanned the room.

It was the study.

Lili recognised the desk she had spied from beyond the garden wall. Pages covered in a small and delicate script were scattered among open books. A large telescope sat on its splayed tripod, pointing at the sky over the lake.

Lili turned with her torch.

Deathly eyes stared back at her.

Eva heard her gasp and followed the beam.

A black face with garish zigzag markings was glaring at them. With straw for hair, a bloody gash of a mouth and blank gums, it looked like the masks they made at carnival time.

Elsewhere on the walls were paintings of familiar scenes.

'Let's go and see what's in the cellar,' said Eva. 'Perhaps he keeps his lunatic wife in chains down there.'

At the very idea Lili felt the hairs on the back of her neck stand up as straight as needles.

A curtain separated the study from the stairs leading down to the cellar. They pushed it half-aside and went down. The wooden door opened with a sing-song creak.

What they saw when they arrived puzzled them. Not because there was no sign of a deranged woman with black teeth, straggly grey hair and wide mad eyes chained to the wall. It was the presence of a large machine.

'It's a torture chamber!' shrieked Eva.

Lili was reminded of the cider press in farmer Ursprung's barn which moaned and groaned when it mashed the fruit at harvest time. As they shone their torches into its cogs and levers, they realised that it wasn't golden juice pressed from apples which poured from its round belly but page after printed page. Piles of these pages covered a desk in the middle of the room. Some had been divided and parcelled up. Nearby there were bottles and suitcases.

The catches opened with an echoing click. Inside were more pages stacked neatly into piles.

Eva peered into the bottles and found yellow sheets rolled up inside them.

'Look. Messages in bottles. I wonder who they're for.'

Lili went over to the table and picked up one of the loose sheets. She shone her torch on the large angry heading.

The Voice of the German People!

Hitler must fall if Germany is to live!

A pile of cloth-bound books sat on a trestle table. Lili held one in the light of her torch, slowly deciphering the title on its cover. The beam followed each letter like the finger of God on the stone tablets.

'Schiller ... Wilhelm Tell ... A Drama,' she read out quietly to herself.

Lili was baffled on opening the book in the middle. Instead of finding the text of a play like the ones they read at school, she discovered the same angry words as before, on every single page.

The Voice of the German People!

Hitler must fall if Germany is to live!

She put the book back on the table.

Every page the same, how boring.

'Let's go back upstairs,' said Eva, putting an abrupt end to any further reflection on these strange discoveries. They returned to the study. The fierce face on the wall now smiled toothlessly at them.

Suddenly Eva cried out.

'Hey, Lili. Look at these books.'

The silver and golden lettering on the leather-bound volumes twinkled like stars against a dark blue sky. Lili stood open-mouthed; she had never seen so many books. She wanted to reach out and run her fingers gently down their spines.

'Aquinasdanteflaubert…gogolhomerjung… spinozatolstoyzola.'

'What's that?' asked Lili.

'Don't you see?' replied Eva, interrupting her incantation. She seemed proud at having cracked an insoluble riddle.

Lili imagined the bookcase about to open in front of their eyes to reveal a secret passage leading to the hidden dungeon where…

'Eva. I'm tired. Let's go home.'

'Wait … Look, Lili. They're in perfect order. Not a single one is out of place.'

Lili followed the names along each shelf.

Eva was right. Nevertheless, she felt some disappointment that this was the extent of the mystery and desperately wanted to go home to bed.

'Let's have some fun.'

Eva was getting more excited.

'We'll change some of the books around. When he goes to find one, he'll wonder what's happened. He'll think he's going mad, like his crazy wife.'

It was pointless objecting. Eva was soon completely absorbed in her mischief-making.

Meanwhile it was slowly dawning on Lili that they were not alone.

Without saying a word to her friend who was giggling to herself as she warmed to her task, Lili turned very slowly towards the curtain behind her.

It was moving.

Someone or something was behind it.

She grabbed Eva's arm and with eyes widened in fright gesticulated wordlessly towards the swaying curtain.

The rings along the curtain rod were chiming eerily.

And there was a strange sound belonging to neither man nor beast.

Lili pointed her torch to the bottom of the curtain. A foot moved.

A single foot.

The hem of the fabric jerked.

It was coming towards them.

'Let's get out of here,' she shouted.

As she turned to run for the door, she tripped and collided with a small table. An ornate vase wobbled and span like a drunken ballerina. Lili watched horror-struck as it eventually lost its balance and crashed to the floor. There it lay in accusing pieces.

She froze.

'Run, Lili! What are you waiting for?'

They ran open-mouthed into the night. With clenched fists, pumping hearts and bursting lungs, they ran and ran until they reached the windows of their bedrooms.

Only then did a sickening realisation hit her.

'Eva …'

'What?'

'My torch … I must have dropped it in the house.'

There was nothing they could do. They certainly weren't going back to face whatever one-legged creature was lurking behind the curtain.

* * *

Lili wrapped herself tightly in her sheets.

Sleep refused to come. She cried as quietly as she could. How soon would it be before the inevitable happened and her part in the crime was discovered?

The shame of it all.

And her father, the village policeman.

Shadows of trees moved in a frenzied dance across the walls and ceiling of her bedroom.

The clock struck two.

What would he say? What would he do to her when he found out? He wouldn't let her off this time.

'It's prison for you, young lady.'

Still sleep refused to come. A cock crowed for the first time.

On the mantelpiece the clock struck four.

As eastern light began to flood her room Lili at last drifted into a shallow sleep.

II

On a glorious Good Friday morning Maximilian Meyer released the rusty chain from an old tree trunk and started to push his boat towards the water.

'Grüezi, Meyer. What a beautiful day!'

Max looked up from his exertions only to be blinded by the brightness of the sun. He squinted as he tried to make out the figure standing on the bank above him.

'Ah, Vogelsang. Grüß Gott,' he replied. 'I didn't recognise you out of your uniform ... Heading for the mountains, I see.'

Max could now distinguish the man, who he reckoned to be in his mid-thirties. He noted that Vogelsang's hair was receding, and his thick shirt stretched over the beginnings of a paunch.

'Do you need a hand there, Meyer? You seem to be struggling.' Vogelsang chuckled and dropped his rucksack in an ungainly heap. His bare, muscular arms betrayed athleticism.

'Where are you going?' Max asked breathlessly as they heaved the boat towards the water.

'To the Säntis range. I'm meeting up with my brother for a couple of days.'

'Leaving the border unguarded for Easter?'

The comment was ignored.

The boat was soon in place. They surveyed the scene before them.

What a serene day the sky foretold!

A moderate wind caressed shimmering furrows into the brimful lake. Blossoming crowns of pear trees hung banner-like against the clear blue sky.

The two men stood awhile in awkward silence. It crossed Max's mind to mention the strange goings-on he'd discovered on returning home from his recent trip, but he quickly thought better of it. The last thing he wanted was a policeman snooping around the house.

'You've made a good job there,' Vogelsang said with a hint of envy. 'She's looking very smart.'

On the previous Sunday, Palm Sunday, Max had started early with a wide brush and painted the wooden planks of his boat green and red as the villagers passed by on their way to church. They greeted him with reserved politeness.

It had taken four or five hours, but the work was done.

Standing next to Vogelsang, Max could now admire the fresh colours glistening in the sunlight.

'Well, I'd better be off,' said Vogelsang, breaking the spell. 'Enjoy your day.'

The border guard instinctively peered into the boat.

'Where's your rod?' he asked with some concern.

'No rods today. Brushes ... I thought I'd do some painting.' Weary from his recent struggles with words, Max was eager for the respite he was accustomed to find in line and colour.

'Well, have a good day, anyway.'

A momentary look of suspicion betrayed itself in Vogelsang's eyes. He would never have passed up an opportunity to pull a few fish from the lake to feed his growing family. There was no accounting for these strangers from across the lake.

As he hauled his rucksack back onto his wide shoulders a scattering of children came down from the village like a flock of hungry sparrows.

'Grüezi Herr Vogelsangs' filled the air.

Max observed the lively scene from the side.

'Salü, Papa.'

One of the sparrows clasped her spindly arms around Vogelsang's wide waist.

'Salü, Lili.'

Aware of the other man's discomfort he added: 'Say 'good morning' to Herr Meyer, Lili.'

The girl turned around, blushing as intensely as dawn across a snow capped mountain. Her head dropped quickly to study her right foot tracing an arc in the dust.

'Grüezi, Herr Meyer,' she mumbled through a thick tangle of hair tinted a beautiful chestnut hue by the morning sun.

'Now then, where are you lot off to?' Vogelsang asked in his policeman's voice.

'We're just going down to the lake to play, Papa,' replied Lili, turning her back on Max.

'Well, make sure you look after your sister.'

'Yes, Papa,' came the drawn out reply as Lili reluctantly took hold of the right hand of the smallest child in the group – the left being attached to her mouth by her thumb.

'And don't forget to help your mother when she gets back from church.'

'Aw, do I have to?'

'Yes you do.' In his policeman's voice he added: 'Or it's prison for you, young lady.'

By now the other children, bored with waiting, had started to wander off.

'Come on Lili,' they called back.

Vogelsang set off on his way. The ice-pick strapped to his rucksack blinked in the sunlight.

''Bye, kids. Behave yourselves. And watch the monster catfish doesn't get you.'

'Papa! Don't scare them,' his daughter remonstrated with a playful scowl, her hands on her hips. The scowl turned into a wide smile.

'Say hello to the Säntis from me.'

As Vogelsang waved goodbye he cast a last uncertain glance back at the boat and shook his head.

*   *   *

Max was alone again.

He clambered awkwardly into the boat. With satisfaction he breathed in the smell of water, fish and reeds. The lake was a mirror alive with all the hues of springtime. Here and there a yellow film sheathed the surface; flowering bushes on the shoreline had cast their seed upon its silken sheets.

After a few tentative strokes, Max looked back to the shoreline and watched as wavelets licked the cool blue and orange pebbles, played with flotsam and jetsam, and hid amongst the reeds.

The oars seemed strangely heavy and cumbersome after so long left idle. The unaccustomed heat of the day and the inactivity of the winter months soon brought on a strange lethargy. Max rested the two frozen wings over the surface of the lake and watched as translucent pearls of water slipped across their polished surface before dropping into an endless blue.

Present moments falling back into timelessness.

Imperceptible waves lapped the hull of the boat as it moved gently away from land.

A peal of bells drifted across the lake.

Max had forgotten. It was Good Friday.

Another drop fell off the wooden blade and was caught by the midday sun.

Max was assailed by a wave of melancholy as he recalled the affectionate scene he had just witnessed. He lifted his head and looked towards the distant shoreline which once had been his home.

Such unconditional love between father and daughter! He thought of Lotte his wife, and of his own daughter Rosa.

She would have been the same age as those village children …

With an irritated wave of his hand he dismissed these unsolicited thoughts as though swiping away a swarm of gnats poised to attack him.

They withdrew for the moment, biding their time.

Max impatiently unpacked his pencils, brushes and colours. The boat was at rest save for the occasional waves sent out by a distant passing ferry. Settling his board on his knees, he made a few hesitant strokes, his pencil barely touching the surface of the paper.

As he glanced up towards the white walls of his house, Max pictured what lay behind the shutters of his study window: the perfectly ordered books serried on their shelves; his desk with its tidy heap of unfinished business.

Chance had brought him to the house by the lake.

Awaiting a consultation with Doctor Jung, he was leafing aimlessly through a journal when he saw the advertisement. It promised a wonderful shoreline, excellent inns, forest walks and beautiful views. Max made the decision there and then to leave the country of his birth and cross the lake to the Swiss shore.

The advertisement had caught his eye for another reason. It claimed the village had a thriving colony of poets and painters.

How could the young writer resist such a lure?

Max arrived to find the painters and poets had packed away their easels and notebooks and moved on, having exhausted the simple delights of the place. That suited him fine.

In the first years he rented a dilapidated fisherman's cottage outside the village and adopted the lifestyle of an impoverished recluse. He was just one more itinerant, uprooted and dislocated by the times, living frugally off milk and rice, fish from the lake and chestnuts and berries foraged from the woods in the autumn. He shunned all human contact.

Then one evening, breaking his firm resolution, he accepted an invitation to dinner from an old friend, a wealthy industrialist and patron, at the Stork Inn in Zurich. As chance would have it, his friend had bought the most impressive of the houses on the lake's shore as an investment.

'You'll be following in a long and glorious tradition if you move in,' his friend said.

Early in the previous century, merchants, recognising the trading opportunities offered by the village's location, had built the elegant houses which dominated the shoreline. Sailing boats crossed the lake transporting fruit, wine, cider, cheese, butter and corn from port to port along its shores.

But then a fresh wind began to blow through Europe. Steam threatened the traditional livelihood of the sailors. The upstart masters of the lake needed a larger port; they also needed a link to the new railways. Several ports along the lake challenged, but in the end destiny chose another.

The picturesque and agile sailing boats disappeared, and the merchants abandoned the great houses they had built.

The village was on the brink of returning to obscurity.

But, as with a sunset on a scorching summer's day, there was one last, unexpected blaze of life and colour.

At the beginning of the new century, the parish council decided with some unaccustomed foresight to construct a jetty for the steamers to berth. Tourists streamed to the village from all over Europe. These were not just day-trippers from the surrounding area. These were travellers from the highest echelons of society in Saint Petersburg, London, Munich and New York. They were lured by the natural beauty of the lake, the tranquillity of the village and, most importantly, the ensemble of beautiful houses left by the earlier entrepreneurs.

These now offered luxury and comfort as their illustrious guests read, attended concerts, promenaded in the lakeside park or bathed in the lake itself. They would dine in the Bellevue on freshly caught fish, and after dinner those seeking company and conversation could find it in the billiard room (for the gentlemen) or in the salon (for the ladies). The local hoteliers competed with each other in offering concerts, entertainers, Venetian nights and regimental bands.

Europe's aristocracy held court there in the years before war tore through the continent. Then the borders closed. Fortunes spent, for many their time was up.

'Well, Max? What do you say? You'll be doing me a favour.'

Despite his friend's insistence, Max was uncertain. He had no desire to compromise his cherished seclusion.

'I suppose I could give it a try.'

'That's settled then. Stay as long as you like.'

* * *

The church bells had fallen silent.

Max sighed as he put the completed watercolour to one side. It was time to get back to work.

As he rowed towards the shore he saw children playing by the water, blissfully unaware of the significance of the day. They were paddling and splashing and throwing pebbles into the water. Though she was transformed into a silhouette by the late afternoon sun, he could discern the lithe figure of Vogelsang's daughter standing apart from the other children.

Her arm was stretched out. A finger was pointing towards the far shore where a tale began.

III

On a summer's afternoon when the fishermen were on the lake, the farmers in their fields and the artisans in their workshops, Maximilian Meyer left behind the empty streets of the village to walk into the surrounding countryside. A tattered knapsack, companion of countless wanderings, held his paints, brushes and water. He carried a folding chair, and his easel was tucked awkwardly under his arm.

His movements had not gone unnoticed.

A spy, hiding behind the wall, gave the signal.

The others picked up their bicycles and set off in pursuit.

Draped stole-like over his shoulders, Hiddigeigei angrily flicked his tail.

Max was oblivious to the warning. His mind was still troubled by the strange goings-on in the house. Unable to provide a cast-iron alibi, Hiddigeigei had himself initially taken the blame for the broken vase. It wouldn't have been the first time the black kitten had left a trail of destruction.

But then he was baffled when looking for certain books on his shelves, only to find they had moved. What was Zoroastra doing leaning against Voltaire? That, at least, was an easy mistake to make. But jovial Juvenal swapping places with stoical Seneca? Sachs the humble cobbler filling the shoes of Goethe? And as for sullen Schopenhauer haggling for his place with humorous Heine? – No, some Dionysian spirit had been at play.

His suspicions were confirmed when he found a torch carelessly abandoned under the heavy cloth covering the piano. Then there was the window to the storeroom his housekeeper had inadvertently left open. Only a child could have got through a gap that small.

Max stopped to observe a stonechat on a nearby post. Behind him there was a squeal of brakes, the sound of skidding tyres and clashing mudguards.

He felt a more insistent flick of fur about his ears.

'What's the matter? Are those ragamuffins bothering us again?' he said in a deliberately loud voice.

Max strode on. He only hoped that the intruders – he was convinced there was more than one – hadn't seen certain things. He was horrified to find on his return that he had forgotten to lock the door to his cellar. Normally he was meticulous about putting things away and locking up, particularly when his housekeeper was around. On this occasion he had been in a hurry. Max was angry with himself. Such clumsiness could have implications for the work of the transport column.

Not for the first time he was sorry he'd let himself be talked into getting involved in all this cloak-and-dagger stuff.

Harry bloody Haller!

What would he have to say about the whole affair?

Probably best not tell him.

Max frowned at the memory of his friend and literary rival's last visit to his house by the lake.

It had been one of those surprisingly warm March days which promise a swift end to winter. After an evening spent in rancorous dispute, they were sitting sullenly in the garden of the Bellevue. The front pages of the newspapers they'd brought with them fluttered on the table, their headlines growling like rabid dogs.

'You know, Max,' Harry had said, lighting up one of his revolting cigars whose smell turned Max's stomach. 'I too would like to write about all this.'

The sweep of his gesture covered the lake, the shore and the forests.

'But since your fellow artist over there has been daubing the streets with blood, how can I? ... How can anyone?'

The playful light in Harry's eyes was extinguished in the silent contemplation of unspoken horrors.

'You know, writing about trees in times like these is a crime.'

Max laughed to himself.

A crime?

He knew perfectly well what Harry was insinuating.

'I've told you, I want nothing to do with it,' he said through gritted teeth.

His friend was visibly struggling to contain his impatience.

'You can't act as though it's got nothing to do with you. It's all very well sitting here in this idyllic backwater writing your poetry.'

Harry leaned forward stabbing his forefinger.

'I wouldn't assume you're safe, Max. You haven't exactly endeared yourself to them. Watch out! The northern wind will blow you away.'

They both studied the shore from where the invoked storm was to come, avoiding each other's gaze. Max was irritated by his friend's certainties. But on this he was certainly right: Max had been publicly contemptuous of the brown-shirted hoodlums. They were unlikely to forgive or forget.

'You've got to make your mind up,' had been Harry's parting words. 'The transport column needs you.'

* * *

Max turned round swiftly.

They were still on his tail. Each with one foot on a raised pedal, as though to make a swift get-away, and with a determined look on their faces.

Over time he had come to an unspoken agreement with this gaggle of dirty-kneed, snotty-nosed kids. He would play along with their little game of cat and mouse up to a point, and they, for the most part, kept a respectful distance. If they overstepped the mark, it was enough for him to drop his folding chair, turn round suddenly and glare at them.

But now that his suspicions had been aroused and all the evidence pointed to child intruders, he was starting to take a closer interest. He let them approach as he set up his easel and unfolded his chair.

His stalkers had by now lost their inhibitions and were gathered in a huddle around him.

They watched as the work emerged, transferring their gaze from the movement of brush on paper to the scene and then back again.

'What colour is that?'

Max carried on painting whilst watching them carefully from the corner of his eye. He completed his stroke, dipped the brush into a small cup of water and sucked it dry before answering.

'It's called burnt sienna.'

'That's a funny name. It's brown, isn't it?' suggested one of the children.

'No, it isn't. It's orange,' argued another, the formality of respectful whispers now abandoned.

Now the ice was broken, comments flowed more freely, but more as a discussion among themselves than directed at the artist at work.

'I like the sky best.'

'The house is good. The roof is very red.'

'There's the sail of a boat on the lake.'

'No it's not. It's a seagull.'

Cicadas ceased their chirruping as suddenly as a child's wound-up toy.

Silence returned as they watched.

'I wish I could paint like that.'

A timid voice, hidden from his view, spoke up.

'Let's go, Eva. It's too hot here.'

Max tried to identify his intruders from among the children now riding away into the coolness of the woods. It was no easy task. They were all scrawny and without scruples. At least he felt safe in the knowledge that, even if they had seen something, they wouldn't say a word to any adult. To do so would be tantamount to a confession that they had broken into his house.

There was no harm done. Harry didn't need to know.

Still, Max was more than interested in finding the little culprits.

IV

It had been Eva's idea, as ever.

Lili could have made some excuse, but her friend had that look in her eyes.

'Come on, Lili. It'll be fun.'

What could happen on a simple bike ride?

The afternoon was sultry. The pale disc of the sun had retired behind an exhausted sky. Out on the water sails drooped like tongues too weary to lap the scarce air.

They set off, Eva leading the way.

Lili pedalled listlessly. A heavy band tightened across her temples. A dull ache was making itself felt in the pit of her stomach.

They cycled for the best part of an hour.

'Let's stop here,' said Eva.

They dropped their bikes and threw themselves into the grass. There they lay staring into the leaden sky.

Eva pulled herself up to pick burrs from her socks.

'Lili ...'

Lili wanted to pretend to be asleep but rolled over onto an elbow to face her friend.

'Yes?'

'Why don't we go and spy on old Meyer?'

Lili swallowed hard. Somehow they'd got away with it last time. This time they might not be so lucky.

Eva was still talking.

'We can climb over his wall and creep through the garden to see what he's up to.'

Lili groped for the first excuse which came to mind.

'I can't. I promised I'd play with Elsbeth.'

She knew as soon as she uttered the words that Eva wouldn't believe her. How many times had she told her friend that *she* was more of a sister than Elsbeth, her own flesh-and-blood?

Her friend's eyes darkened in jealousy.

'She's not really your sister, you know.'

Lili gulped.

'What do you mean? Of course she's my sister.'

Eva picked up her bicycle from the long grass where they sat. Lili squinted as she fixed her in her sight astride the saddle.

'She's not, Lili. I heard my aunt talking about it. She said how awful it was when your mother died ... how very young and beautiful she was.'

The spite was gone from Eva's voice.

Lili felt a sudden pain in her stomach. Her head was spinning. She gasped for breath. She wanted to cry out but the words stuck in her throat.

'Your real mother died after giving birth to you. Elsbeth's only your half-sister. Anna's really your step-mother. She looked after Helena when she was ill, and then your father married her.'

Her words were suffocating Lili.

'Everyone called her Leni. She was only twenty.'

The blockage in Lili's throat suddenly cleared.

'I don't believe you. You've made it all up because I don't want to come on one of your stupid adventures. Your aunt is a liar. She's a wicked gossip!'

Lili let out a cry as she picked up her bicycle. In her rush to escape she gashed her shin painfully on the pedal.

She dropped her bicycle and hobbled to one side looking down at the cut as it opened up and blood started to run.

Lili stopped crying. Fascinated, she followed the thin trickle tracing its course from her shin to the top of her sock. There it hesitated a moment, as though deciding which further path to take, before spreading out like red ink on blotting paper.

She looked up at Eva. Her friend's jaw was locked in horror.

'Are you alright?'

The pain reasserted itself. Eva's parting words rang in Lili's ears as she rode off.

'It's all true. Cross my heart and hope to die.'

Fresh tears streamed down her face as she pedalled as fast as she could. Eva was still calling after her.

*   *   *

The spinning wheels of her bicycle whirred as Lili threw it down by the door. She rushed inside and hurled herself onto her bed weeping uncontrollably.

Her sobbing filled the empty house.

'How could she be so mean? How could she tell such nasty lies?' she cried, thumping her pillow in exasperation. Try as she might, Lili couldn't rid her mind of the things Eva had said about Elsbeth only being her half-sister and her mother not being her real mother.

A doubt was whispering in her ear: Why would she make such things up?

Slowly her rage subsided. Lili began to think about what Eva's aunt had said about her father.

Then she remembered.

She remembered an evening when she was with him on the lake waiting for the fish to bite. The air was still. Music drifted from the window of an upstairs room in the Schuberts' house. Frau Schubert was playing the piano. Lili remembered the look of sadness on her father's face, then the tears rolling down his cheeks. He made no attempt to hide them from her. Why had he been so sad?

There was no-one at home.

Lili got up off her bed and dried her eyes. She winced with pain as she felt the cut on her shin. Wiping away the blood she made up her mind.

She crept into their bedroom. It was in darkness; the shutters were closed against the afternoon sun.

If what Eva said was true, there had to be something belonging to her.

'Helena.'

Lili spoke her name for the first time.

The photographs on the chest of drawers were all of long-deceased grandparents and great-grandparents.

Yet the evening on the lake convinced Lili her father would have kept something belonging to his young bride. She delved into the dark shadows of the wardrobe, breathing in the pungent whiff of mothballs. She searched through the heavy chest of drawers, lifting her mother's carefully folded white blouses.

Nothing.

On the side of the bed where her father slept stood a small table. Lili opened the drawer carefully, listening for the sound of a door opening. Inside she found male clutter: cufflinks, an old pocket watch, badges, documents, a few old coins, spent cartridges.

She rummaged at the back of the drawer. Her fingers touched the velvet surface of a small box carefully hidden in the corner. She lifted it out slowly, scarcely breathing.

Lili hardly dared open it.

Her eyes were squeezed closed. Her fingers felt a ring. She took it between her thumb and forefinger and traced the incisions with her fingernail.

A for Anna. O for Otto; her mother and her father.

She felt again. Something wasn't quite right. She opened her eyes.

Not A –

It was H.

H for Helena.

Eva had been telling the truth!

It was her father's wedding ring. Their ring. He'd kept it.

Lili investigated further.

There was something at the bottom of the box, folded tightly.

With a fingernail she peeled it out, carefully revealing it to a pencil light slipping through the shutter. The photograph was creased and worn at the edges, but the faces in it were clear to see.

There she was. There they were, smiling at the camera. They were wearing sturdy boots and carried ropes slung across their shoulders. The snow-capped mountain rose high in the background. Were they about to climb it? No, she concluded. They'd just got back down. Their tanned faces were shining with fulfilled adventure.

Lili stared at the photograph. She studied every detail: the look of delight on her smiling face; thick hair falling freely over her high, handsome brow; the determined arch of her eyebrows, and cheeks flushed by the exertion of the climb.

The scratching of a key in a lock startled her. In panic she fumbled with the little box containing the ring. The photograph was refusing to go back in.

A door creaked open.

With the evidence of her latest crime cutting into her palm, Lili stole out of her parent's bedroom.

'Now I'm a thief as well,' she thought.

* * *

Occasionally she would still play with Eva, out of habit, but without any real joy. Soon Eva gave up calling for her and turned to other friends. Lili was left alone and withdrew into herself.

The scales had fallen from her eyes. She began seeing things that had been hidden from her until that time. She watched her father playing cards at his regular table in the Bellevue. He seemed the same, laughing and joking with his drinking companions. But in unguarded moments Lili detected the sadness she'd seen in his eyes that evening on the lake.

Why hadn't he told her? Why was he keeping this painful secret from her?

She was waiting for a sign. She was waiting for him to call her over and say: 'Lili, I need to speak to you ... It's something very important.'

Surely he'd discovered the photograph was missing by now.

But the moment never came.

Perhaps he couldn't bear to be reminded of Leni's face. Perhaps he wanted her to remain buried in her little box, eternally hidden away in the shadowy corner of his drawer.

In the meantime, he was slipping away from her, and Lili was struggling to understand how or why it was happening.

Sadness and confusion were her constant companions over those months. After she finished rowing students from the nearby university town out on to the lake, where she watched them canoodle and pet, she would sit at the end of the jetty and study the shoreline in the distance as it approached and withdrew according to the season, the time of day, the weather and the play of light.

She took the photograph from her pocket, carefully unfolded it and studied the face gazing at her. It was as though she was looking at her own likeness.

She spoke her mother's name: Leni. She spoke her own name.

Lili raised her eyes to follow the path of the Zeppelin, glowing in the silvery light of the föhn, as it lifted above the distant hills, turned to cross the lake and headed towards the mountains.

She wished she could fly away in the airship and never come back. She wished she could be transported over deserted islands lapped by the white surf of the Atlantic. She wished she could put thousands of miles between her and her unhappiness and let outstretched arms welcome her to a new and better world.

V

A smart green sports car arrived in the village square with a screech of brakes and an impetuous sounding of the horn, announcing someone important.

Lili saw a short stocky man get out. He wore a leather jacket, had a closely shaven head and looked like a boxer.

Not long into his visit, Lili was walking home after an early evening swim. The freshness of the water had cooled her skin after the oppressive heat of the day, and her tongue could still taste the tanginess of the lake on her lips. From among the heavy boughs of a tree which cast deep shadows on the path came a fearful wailing. She could just make out – where the sky started to pierce the canopy with shards of ultramarine – the black shape of a cat. A dog must have chased it up there, and now it was stuck and in obvious pain.

There being no sign of its master, Lili thought of shinning over the garden wall and climbing up to rescue the distressed animal. She'd almost forgotten the time she and Eva had climbed through the little window into the house; the shame she used to feel every time she passed by had subsided. Plucking up her courage she went to the door.

The boxer answered her timid knock and called back grinning: 'Max. Come quickly. There's a beautiful female admirer at the door.'

Holding a stubby finger to his lips he smiled conspiratorially at Lili, who shuffled in embarrassment.

'She craves an audience with the great writer.'

After a moment which seemed like an age, a tall figure emerged from the shadows of the house. He seemed to be struggling to recognise her.

'Good evening…. I'm sorry, do I know you?'

'I'm Lili … Lili Vogelsang. My father is the border guard. We live here in the village.'

'Yes. Yes … Of course.'

Max carefully put on the spectacles Lili only now noticed he'd been cleaning absent-mindedly on an ink-stained rag.

The three stood in an awkward silence at the door. Max looked to his guest for guidance and was answered by a slight shrug of his heavy shoulders.

'How can I help you, Lili?'

'The young lady wants you to sign a copy of your latest masterpiece,' the boxer suddenly announced.

'No, I don't … I mean …' Lili felt the redness flooding to her cheeks.

'It's your cat. She's stuck up a big tree in your garden. I think she's hurt and can't get down. I was walking past when I –'

'Oh, Hiddigeigei?'

Lili must have looked puzzled at the strange sounds coming from Max's mouth, for the boxer quickly provided an explanation.

'That's the cat's name ... She is a he, by the way. Max calls him Hiddigcigci. A very literary allusion, as befits a writer of his standing. Some tale about a trumpeter who falls in love with an aristocratic maiden, if I recall correctly. And a cat which spouts homespun wisdom. Am I right?'

'Too bourgeois and sentimental for your taste, I expect. But yes, Harry.'

As far as Lili was concerned they might as well have been speaking Chinese.

'Well, we'd better go and get your philosophical pussy cat out of his tree. Come along, young lady. You might be able to assist in some small way,' said the boxer.

A scent of soil and vegetation released by the earlier storm lifted off the carefully tended plot; tomatoes hung suspended – bright red planets in a universe of green. When they reached the tree, the black cat started yowling again in pain.

'Leave it to me,' ordered the boxer. 'I always loved climbing trees. D'you know my poem, Max? *The evening trees?*'

Max shook his head.

'I'm not sure I do, Harry.'

He took off his glasses; his eyes narrowed into a penetrating, searching gaze.

'Anyway, I thought you said writing about trees was
...' Max paused as though waiting for Harry to finish
his sentence for him.

'What Max? What did I say?'

Lili felt a strange tension between the two men; she
averted her eyes.

Another yowl came from high in the tree.

'Oh, never mind,' Max was smiling. 'You'd better
go and rescue Hiddigeigei.'

A large foot was placed decisively onto the trunk of
the tree.

'When evening falls I climb the tallest trees ...'

The first line of Harry's poem resounded through
the garden in a booming bass. He was pulling himself
up on to the first available branch.

'Where bats and birds fly across my brow ...'

There was a semi-audible expletive as he caught his
shaven head on a jutting bough. The fist-fighter's fat
bottom vanished from view.

'Leaves give answer to the whispers of the breeze
...'

He was almost out of sight. There was a rustle and
a small groan.

'As I stand triumphant on the highest bough ...
Nearly there.'

So the boxer was not a boxer after all, thought Lili.

'We'll soon have metaphysical moggy back on terra
firma.'

The boxer-poet had disappeared into the canopy.
Occasionally his feet reappeared as they sought a new
branch; occasionally there was a more audible curse, as
the branches grew thicker.

'Come on puss! Uncle Harry's here … There's a good cat … Come to Harry.'

The booming bass softened with his blandishments.

Another rustling of leaves.

Silence.

'Owwchh! … Fucking hell! You vicious little shit!'

The obscenity echoed around the garden, bounced back off the lake and reverberated round the trees and plants, like the curse of some primitive god. The tomatoes in the vegetable patch trembled on their stalks.

'What is it, Harry?'

'Your flea-infested shit-bag of a cat just scratched me –'

The loudly uttered accusation changed immediately into a cry of pain.

'I'm bleeding … Jesus Christ, he's drawn blood.'

Harry's descent from the tree was punctuated by uninhibited obscenities the like of which Lili had never heard before in all her life.

'Well fuck you, fucking-Hiddi-fucking-geigei!'

'Harry!'

'Christ almighty! You can stay in your fucking tree, for all I care, you ungrateful streak of black piss.'

'Harry… Please …'

'Bastard cat.'

'Harry … language … there's a chi –'

'Your cat's a –'

'Harry!'

The exchange of vile oaths and pleas for calm continued until Harry was once more visible, clutching his bleeding forehead.

Back on solid ground, the poet's anger turned into self-pity as the garden filled with a curious mixture of wails from both the poet-pugilist and the philosopher-tomcat.

'Shall I have a go?' asked Lili quietly.

Max looked like a priest giving absolution to a sinner as he inspected Harry's forehead.

'I think Hiddi... Hiddi...'

'geigei...'

'I think he's hurt. That's why he lashed out and scratched your friend. I can easily get up there.'

Max looked up at the tree and then down at Lili.

'I've climbed much higher trees,' Lili assured him.

'Have a go if you like. Meanwhile I'd better see to Harry's injuries.' Max began to escort his wounded friend from the battleground.

'Be careful. I think Hiddigeigei is upset.'

At this, Harry opened his mouth to utter another obscenity, but for once words failed him.

Lili shinned up the trunk of the tree, twisted through the awkward branches and in no time at all hauled herself up to where the black tomcat was stuck. From her position high in the tree she looked back through the thick leaves and was surprised to see Max had come back into the garden.

'Lili?'

'I'm up here!'

Max peered into the high branches. There was a look of astonishment on his face which quickly turned into a thin smile.

Has he never seen a girl climb a tree before? Lili thought.

Hiddigeigei meowed plaintively. Two pairs of green eyes met across a heavy bough.

'Hiddigeigei. Come on, Hiddigeigei. Come to me ... Lili'll help you.'

Lili stretched out her hand slowly and stroked the cowering animal. She felt a sticky dampness on his paw. Reaching under his belly, she gently lifted the suffering creature off the bough and snuggled him to her chest. Hiddigeigei was purring; his eyes closed in trust.

*　　*　　*

'His paw's cut. We need to bathe it.'

Max's study resembled a field hospital. For a second time he was attending to the wounded, though on this occasion the injured party showed considerably more patience.

'He'd love some fresh milk – Hiddigeigei, that is. Harry prefers something stronger. Unfortunately, I've none in the house.'

'I can get it,' Lili shouted, barely able to contain herself at the chance to make up for her earlier transgression.

'Herr Ursprung'll let me have some straight from the cows. They'll have just been milked.'

She sprinted to the farm, poured the still warm milk into a kettle and ran back as quickly as she could, without spilling a drop.

'Lili ...'

Max turned to her as Hiddigeigei greedily lapped up the fresh milk from a bowl placed among books scattered on his desk.

'You know, you can bring Hiddigeigei milk from the farm whenever you like. Stay and play with him. He obviously likes you.' Max fired an ironic glance at Harry, who was strangely subdued as he held a slightly bloodied cloth to his brow.

'He's lots of fun.'

He was running his long, elegant fingers through his thin hair. 'He loves climbing up and down this curtain…'

Max laughed as he shook the fabric, recreating the eerie jangling sound.

'You know, Lili, he even slides around the floor in one of my slippers.'

Lili gulped: the strange sounds; the rustling of the curtain; the one-legged monster coming towards them that night.

'But he can get up to mischief sometimes … You'd never believe what he does.'

A smile was playing around the corners of his mouth.

'When I got back from my last journey, I found he'd jumped up on to a table in the living room and knocked over a vase an old friend had given me. It was in pieces on the floor.'

His face clouded with sadness at the loss of a precious object. Lili felt her cheeks burning.

'Oh, it didn't matter,' Max quickly added. 'I never liked it anyway … I think he knew that. Hiddigeigei's a clever cat. He's a philosopher-cat, you see.'

Max paused. He had taken off his glasses.

'He even appears to have been reading some of my books.'

His blue eyes were gazing straight into hers with the same searching look she'd seen directed at Harry in the garden.

Lili swallowed hard. Confused thoughts raced through her head.

He knew someone had broken into his house. The shattered vase and the misplaced books provided the evidence. Surely he'd found the torch she'd dropped and the window they'd left open, too? He must have worked out that was how they got in.

Lili felt the colour draining from her face.

That was why he watched her climb the tree with so much interest. She'd just been stupid enough to confirm his suspicions before his eyes.

It was a matter of time before he told her father.

It was Eva not me, she wanted to shout out. I never wanted to do it. She made me. I never touched any of your books. And the vase ... it was an accident.

Her lower lip quivered; her gaze drooped to the floor like a wilted flower.

When she dared to raise her head again, blinking away hot tears of shame, Lili saw a fleeting, gentle smile on Max's lips.

'You won't forget milk for Hiddigeigei, will you Lili?'

VI

Lili placed a hesitant hand on the iron gate; the rust flaked under her touch. The absence of the sign warning off unwanted visitors gave her some encouragement as her feet crunched into the gravel path. Her timid knock echoed through the afternoon stillness of the garden.

She stood at the door and waited. Between her hands she held a kettle; she seemed to be searching the creamy liquid it contained for something she'd lost.

She'd put off this moment. But the last words he'd spoken to her that evening worked like a spell. It was as though he'd wrung a promise from her which she felt compelled to keep as part of some unspoken bargain. In the intervening days the beating she expected to receive from her father never came. If the owner of the footsteps she now heard approaching knew she was in some way responsible for the broken vase and maltreated books, he wasn't telling. The least she could do in gratitude was to bring his cat some milk.

She held out the offering in anticipation. Suddenly Lili's eyes fell on the unravelling ends of her cardigan sleeves. She coloured in embarrassment but was powerless to hide them, for at that very moment the door opened.

'Ah, Lili.'

'Grüezi, Herr Meyer ... I've got some milk for Hiddigeigei,' she said in a faltering voice.

'That's very kind of you.'

Lili was caught between opposing forces: her arms wanted to push the kettle of milk to meet Max's outstretched hands, but in the very same instant they retracted in shame at her frayed sleeves. The intended recipient of her gift was left nonplussed and empty handed.

'Tell you what,' said Max in an attempt to relieve the apparent stalemate, 'Why don't you give Hiddigeigei the milk yourself? He's at a bit of a loss how to amuse himself since his arboreal adversary left the scene ... I mean Harry, the man who climbed the tree,' he added quickly.

'Oh, the boxer,' Lili murmured involuntarily.

Max laughed a full, friendly laugh.

'Harry, a boxer? He'd be flattered at the description. Now, let's go and find your friend. Last time I saw him he was in the garden enjoying the sunshine ... Oh, and by the way,' he added with a frown, 'you don't need to call me Herr Meyer. Call me Max.'

Lili often found herself at Max's door over the next weeks and months. The house by the lake became a refuge. She'd lost track of her old world; the familiar world where she'd spent her thirteen years had become strange to her.

She was not alone in finding escape there. During that summer and autumn, the guests kept coming.

They arrived unannounced, sometimes in the middle of the night. Some came with just the clothes on their backs, others carried heavy suitcases. More often than not, they stayed for only a few days before moving on.

Who were these people? Lili wondered. They didn't seem to be old friends come to share joyful times with their host. They looked sad, confused and lost. Occasionally she would overhear them talking darkly about what was happening 'over there'. Whatever they had suffered was far weightier than her own worries.

Max treated all of them with great kindness, giving them shelter and words of comfort before they continued their uncertain journey. He was different here in his own house; he was no longer the stern and remote figure who fascinated and frightened Lili and the other children in equal measure.

One hot day Lili took milk for Hiddigeigei and was sitting with him in the shade. A taciturn, serious man was the latest visitor to the house. He showed not the slightest interest in Lili, Hiddigeigei, or anyone else for that matter.

Max was weeding his vegetable plot. He wore his wide-brimmed straw hat. Lili saw a dark movement of sweat spread across the back of his tattered shirt.

Hiddigeigei sat in the shade. Lili watched the patterns of butterflies flitting across his eyes. Common blues, painted ladies and red admirals caused a lazy flick of his tail; at the sight of swallowtails his ears twitched. But whenever wings marked in black and white entered his field of vision, he would spring up in determined pursuit.

But today he had no thought of the chase. It was even too hot for him to go and patrol his patch and disturb his friend the hedgehog who'd built his nest under the wooden floor of the summer house.

There was hardly a breath of air.

The earnest guest sat at a table in the garden under a large parasol. He had spread out in front of him a collection of newspapers. Lili watched as he opened a large red notebook, wrote a few sentences, stopped, selected a newspaper, studied its contents, found what he was looking for, and with a pair of scissors cut out a small section. The cuttings were laid out carefully on the table.

The sound of the spade piercing the dry earth slowed.

The day's heat intensified.

Suddenly Hiddigeigei's ears pricked up.

Out of nowhere, as sometimes happens on hot days by the lake, came a sudden, strong gust of air.

The leaves on the trees shivered.

'Oh, no.'

A polite cry of dismay broke the silence.

'Max, come quickly. Help!'

The painstakingly assembled cuttings on the visitor's table took flight and were sent spinning through the garden. On seeing the small white shapes with black markings Hiddigeigei jumped up and gave chase. So many butterflies at one time! He didn't know which way to turn, as the wind blew the fragments around the garden.

Max fetched his butterfly net, which only added to the illusion in Hiddigeigei's mind that he was chasing live creatures. When he caught one, he held it down with his paw, sniffing it. But something wasn't quite right. These did not smell or taste like the butterflies he knew. He lifted his paw. The shape took off once more. He chased it down. Still it didn't smell right. Hiddigeigei lost interest and went back to his shady tree; these butterflies were far too easy to catch.

Meanwhile Max and Lili continued the chase.

'Here's one!' shouted Lili as she caught a white-winged shape in mid-flight.

'I've got one too,' countered Max, scooping one off a rose.

Laughter filled the garden as they ran round madly in a competition to find the last of the prodigal cuttings.

Eventually they were returned. Lili and Max watched in breathless bemusement as the stranger feverishly and randomly stuck them into his notebook.

'I am most grateful to you both.'

They were the only words Lili heard him utter during the whole of his stay.

*   *   *

As the summer began to fade an odd couple arrived at the villa.

She was tall and beautiful, her eyes an almost violet colour Lili had never seen before. She laughed a thick laugh full of the smoke of the city. Her ash-blonde hair was short and flattened down, with a lock falling over her pale forehead. Her whole face was white, far from happy, but strangely appealing. An occasional light grimace betrayed bitterness.

He was short and bald, hunched and nervous as though expecting to be beaten at any time. His round glasses glinted in the sun as he scribbled madly while she looked over his shoulder, occasionally pointing to something he had written and making him change or cross it out.

On an evening when sounds carried for miles and miles on the slightest of breezes, Lili was walking home past the house. Music drifted across the garden. The French windows had been thrown open, and at the piano, previously kept under wraps, sat the odd little man with the round spectacles. By his side, wearing a long, straight, black velvet gown, which exaggerated her slight figure, stood the lady with the white face, her vermilion lips a slash of blood across a pale mask.

Enraptured, Lili watched as the scene unfolded. Stood next to the piano with a cigarette burning between her fingers, the pale woman raised it dreamily to her lips.

Lili imitated every gesture with a stalk of grass. She put it in the corner of her mouth and let go. With the tip of her finger she removed a stray fibre from her bottom lip. When the woman took a long draw on the cigarette, Lili did the same, removing the stalk and pretending to blow smoke from the corner of her mouth.

The cigarette, still burning, was placed carefully on the edge of the piano. The blonde head nodded almost imperceptibly to the pianist to begin; the violet eyes shut as though in a dream. Perhaps intimidated by his partner, the nervous pianist messed up the introduction to the song.

In irritation the singer opened her eyes, picked up her cigarette and flicked the accumulated ash on to his bald head, before cuffing him.

'You call yourself a musician.'

To Lili's astonishment she then climbed discordantly over the piano to sit on top of it. Her crossed legs revealed a long slit in her dress which reached from her feet to her upper thighs. She crossed and uncrossed her long, beautiful legs, placed the cigarette back down on the piano as the pianist began playing once more. Her eyes lit up in pleasure.

Even from afar her face was surprising in its expressiveness. Her voice was passionate and intense, with sudden unexpected bursts of feeling. The songs she sang were utterly different to those Lili was used to hearing from the radio in the Bellevue. At times they were coarse and raucous. Then quite unexpectedly the music would become soft and longing before ending with a sob or a cry which seemed to tear through the singer. Both of them, man and woman, seemed transformed by the music. Earlier disharmony was replaced by sweetness. She glided off her perch and went to lean over his shoulder between the verses of the song, looking at the music; he gazed back admiringly at her while she sang.

She sang of the sea and sailors, ships and pirates, of traitors and lovers, of treasure, and the poor people in the cities. The words evoked ports with exotic sounding names and nostalgia for a lost world. The singer became a woman of the streets and docks, in love with a sailor, a waster and gambler. She believed she could escape the misery of her life with him. But he was fickle; he abandoned her to despair and the gutter.

You said you'd be true, Joe,
You said you'd be mine,
You took all I had, Joe,
You lousy, cheating, little swine.

As Lili listened to these dark intimations of adulthood she was once more disturbed by a scene she had witnessed the evening before. Walking back from the lake she had spotted Eva ahead on the path. Lili was on the point of calling out to her but then saw she was with a boy, so hid herself quickly behind a tree. Her childhood friend was laughing in a strange way as she took the boy by the hand. Suddenly, to Lili's consternation, Eva pushed the boy's hand between her legs. The laughter stopped, and she led him into the bushes.

* * *

Autumn days presaged the onset of winter.

Scudding grey waves bobbed the fishing boats like corks. Mists shrouded the water. The groans of steamers and the ringing of bells were at times the only guides to where land ended and water began. In the garden of the Bellevue the white tables were covered by fallen leaves from the chestnut trees.

Lili sat on the shore and watched the Zeppelin rise into the sky. It hesitated, hovered for an instant as though unsure, before heading in a westerly direction.

She wondered what it would be like to look down on her world from the Zeppelin. All that was great would be humbled: cathedral-like forests of beech trees; the green onion-towers of pilgrimage churches; tall poplars with their dark tongues licking the sky; lighthouses, castles and even the mountains. In her mind's eye she saw the ferries crawling across the lake pursued by sailing boats; they were like insects scattering white larvae. She saw the shorelines edged by shallow water, a white hem on a beautiful gown of jade. All that once sped now slowed: the darting flights of kingfishers were frozen in time; cormorants were caught in the act of stealing from fishermen's nets; a car speeding down a country lane was overtaken and devoured by the shadow of the Zeppelin's belly.

A choking sound interrupted her reverie.

Lili got up to see where it was coming from.

A contorted shape, wrapped in a long thick pullover sat on the jetty; her knees were pulled up to her face. She must have been there for some time without Lili noticing.

Lili stood rooted to the spot. She felt as though she was a witness to someone dying in the street. Should she offer to help? Should she just go away quietly and leave the poor woman to her private grief?

The woman's head turned towards her.

Lili immediately recognised those stunning violet eyes, reddened with crying and smeared with sadness. She looked so small compared to that summer's evening when she'd moved so gracefully around the piano and sang with such strange power and beauty.

'I'm very sorry. I didn't mean to …' Lili said.

'Don't worry, darling.'

The singer smudged her mascara with the back of her hand. Now she looked like a vampire.

'Are you alright? Is there anything ...'

'It'll pass,' she croaked.

Lili had no idea what she was talking about.

'Everything passes.'

The smeared face turned back towards the opposite shore veiled in mist. The violet eyes seemed to be staring beyond the villages and towns, hills and rivers, forests and valleys to a place lost in the far distance.

'The night has twelve hours. And then it is day,' the singer half-sang into the autumnal air.

VII

Winter returned. The flurry of visitors ended.

Contrary to all his expectations Max started looking forward to Lili's visits as much as Hiddigeigei. On gloomy afternoons they sat together in his study looking out at the grey lake.

The black tomcat lay asleep on Lili's lap. He had placed his once injured paw between the thumb and forefinger of Lili's left hand; his other paw seemed suspended in mid-air. Lili's right arm had fallen lifelessly into the lap of her blue skirt.

She seemed asleep too; her eyelashes were closed tight and her lips slightly parted. Max observed Lili's tilted head. Perhaps it was a trick of the light or the reflection of Hiddigeigei's coat, but her hair, tied back by a blue ribbon, seemed to have turned a darker shade. He admired her high forehead and cheek-bones, lit by the pale yellow flood of winter sunshine suddenly entering the room, and the arches of her resolute eyebrows.

'Max,'

He started slightly as she looked up, revealing beautiful green eyes, a delicate, slightly up-turned nose and full lips widening in a smile.

'Yes, Lili?'

'Why do you have so many books?'

'They're my friends, Lili.'

'It must be nice to have so many friends.'

Max felt the sadness in Lili's voice.

'Would you like me to tell you one of their stories?'

Lili nodded.

Max smiled. He stepped towards his library and slowly scanned a row of books, since returned to immaculate alphabetical order. His fingers swept across the shelf before coming to rest on a volume; he hesitated before removing it. He stood for a moment, carefully examining its cover.

'What is it?' asked Lili.

'It's called the Legend of the Lake. I've just realised, I haven't read this since I was a boy. Would you like –'

'Oh, yes. Please read it to me!'

Max turned to the opening page and began reading the tale in his melodious baritone.

'A storm speaks angrily with the trees. The sound of a horse's hooves can be heard in the forest. A rider is trying to find his way out on the snow-covered path ...'

Lili sat stroking Hiddigeigei to the rhythm of the story. The reader was quickly absorbed in the legend and oblivious to his surroundings.

The words seemed strangely familiar to her. There was something about the scene of snow and storm, the darkness of the fir trees in the forest; something about the tale of a rider reaching the forest's edge.

'... Now he gallops through a valley, sweating as he races through the fallen snow, under a pale winter sun. He wants to reach the other side of the lake before nightfall.'

With a sudden jolt which sent Hiddigcigei scuttling for cover Lili sat upright in her chair.

'How is he going to cross the lake?'

'He'll take the ferry, Lili.'

Max's lips were still moving; yet it was her father answering her from across the years.

'Like our ferry, Papa?'

'No, Lili. Long ago a ferryman rowed a small boat across the lake.'

'Like your boat?'

'Yes ... a bit ...'

'That takes a long time.'

She was there, sitting on his shoulders again, kicking her little feet against his chest, spurring him on. The night was cold. Fresh snow lay on the ground. It was late; they had just left the warm glow of the Bellevue to walk home.

Max had half-turned away from her. He was looking across the lake as though trying to spot the rider coming from the other shore.

'... The way is hard, over stones and through thick thorns. He goads on his horse. He can see the snow stretching like a desert from the distant mountain peaks ...'

Lili felt a sudden chill; it was the chill of that faraway night. She closed her eyes tightly to hold on to the inconstant scene.

Max's voice faded; her father's became stronger.

The rider digs in his heels. Dogs are barking. In the village he sees the light of a fire. A window opens.

"Good eve, fair maiden! Tell me, how far is the ride to the lake and the ferryman?"

The maiden stares at the rider, looks behind him at his path, and smiles.

"Good sir, both lake and ferry are whence you came. Truly, you and your horse would both be drenched through and through, were the lake not sealed with ice …"'

'Papa?'

'Yes, Lili?'

'Does the girl not believe him?'

'No, Lili … At first she thinks he's teasing her. She can't believe he's come the way he said. The ice is too thin.'

'How thin?'

'Oh, I'm not sure, Lili … perhaps a foot or so …'

Lili felt the warmth of his ear against her cheek.

'What happens next?' she whispered.

'The rider stares at his horse...'

'...The rider stares at his horse. He hears only the first few words. His hair stands on end; his heart beats wildly.'

Max's voice was gathering pace.

'Behind him he sees danger grinning at him through the gloom. In his mind's eye he sees the dreadful depths of the lake. Thundering in his ear the ice cracks; waves of cold sweat wrap around him as –'

Suddenly he faltered; the final, awful sentence was left hanging in the air.

There was silence.

Lost in memories unlocked by the words of the story, both story-teller and listener had, until this moment, been blind to the powerful emotions sweeping over the other.

A voice was calling Lili back to the house by the lake.

'Lili? … What's the matter?'

She buried her face in her hands.

'N-n-nothing. I've got to go home now,' she sobbed.

'Of course,' Max said sadly as he put his hand on Lili's shoulder and walked her to the door.

* * *

Lili stopped coming with milk for Hiddigeigei.

Max caught sight of her very occasionally in the street. She kept her head down when he waved. When being honest with himself, he knew that the young intruder had found a way into his heart.

1936

VIII

A train rattled through the peaceful countryside.

In a compartment two men sat next to each other. The only other passenger, a young girl on the seat opposite, had been sound asleep ever since they had boarded. Like a marionette with its strings cut, her arms dangled loosely by her side. Her fingertips all but swept the dusty floor of the carriage. With every jolt of the track her head lurched suddenly to one side, giving the alarming impression it was about to roll off her neck.

The younger of the two men, hatless and wearing only a thin jacket, had turned his back on his fellow passengers and was studying, from his window seat, the trees, fields and farmsteads as they flew past. Whenever the train raced through a deserted station, his head twisted to allow his eyes to fix on the name of the insignificant place. It was a futile task.

The man in the hat and overcoat had stretched his legs out like a barrier. His bored eyes followed the fitful course of an empty bottle as it travelled across the compartment. His sole interest seemed to be whether it would reach the other wall of the compartment and finally come to rest. But every time the train steered itself into a curve, the bottle hesitated, came to a momentary standstill and turned back on itself. It seemed destined to zigzag perpetually across the compartment as the train wound its way through one valley after another.

At some point the man in the hat tired of even this insipid diversion. With a stifled yawn he stood up, bent down and picked up the bottle. A sudden, noisy gush of air filled the compartment. He hurled the bottle with a groan through the open window.

The younger man saw the sun catch its flight. Sweeping his thick, black hair from his brow he turned towards his fellow passenger, slumped once more in his seat following his exertions, and gave him a look as if to say: What did you do that for?

His dark eyes moved anxiously from the man's outstretched legs to the girl's lifeless arms; from there they briefly settled on the window, now closed again, before fixing on the door of the compartment.

Then he leant over and whispered – though the girl was in such a deep sleep even the sudden loud screech of brakes didn't stir her –

'Excuse me, Konrad ... I need to ...'

The other man pulled in his long legs and stood up again with a look of mild irritation.

'Thanks,' said the dark-haired man, struggling to negotiate the contorted configuration of the girl's limbs. 'I won't be long.'

He pulled open the door of the compartment and staggered out into the corridor. Something made him cast a glance back over his shoulder.

'You're surely not going to follow me in there, are you?'

'I have my instructions, Herr Engeler.'

'Look, I've told you to call me Freddi ... What d'you think I'm going to do? Jump off a moving train?'

'It makes no difference, Herr ... Freddi.'

It was an option Freddi had considered, along with others. When his plain-clothes shadow was walking him through the busy streets of the city to the station he thought of shouting for help. But what good would that have done? Bystanders would simply have taken him for a common criminal. No one would have lifted a finger. In the train he also thought of pulling the emergency cord and making a dash for it. How far would he have got? His minder was sure to be armed.

Freddi attempted to close the toilet door. Something was blocking it. He looked down and saw a shoe.

'For Christ's sake, Konrad. I need a shit.'

The door eased into place.

'Don't lock it.'

Freddi thumped his fist in frustration against the wall. He attempted to take a few deep breaths to counter the onset of panic, but a pungent malodour caught in his throat and made him gag. He fell to his knees and vomited into the filthy bowl. An uneven stream of fear disappeared down the soiled pipe and back along the track.

He stood up and wiped his mouth. There was a tap at the door.

'Are you alright?'

'Wonderful, Konrad. What do you think?'

He didn't feel particularly bitter about his police escort, even though he was taking him to a place he had no wish to go. At least this one was a human being you could talk to – not like those bastards who had arrested and interrogated him.

He'd unfortunately fallen into the hands of the Swiss border police. The treatment they meted out to him struck him, a veteran of Gestapo prisons despite his youth, as strangely familiar. He was made to face the cold wall of his interrogation cell for hours on end. They abused him verbally. 'Communist spy', 'Jewish pig', 'Gypsy criminal', were some of the less demeaning insults to which he was subjected. He was forbidden any contact with the outside world – not that there was anyone who could have helped him anyway – and thrown into a cell with a prostitute and a violent drunk. There was only one wooden board to sleep on, the bare bulb shone all night and he was regularly hauled out for questioning.

During his last interrogation the police officer had bawled at him in his coarse dialect.

'Why have you come here? Why didn't you stay where you were?'

'I'm seeking political asylum.'

'That's what they all say. You've got no right to asylum here. You were arrested near the German border. That's where you came from, isn't it?'

'I had to leave.'

'Why? Things are going well over there. Why would anyone want to leave? What crime did you commit?'

'I'm not a criminal.'

'If you weren't a criminal, you wouldn't have to leave. If you were law abiding, you wouldn't have problems with the police. So why didn't you stay in Germany?'

Freddi remained silent.

'How much money have you got?'

'What's that got to do with it?'

'Answer the question!'

'Not much. About twenty Reichsmarks. I had to leave in a hurry.'

'So you've come to sponge off us. We don't appreciate leeches. Why should we have to provide bread for you?'

'I've no intention of sponging off others. I can earn my living.'

'Oh no, you don't! Why should you take a job from one of our own people? You'll be a burden. We're sick to death of all you beggars, swindlers and criminals taking us for a ride.'

'I'm not a beggar and I've never swindled anyone.'

'That's what you say. So why are you here?'

Freddi hesitated as he considered his next response.

'I thought your country had a long and noble tradition of welcoming victims of political persecution and giving them asylum.'

'Oh, you did, did you? … Show us the scars.'

'Scars? What scars?'

'If you've been tortured, you'll be able to show us your scars.'

'It doesn't work like that. You of all people know that.'

His interrogator turned puce with rage.

'Cut the fucking impudence! What crime did you commit?'

'I've already told you. I haven't committed any crime, unless having Jewish parents is considered a crime.'

Freddi knew immediately he'd made a big mistake.

'So you're a Jew, are you? Jews are cowards. Jews are only coming over here to make money. If they behaved decently there would be no need for them to leave.'

Freddi could see which way the wind was blowing.

'You belong back in Germany. And that's precisely where you're going. And don't fucking come back.'

* * *

The train slowed.

'We're here.'

From the expression on the policeman's face when he opened the toilet door, Freddi concluded he must have looked pretty dreadful.

'Where?' he asked.

'Our destination.'

'Not exactly a mine of information, are you? ... Don't tell me: "you're only following instructions".'

His minder attempted a smile.

'Let's go.'

The station was deserted. It was in the middle of nowhere. They left the platform and walked down a track. Freddi cleared his still stinging nostrils with a few draughts of country air.

They walked in silence for about fifteen minutes and reached a small village. There were a few houses and a restaurant.

'Can we go in and get something to eat?'

'Stop playing for time. It's no use.'

'I need something in my stomach ... for what's awaiting me.'

The policeman nodded his agreement.

The restaurant was empty apart from two old men sat in a corner. They didn't look up from their glass of beer and game of cards.

'Grüezi, Fräulein.'

'Grüezi, miteinand' ... What can I get you?'

Freddi only had a few coins in his trouser pocket. He took them out and placed them on the counter.

'What I can buy to eat for this?'

The barmaid looked him up and down. There was pity in her eyes. She must have known where he was going. Without saying a word, she went out into the kitchen and came back with cold sausage, bread and chocolate. She refused to take any money.

They left the restaurant. Freddi knew time was running out.

'Tell me, Konrad. Do you often bring people like me to the border? You saw the look in that barmaid's eyes ... You know it means death, don't you?'

'I'm only obeying – Look, Freddi. I'm sorry. You haven't given me any trouble, and I'm grateful for that. What else can I do? Put yourself in my shoes.'

'You can let me go,' said Freddi.

They were walking through fields. The sun was sinking quickly in the sky. The policeman stopped. He pointed ahead.

'This path leads through the woods to the border.'

Freddi felt his stomach turn. He decided to try a different tactic.

'Wait!' he said. 'I can't do it. I haven't the courage to go back there. You don't know what they'll do to me ... Perhaps it'd be better for me to end it all in those woods.'

His escort's mood changed.

'Don't fuck me about. You just walk through the woods and get yourself across the border. And don't ever think about coming back.'

Freddi realised that the policeman wanted to be rid of him as quickly as possible and with the minimum of fuss. There was no one around to make sure he'd carried out his orders to the letter. He didn't want any ugly scenes at the border itself. This was as far as he was going to take him. After a while he would leave, thinking his prisoner had crossed back over. And now Freddi had put the idea in his head, Konrad certainly wasn't going to come looking for him in the woods, just in case he did have to cut him down from a tree. He didn't want all the bother. It was getting late. All he wanted was to get back to his wife and kids and a good supper.

'Ok, Konrad. I'll do what you say.'

The policeman studied Freddi with an anxious expression.

'Straight through the woods ... and don't fuck about.'

Freddi walked away from him without looking back and followed the path towards the woods as instructed. A signpost indicated the border was not far. He felt a chill as he entered the woods. Darkness was falling. Freddi reckoned it must have been eight o'clock when he set off on his own. Once in the coolness of the forest he waited and waited. When would Konrad decide he'd had enough?

A nightjar's churring came from the clearing.

A good hour must have passed. Freddi crawled out of the forest on all fours. The grass was high, and it was hard to see anything. It was so dark by now, it would be almost impossible for the policeman to find him again – if he could be bothered.

The stars came out. His heart stopped thumping and he calmed down. In the distance a church clock struck ten.

He lay down in the grass and looked up at the stars. He remembered when he was a student in Tübingen. He and several fellow students had gone hiking and camping in the Black Forest. In the evening they drank and talked by the camp fire. Intoxicated by wine and conversation they lay on their backs and looked with awe at the night sky.

Freddi studied the constellations. He had no idea where he was on Earth but he could locate his position in the universe against those bright sprinklings of light.

A shooting star flared and quickly faded.

Mortal danger heightened the beauty of the moment. He felt as though he was hovering above the dampening grass.

He was lost and alone; an orphan in this vast universe.

He thought of his parents. They had taken a swift exit from this vale of tears. They couldn't understand what was happening. His father had fought for the Kaiser in the trenches alongside friends and neighbours. His mother wept when he abdicated and kept a photograph edged in black ribbon. They even converted to Christianity and worshipped in the Lutheran church in their home town. Then the rocks started flying through the windows of their jeweller's shop. 'It's just a few hotheads,' his father said to his anxious mother. But it wasn't. Their shop was daubed in insults, lifelong clients stopped coming, and they were shunned in the streets of their home town.

Freddi had no family; he was an only child. And now he had no country too. They had stripped him even of that tenuous sense of belonging.

He had to make a decision. He couldn't lie there all night. But he had no idea where he was. If he wasn't careful, he could end up walking back to the border.

He thought about making his way to the railway station. Not to get on a train. The policeman might have been there waiting for his train home. But just to get his bearings. He wandered around on several paths but couldn't find it. Nor could he see any signposts. Then he came across a country road. He followed it to a junction.

There was an inn. In front of it was one solitary car. Freddi considered waiting for its owner to come out of the inn. He planned to set off in the direction the car left.

Shit! What if he's heading back to the border, he thought.

It was too dark to see the number plate.

A wave of despair overcame him. He was lost in the middle of nowhere with only a few coins in his pocket. The hounds of the Swiss border police were on his heels, and the bloodthirsty henchmen of the Gestapo lay ahead in wait. There was no escape whichever path he chose. He might as well lie down in a ditch and die.

He had no-one. If it hadn't been for Harry...

'Come on, Freddi. Never say die. Remember where our strength lies.'

That was one of the things Harry used to say to him.

Freddi smiled and hauled himself back on to his weary feet.

He searched for signposts. The moon now came out from behind the clouds to assist him.

At last he found one. The lettering was faded and it was difficult to see by the weak moonlight, but he could just about make out the place.

Sankt Gallen.

He jumped for joy when he saw the name. Apart from giving him encouragement, Harry had made sure Freddi memorised the address of a safe house in the town.

He ran off along the road in the direction it was pointing. Every time he saw the lights of an approaching car or motorcycle he dived for cover in ditches or behind piles of manure.

It took all night to get there. He entered the deserted town before first light and found the safe house.

Freddi knocked. Through the crack of the open door a sleepy voice asked what he wanted.

'Oskar sent me,' he answered.
'Come on in.'

IX

'What exactly do you get up to down there?'

Max was caught off guard by the question. 'What do you mean?' he stammered.

'In that cellar of yours?'

He decided there wasn't any point in trying to hide his activities from his young house guest any longer. Given his situation, Freddi wasn't about to be leaving in a hurry. It was a matter of time before he worked out what was going on.

Max went over to his desk, unlocked a drawer and took out one of the carefully crafted appeals to the somnolent population across the water he had recently run off on his temperamental printing press.

'Here, take a look.'

Freddi began reading. He stroked his chin earnestly.

'It starts well, Max. I like the title. *The Voice of the German People!* That's nice. An exclamation mark ...

Hitler must fall if Germany is to live! Good ... another exclamation mark ... in case we missed the first.'

The writer of international renown was starting to feel like a novice submitting his first manuscript to a hard-nosed publisher.

Freddi read on. After a few moments he glanced up quickly to look at Max with a frown before concentrating again on the page in front of him.

'I dunno, Max. I'm probably not really qualified to comment, but ...'

Freddi paused. He was scratching the back of his neck. This wasn't exactly the reaction Max was hoping for, given the hours he'd spent drafting and redrafting the text.

'I think – and it is just my opinion, of course – that there may be too many, erm, too many ...'

What? thought Max. Too many literary allusions? Too many flourishes? Perhaps he had gone a bit over the top with the rhetoric.

'... too many words. That's it – too many words.'

Too many words indeed! Max was starting to feel hostility towards his young critic coursing through his veins. Didn't he know who he was? His books had struck a chord with a whole generation and brought him fame at home and abroad. Who did this cocky undergraduate think he was?

'And I think on occasions, well perhaps a bit more than that, you also tend to use – how shall I put it? – the *wrong* words.'

Max was about to explode when he noticed Freddi grinning from ear to ear.

Writer and critic were joined in laughter.

'I'm sorry, Max,' Freddi said, wiping away tears of joy. 'I couldn't resist it. Harry told me I should wind you up, and I'm afraid you presented me with a golden opportunity.'

'I might've known he'd be behind it,' said Max with begrudging appreciation.

'So are you going to let me help you?'

Max frowned.

'You know the situation, Freddi. If they find out you've been involved in anything like this, they'll throw you out instantly.'

'C'mon, Max. How're they going to know I've been polishing up your texts?'

Max knew it wouldn't stop there. He'd already worked out that his young friend possessed that rare combination of intellectual sharpness and a complete disdain for danger.

* * *

Weeks had passed since he'd taken in his latest guest. Max had quite got used to being alone again when out of the blue a letter arrived from Denmark. Harry was asking for his help. One of his comrades, a young man called Freddi Engeler, had fallen foul of the Gestapo. After spending several hellish months of 're-education' in a Nazi jail, he'd been released under the threat that no mercy would be shown if he ever dared to tread on German soil again. Fearing for his future safety Freddi fled over the border under the cover of darkness only to fall into the hands of the Swiss police.

Max smiled at the characteristic flourish with which Harry's letter ended: Remember where our strength lies, Max. Solidarity!

He imagined Harry's fist punching the air defiantly.

Max missed his old friend. He smiled at what Harry had once told him: 'It's a crime to write about trees in times like these.'

He'd be pleased to know that the rickety old printing press in his cellar hadn't churned out nature poems for ages.

Harry gave him a contact name, another link in the chain of solidarity they knew as 'Oskar's transport column'.

Freddi had been located.

Using his influence as an internationally famous author Max was able to convince the authorities that he'd provide for the emigrant's welfare at no cost to the state, vouch for his good behaviour and guarantee that his guest would stay clear of any political activity likely to jeopardise the neutrality of the country. Notwithstanding all these efforts, Freddi was only granted temporary residence which had to be renewed and approved by the local police every three months. The expectation was that at some point he would, like so many other emigrants, leave the country for a more permanent refuge.

For his part Freddi had no desire to renew his acquaintanceship with the Swiss police.

'They were perfectly happy to send me back into the hands of Hitler's executioners.' Freddi swallowed hard as though struggling to overpower a painful memory rising through his throat like nausea.

'You know Max, while in prison we got to hear about what happened to some of those arrested at the same time we were. They had been condemned to death by the Nazis on completely trumped-up charges.'

Max had lately heard enough from reliable sources to need no convincing of the abuses taking place in the country of his birth.

'Their preferred method is the guillotine ... But for some reason on this occasion the executioners decided otherwise. When our comrades entered the room they were met by the sight of a bench and block. Their executioner was waiting for them with an axe in –'

Freddi stopped.

Max suspected that the scene was now being played out behind those impenetrable dark eyes. Involuntarily anticipating what he was about to say, Freddi's hand swept his thick hair off his forehead.

'The prisoners' heads had been shaved – women too –, and their necks were freed from their clothing. They were paraded before their accusers and told their appeal for clemency had been rejected ... The first victim was seized and hauled over to the block. With a single blow of the axe she was beheaded.'

An oppressive chill suddenly filled the room. Freddi's eyes were searching for an escape from the monstrous phantoms of this terrifying nightmare. Max wanted to go and put his arm around the young man's shoulders but could only sit there and impotently watch the pitiless struggle Freddi was waging with his memories.

Several times it seemed as though he was on the brink of taking up his story once more, only for the words to dry on his lips.

Max stood up. The everyday sound of water being poured into a glass brought his young friend back to the present moment.

'Here … have a drink.'

'I'm alright …It's just …'

'Look Freddi, you don't have to tell me all this.'

'But I do, Max. I want you to know my debt to you. I want you to know the fate you saved me from.'

Max looked out of his study window. A ferry making the crossing slowly shrank from view. The ease with which it transported its passengers from one shore to another, from one country to another, struck Max as strangely incongruous at that moment.

Freddi took a sip of water and cleared his throat. He put down the glass with a shaking hand.

'Two other comrades were beheaded in the same fashion, with one blow from the axe. But then the fourth was forced onto the block. The executioner had been drinking large quantities of schnapps along with his murderous henchmen … his blow missed the neck. The axe was buried in his victim's skull. The drunken butcher tore it out and raised the axe again. Once more he missed his intended target. Only on the third attempt did the blade divide the head from the rest of the body.'

Freddi put his hand on Max's shoulder.

'So you see, Max, when the border police said they were sending me back, I knew what was awaiting me.'

* * *

Max tapped away on the battered typewriter on his study desk. Freddi was washing. He had become a tireless assistant in the work of 'Oskar's transport column'. They had to exercise extreme caution, and Freddi had to keep his head down. Fortunately for them Vogelsang wasn't the most conscientious of border guards. They soon worked out his routine which involved most evenings spent at the Bellevue drinking and playing cards.

Max eased his latest effort from the typewriter and recited it, unwittingly adopting the mannerisms of his tree-climbing friend.

> *What is to be done?*
> *Trades unionists arrested and imprisoned!*
> *What is to be done?*
> *Comrades beaten up in the streets!*
> *What is to be done?*
> *Workers' newspapers closed down!*
> *What is to be done?*
> *Brothers and sisters tortured and killed!*
> *Wake up, fellow Germans, before it's too late!'*

'Sounds fine, Max.' Freddi had been standing behind him listening. A towel covered his bare shoulders, and he was tightening a thick leather belt around his waist. 'I'm sure Harry'd approve. You're getting pretty good at this propaganda lark.'

'We need to get it printed and take it across. There's been a call from grandmother,' said Max.

The two men worked through the night rolling sheet after sheet off the press. They bound the pages into books taken from Max's extensive shelves and eviscerated to provide the necessary camouflage. Under the cover of darkness they loaded the boxes, with fishing rods and tackle, onto the motorboat Max had acquired for transporting the material across the lake.

Before day broke, they set off.

Mid-lake they met up with fishermen from the other side.

'Heil Hitler!' came the greeting from the German boat.

'And a very good morning to you too,' was the sarcastic riposte.

'So what've you got for us today?'

'Oh, some Goethe and Schiller ... Looks tasty – food for those in desperate need of enlightenment.'

'Let's be having it then.'

The exchange was made for trout, whitefish and zander, with an eel thrown in for good measure.

As the fishermen were lifting the boxes into their boat, one of them called out to Max and Freddi.

'Hey, have you heard the latest?'

There were grins of anticipation from the German boat. Max and Freddi glanced at each other.

'Don't worry ... Even the Gestapo don't have fish for spies.'

'Slimy eels they'd be.'

Nevertheless, a reflex instinct for self-preservation made the would-be joke-teller cast a nervous look over his shoulder before launching into his story.

'Hitler's driving in the countryside with his chauffeur. Suddenly there's a screech of brakes and splat! They've hit a hen. Who's going to tell the farmer? "Leave it to me. I'm the Führer. The farmer will understand," Hitler says generously to the chauffeur. No sooner said than done. Hitler disappears into the farmyard and returns breathless and running after a couple of minutes. He's got a black eye, a bloody nose and he's rubbing his arse. "Shit!" he cries, "get me out of here quick!" They drive on a while. Suddenly there's a screech of brakes. Splat. They've run over a pig. Hitler looks at his chauffeur and says: "I'm fucked if I'm going again ...Your turn." The chauffeur goes to the farmyard. Hitler waits ... ten minutes ... thirty minutes ... After an hour, the chauffeur returns singing, beaming with joy, his pockets full of money and a fat ham under his arm. "My God," shouts Hitler, "What did you say to him?" The chauffeur answers: "Heil Hitler! The pig's dead.'"

The lake echoed with laughter. An ancient fisherman smiled a toothless grin.

'I've got one too,' Freddi revealed.

Max admired the confident ease with which his young friend spoke to these storm-hardened smugglers.

'Go on, then! What're you waiting for?'

The fishermen ignored the crates of fish and books. Freddi smiled.

'The Führer was making his first flight in an airplane and was very nervous. So nervous, he was about to shit himself.'

He looked around briefly. He was surrounded by grins of anticipation. They hadn't heard it.

'There's no toilet on the plane. Fuck me, he says to himself. What am I going to do now? He looks around in blind panic – there's nowhere he can go ... Then he sees his hat. In his desperation he shits in it and tosses it out of the window. The plane lands. Everyone on the ground is singing and dancing and cheering. Hitler's puzzled. He sends one of his men to find out why they're all celebrating. "What's going on?" his lackey asks someone in the crowd. "Haven't you heard?" comes the reply. "Hitler's dead. We've found his hat … and all that's left of him is inside it.'"

*   *   *

On the journey back home the refreshing breeze blew tears of joy across Max's cheeks as he relived the punch-lines of the jokes.

He looked across to Freddi; he was pushing the bouncing motor boat to the limits of its capabilities. Max felt alive in his company. His heart swelled with pride at the thought that Germany's great writers were the cover, literally, for hundreds of forbidden propaganda leaflets.

They entered the small harbour.

'An impressive catch once more, Meyer.'

It was Vogelsang the border guard, waiting and watching as they landed in the small harbour.

'Remember to leave some in the lake for me. I've got a wife and two kids to feed.'

'Ah, Grüß Gott, Vogelsang. Would you care for a nice fat trout for yourself and the family?'

'Merci vielmol. I don't mind if I do.'

Freddi handed Vogelsang the biggest fish he could find before leaving the scene weighed down with rods and tackle.

'How's that lovely daughter of yours, by the way?' asked Max.

'Lili? ... Oh, she's fine.'

'It's been a long time since I've seen her.'

Vogelsang cleared his throat.

'She's very busy working at the Bellevue helping her mother ... and what with her school work too.'

It was only half the truth.

'Well, tell her Hiddigeigei misses her,' said Max, also telling a half-truth.

There was an awkward silence between the two men.

'Well, I'd better be getting along now, Meyer. Thanks again for the trout.'

X

'Lili! Lili, where are you?'

'Fräulein!'

'Just a minute ... Where is that girl? Otto, have you seen –?'

'Mama?'

'There you are! What's happened to the felchen for table sixteen?

'It's coming.'

'Well, get a move on. They've been waiting for over half-an-hour.'

'Anna, can we get four more of the same over here, please?'

Lili turned with a sigh towards the kitchen; her notepad was swinging from the cord around her waist. The familiar sound of folk music accompanying the traditional fare swelled at that moment.

'Everything alright, Lili?'

'Fine, Herr Gruber,' Lili said to the asthmatic landlord who was standing by the door and wiping the sweat from his face with a grey dish cloth. 'Why is it so busy this evening?'

'They've come to listen to (wheeze) the funeral. Good for business, (wheeze) a funeral.'

'Funeral? Who's died?'

'Food for table sixteen.'

Lili took delivery of the plates of fish and set off on her zigzag course through the crowded restaurant.

'No one we know, Lili. A man called (wheeze) Gustloff. Wilhelm (wheeze) Gustloff,' Gruber answered behind her. 'It'll be on in a minute.'

Lili stopped off at her father's table.

'Papa?'

'That's good timing, Lili. Same again here.'

'Papa, who's Wilhelm Gustloff?'

Her father's eyes narrowed.

'Be a good girl and go and get our drinks.'

On her way back to the kitchen she scanned the room again: still no sign.

There again, he only ever showed up when it was quiet, and this evening was busier than she could remember. He must have been an important man, this Gustloff.

* * *

At first she hadn't been aware of the latest visitor to the house by the lake. So many had come and gone in the last two years that she assumed this one too would only tarry a while before moving on.

Months passed. Now that his presence seemed more permanent her interest in the young, dark-haired stranger grew. At first he hardly stepped out of the house, but now he came with greater regularity to the Bellevue to drink a cup of coffee and bury his head in a book. When he read, his thick black hair fell over his eyes; occasionally he would quickly sweep it aside.

He ordered his coffee from her as though he had no right to do so and was causing her inconvenience. When she stood close to him to take his order, Lili noticed scarring on his brown face.

If the restaurant was deserted he stayed longer, reading and occasionally scribbling something into a small black notebook. Whenever Lili had nothing to do she spied on him from behind the kitchen door. Occasionally he looked up, and his dark brown eyes caught her watching him. She then quickly busied herself with some meaningless task, and he would smile to himself.

*　　*　　*

The accordion on the radio broke off in mid-chord.

A chill filled the restaurant. A grim presence plunged the noisy room into silence. The music turned solemn. It was music for a funeral, although no one there knew the deceased in person.

A disembodied voice started speaking from high up in the corner of the room.

And so, following the long journey through the Reich, Wilhelm Gustloff, martyr to the cause in Switzerland, reaches his last resting place. The black uniformed soldiers of the

Führer's personal bodyguard stand to attention, a testament to the closeness of these two great men ...

The words filling the restaurant held menace within their grief. All eyes were fixed on the wooden box.

The world seemed to have stopped turning.

Lili looked at the people around her, at the villagers she'd known all her life. They were like puppets; their movements were unnatural, as though controlled by some invisible force.

... His journey is over. On a gun carriage illuminated by floodlights and surrounded by a forest of swastikas the coffin now rests, covered with the flag of the German Reich. A guard of honour stands immobile by the coffin ... The veiled widow of the leader, heinously cut down by the treacherous Jew is being led into the hall ...

A fist slammed in anger on to the table where a party of wealthy business men from the neighbouring town sat. Small, silver badges on their lapels twinkled in the dull light of the room.

Lili tried to avoid them. Of late she had started to feel uncomfortable about the compliments they paid her. She shuddered as she anticipated the unwelcome pats coming her way as she walked past them, swerving to avoid the sweaty stench of their corpulent bodies and the revolting vapour of beery cigar smoke leaving their fleshy, faces like mist lifting off a fetid bog.

There was always one who would try to look down her blouse when holding out the tip for her at the end of the evening, refusing for a few dreadful seconds to let it drop from his puffy fingers.

... A procession of officers bearing wreaths follows the loyal companion of the martyr. The highest in the Reich are among the four thousand mourners gathered here today. With those mourners we now observe respectful silence ...

The air crackled.

Through the silence an unuttered threat drove an icy fist into the hearts of all those assembled.

There was a cough, a shuffle and a curse aimed at the race whose member had committed the outrageous crime.

Normal life slowly returned. Chairs scraped and glasses clinked.

'Hey, Vogelsang!'

Lili quickly stepped behind the kitchen door as she saw the businessmen get up from their table.

'Where's that pretty daughter of yours? We need her for our game,' one of the toad-like men called out.

Lili sometimes helped in the skittle alley, though what was fun when she was a child had now become a chore. She tried to excuse herself when the players sought her out. They appealed to her father at his table in the corner.

'She's so quick-fingered,' croaked another toad with a phlegm-filled laugh.

Her father gestured with the back of his hand that he'd got the message. But he didn't look up from his cards; he was abandoning her to her fate. He was no longer her protector.

Gone were the days when he would hide her from her mother under the table where he was playing cards. It would be well past her bedtime. 'Lili? No, I haven't seen her,' he'd say, reaching his hand under the starched table-cloth to reveal to her the cards he'd been dealt. Suppressing a snigger, she'd knock on the underside of the table: three times, and hear a jangle of coins jumping up and down and three knocks back: all clear.

He was no longer her protector. There were forces in the world which exceeded his powers. She would have to look after herself.

'Don't you worry, Vogelsang ... We'll take very good care of her.'

'And there'll be a nice tip for her too if she's good.'

Two of the players smirked at each other.

'By the way, you are keeping a good watch on our borders, aren't you, Vogelsang? We don't want any water rats getting in.'

The players chortled.

'I hear there's a plague of them at the moment. The vermin are infiltrating from all directions.'

Without turning round her father gave his assurance.

'You've no need to worry on that account,' he said, pressing the words through gritted teeth.

Lili slipped quickly past the four businessmen, avoiding their leering gestures and bloated hands, and set up the skittles for the game. Fortunately, she spent most of the game at the other end of the alley picking up the downed skittles and returning the heavy balls. They had taken off their jackets and rolled up their shirt-sleeves in readiness for action. As the evening progressed and glass after glass had been emptied, their aim became more erratic. Her job was easier, as fewer of the heavy wooden skittles were sent reeling and spinning to the floor.

'He's done a good job over there, the Führer.'

'He's certainly sorted the unions out ... put the trouble makers in their place.'

'You mean Dachau?'

There were grunts of mocking laughter.

'Six. You need eight to level the scores,' called out the player scratching up the score in chalk.

'He's got rid of unemployment, cleared the scavengers and beggars off the streets ... Business is good.'

'And the Jewish pigs have stopped their squealing recently.'

'Oink, oink!'

'Fräulein! Another round of the same in here.'

A heavy black ball thudded into the tarpaulin.

'Shit!'

'Now, now. There's a young lady present.'

The men stopped and looked at Lili. She avoided their grotesque smiles and – with one hand clutching the neck of her blouse – bent down to pick up the ball, staring at her from eyeless sockets.

'You're losing your touch.'

'I wouldn't say that ... There's life in the old dog yet.'

There was a pause in the game as the drinks arrived.

'What do you think? Should we ask the Führer if he can spare the time to come over and sort out our own little pest problem?'

'We could certainly do with some assistance.'

A heavy black ball sent rolling down the wooden alley lurched drunkenly off course. There was a thin clatter.

'Three. Damn! I think you might be out of reach.'

'The only problem is: he's getting rid of his Jewish leeches, and where are they ending up?'

'And now one of the little bastards has seen off Gustloff.'

Their mood changed.

'It's intolerable.'

'He was a great man. One of us.'

'He'll be sorely missed.'

The four players were standing in a circle, staring into space; none stepped forward to release a ball.

'Something has to be done ... and soon.'

The last balls raced along the wooden channel back towards the players with a fury that made them leap to avoid serious injury to their ankles.

They looked up to see Lili, hands on hips, scowling back in their direction.

XI

Freddi sat impatiently on the quay side. The lake stretched out before him as smooth as a pebble. Sails danced in and out of each other like lovers; fishing boats bobbed slightly as the day warmed. And on the horizon a speck was gradually taking on the recognisable shape of a ferry.

He was inconspicuous among the army of travellers. Everyone was on the move. Freddi identified smiling honeymoon couples on their way to a romantic destination, families out for the day, businessmen striding purposefully to make their connections, and climbers with rucksacks, ropes and ice-picks back from conquering mountains.

He joined a group of cyclists pushing their heavily-laden bicycles up the gangplank.

As the ferry sailed out of the harbour Freddi watched the vivid colours of the shoreline being extinguished by a veil of soft blue. Houses slipped out of sight to be replaced by ploughed fields, meadows, orchards and forests. Beyond the forests were the foothills and, lit up by the sun, a glorious mountain range, glistening with glaciers of pure silver.

'Look! That's the Säntis. There's the Altmann. That's the Hoher Kasten and Rätikon. No, that one's the Hoher Kasten. And there's the Silvretta and Scesaplana.'

At his side a father was pointing out the peaks to his young child and reciting their magical names.

As one shoreline paled and vanished, the other came to life, unwrapped itself and filled with colour.

A heron rose far into the sky, vying for height with the strong shoulders of the Säntis.

Freddi turned around to look towards his destination. From midway across the lake, the brand new harbour building disguised itself as an ocean-going liner. Now he could make out a terrace with tables and umbrellas; people were eating and drinking as they watched the ships coming and going.

He wheeled his bike down the gangplank off the ferry onto the harbour front. In his left hand he held his new identity in the form of a Swiss passport, courtesy of Oskar. With a curt nod from the official he was on his way.

Max wasn't happy about him going, but Freddi had insisted. The network in southern Germany needed to be extended. He still had contacts with fellow students in Tübingen and was sure they could be brought on board. If nothing else, it would give him the chance to breathe in once more the atmosphere of the beautiful medieval market square and sit down under a willow tree by the river with a book of poetry and watch the punts go by, as he had often done in his undergraduate summer months.

The morning's promise had not disappointed. It was a fine day. The roads had been recently tarred, and the fields were in flower. There were plenty of other cyclists out for a ride; he exchanged friendly greetings with them. He was making such good progress that he decided to ride into Donaueschingen to drink at the Danube's spring.

The old town was decorated with swastikas hanging from all the rooftops and windows. People were going about their business or chatting to each other in the squares. After a short walk through cobbled streets full of new-found prosperity he left the bustling scene behind him.

Back on the open road he was joined by another cyclist.

'Grüß Gott! Where are you heading?'

'Grüß Gott! To Tübingen.'

'Do you mind if I ride along with you for a while?'

They passed the time of day as they cycled through the serene countryside.

'So, what are you planning to do in Tübingen?'

'Visit old university friends. I studied there.'

'Really? What did you study?'

'Philosophy and history.'

After a couple hours of gentle cycling they came to a crossroads.

'Well,' said his companion, 'I'm afraid this is where I have to say goodbye. It's been nice meeting you, my friend.'

Freddi watched him disappear into the distance.

Shortly afterwards he had a puncture. With the unscheduled stop in Donaueschingen, the unhurried ride in the afternoon spent more in conversation than in making progress, and now the puncture, Freddi realised he wasn't going to get to Tübingen before nightfall.

It was already getting dark, and he began wondering about where he was going to sleep. He saw a farmhouse and plucked up the courage to ask for a bed for the night in a barn. The farmer's wife eyed him suspiciously at first, but agreed when he told her he had ridden from the Swiss border. She showed him where he could lay out his sleeping-bag and to his surprise invited him to supper.

'Are you enjoying the food?' the woman asked with maternal concern.

Freddi looked appreciatively at the home-made bread, butter, jam and cheese spread out before him.

'Yes, very much. Thank you.'

'Help yourself to more. You must be hungry after a long day's ride. Fancy that – all the way from Switzerland.'

There was a look of admiration on her worn face as though he'd cycled all the way from China. He smiled modestly while his gaze scanned the homely dining room.

On the wall were photographs; Freddi assumed they were of her sons and daughters. The photograph of an older man edged in black ribbon reminded him of the photograph of the Kaiser his own mother kept in pride of place. But the man in the picture wasn't the Kaiser but a farmer; he concluded that the woman was a widow. Next to the deceased was a picture of Hitler, framed with cornflowers and poppies. His eyes must have lingered on it.

'What do you think of him? The Führer?'

Her question caught him off guard. Freddi hesitated. The enthusiasm in her voice made it obvious she was an admirer.

'Go on, young man. You can say what you really think.'

She stood awaiting his answer with his empty plate clasped between her hands. Freddi wiped his mouth on a napkin.

'I really don't know…'

The widow went over to the collection of photographs and took a couple off the wall, giving them a gentle polish with her sleeve.

'That's my boy Hans. He's in the labour force,' she said proudly.

Freddi looked at the young man carrying a spade over his shoulder. He had a determined look in his eyes.

'He's healthy and satisfied. He's learning discipline … The pay's not great, but at least he's got work …'

She handed him the other photograph.

'And this one is my other son, Martin. He's got an apprenticeship. Things are much better now. Everyone gets work. It's the same for the other lads around here. The main thing is that they don't waste themselves doing nothing. Young men need work, or else what is to become of them?'

Freddi nodded and handed back the photographs. She walked over to the wall and replaced them, standing for a moment with her back to him to admire them.

'The Führer's made all this possible,' she said in a whisper full of awe.

Freddi took a sip of freshly brewed coffee.

'So what do you do in Switzerland?' the widow asked brightly, breaking the ensuing silence.

'I'm a student.'

'Come on then! You're an intelligent lad. You can tell a simple soul like me if I'm wrong,' the mother said with a warm smile.

Freddi shuffled in his chair.

'What do they think of him over there?'

She was offering him a way out of his dilemma. Freddi cleared his throat.

'Different people think different things. Many admire what has happened here in recent years. Jobs. Prosperity … But some are worried about the number of weapons being produced. I suppose they think that it could lead to another war –'

'War?' she interrupted with dismay. 'What war? We don't want war. That's nonsense!'

Freddi held up his hands in apology for the offence he had given.

'It's an impression some have,' he said meekly.

'No, no. The Führer doesn't want war. He's for peace. Without a shadow of a doubt. He's always saying it.'

She seemed to want to reassure Freddi.

'We always listen to his speeches on the radio … No. He just wants to make sure Germany isn't weak again. Other countries have armies, why can't we?'

Freddi could see the mother was getting agitated.

'Some are afraid –'

'What? Afraid of us? Why? Do we want their land?'

Freddi shrugged his shoulders.

'Look at all the land we have here,' the mother said with a laugh.

He smiled and resolved to say nothing more which could upset this kindly widow who had welcomed him into her home.

'Nobody wants war, do they?'

* * *

Freddi slept unsoundly on his bed of straw. The conversation with the mother kept going around his head. What could anyone do or say to convince these people of the path they were on? It was as though they'd been hypnotised.

It was six o'clock when he rubbed the sleep out of his eyes. He wanted to get on his way, but the mother wouldn't let him go without breakfast. Over coffee she told Freddi about the hardships she'd endured. She spoke tearfully about the death of her husband, the time they had to sell livestock to survive, and the struggle to find jobs for her sons. Freddi could see how hard things had been for her.

'But now the worst is behind us. We can look forward to a brighter future,' she said.

He watched the good woman as she cleared away the breakfast. She reminded him of his own mother. Like all mothers she only wanted the best for her children. Wanting the best could make them blind.

Throughout their conversation the eyes of the Führer were looking down on them.

'That was delicious. Thank you again. You must let me give you something for the food and drink,' Freddi said as he got up to leave.

'I won't hear of it. It's been a pleasure welcoming you. You're a fine young man, I can see that.'

She had placed a wrinkled hand on his sleeveless arm.

'It's really beautiful here on your farm,' he said to hide his embarrassment.

'Yes, it's true. Our homeland is beautiful.'

She waited a moment before revealing thoughts that were still troubling her deep down.

'And all that talk about war. Forget it. You really don't need to be afraid. You can surely see that we're peace-loving people. The Führer wants peace. You will tell them that when you go back, won't you?'

* * *

Freddi rode away from the farm, giving the mother a last wave. He cycled hard all morning, dwelling on what she'd said. In the next small town he went into a cafe on a street corner and ordered coffee with rolls, butter and jam. The coffee was wonderful, the white bread smelt divine and there was plenty of jam. He felt as though he was in heaven.

An earlier customer had left a newspaper on the table next to his. The headline caught his eye. He read the article with growing excitement. The Führer was due to speak to a big crowd at the city hall in Stuttgart that evening. The speech was to be broadcast all over the country.

Freddi thought about his conversation with the mother. It was the radio that was hoodwinking people like her into believing in the good intentions of the murderous regime he'd had the misfortune to experience at first hand. She and her neighbours were simple folk who'd lived on the land for generations. What did they understand about the machinations of the powerful? He made up his mind. He was going to forego the pleasures of his old university town. He was heading for Stuttgart.

It was still some way to go, but a farm truck overtook him at a moderate speed and he was able to hitch a lift for a good part of the way. He arrived in the late afternoon to a city full of life. Trams rolled gently through the streets, and a blue sky spread out over the sea of houses. There were flags and banners of celebration hanging in every street.

Freddi cycled out a way into the suburbs and found a small ironmonger's. He bought an axe, wrapped it inside the newspaper and hid it inside his rucksack. He spent the rest of the afternoon in the park, dozing and sunbathing.

When the time came, he left his bike in the park and walked to the city hall. The front of the building was swarming with police but around the back, where the broadcast truck was parked, it was quiet. He followed the cables to a corner hidden from view.

From his location Freddi could see the party members parade in, dressed in their finery, looking as though the world belonged to them. The loudspeakers began to carry frenzied cries for the Führer.

There was no time to dwell on the scene as the Führer arrived.

The cables were there in front of him.

He opened his rucksack and unwrapped the newspaper. He held the axe in his hand.

Freddi thought of his comrades brutally beheaded by Hitler's henchmen. He waited for the speech to begin.

Hesitant and faltering at first, a crescendo was building.

'I have this to say to my enemies. Our struggle against –'

The loudspeakers hummed and buzzed.

There was silence.

Freddi imagined that mouth still moving and those arms gesticulating wildly. But there were no words.

It took some moments before anyone realised what had happened. Leaving the axe between the broken ends of the cables, Freddi beat a hasty retreat.

He slept in a forest that night and next day put as many miles as possible between himself and Stuttgart.

* * *

Max was tending to a disappointing proliferation of weeds in his vegetable plot when he heard the screech of brakes on the dusty path and the exaggerated tinkling of a bell. He looked up to see his permanent house guest, thick black hair flopping over his forehead, leaping off his saddle to dash through the garden gate.

'Ah, Freddi!' he called out in genuine joy and affection. 'Welcome back. Did you have a good trip?'

He put his soil-stained hand on the younger man's shoulder.

'Hello, Max. Great! Another triumph for 'Oskar's transport col –''

Max frowned in warning to his friend to curb his enthusiasm for a moment or two. You never knew who might be listening. Away from the inquisitive glare of the sun, Freddi could give full expression to his delight in the success of his latest venture.

'So, you took the words right out of his mouth,' Max announced with admiration once they were inside.

'How on earth did you know?'

With an ironic smile on his face, Max offered his young friend a drink.

'I was listening to the broadcast when it happened. I had a feeling you or 'Oskar' might have been involved. We need to get a leaflet across tonight … How does this sound to you?'

Max walked over and with a flourish pulled a sheet of paper from his typewriter.

We have taken the words out of the Führer's mouth.

We call upon all to resist this reign of terror.

We call upon all to resist this band of criminals leading our people to disaster.'

And as an afterthought he added:

'Remember where our strength lies. Solidarity!'

'I like it, Max.'

XII

All good gifts around us
Are sent from heav'n above,
Then thank the Lord, O thank the Lord
For-or-or all His love.

As the last chorus of the harvest hymn faded within
the walls of the simple village church, Lili became
aware of a mild commotion behind her. A latecomer
was squeezing past an elderly couple to find his place.
Lili looked over her shoulder and caught his eye; he
smiled back at her and apologetically took his seat.

'Turn round,' her mother whispered sternly. 'And
don't raise your eyebrows at me, young lady.'

Lili resigned herself to the next hour of her life
drifting by in a day-dream.

The congregation stood in prayer.

Our Father who art in heaven...

From her half-closed eye she saw her mother blindly tucking a strand of hair into her bun during the lugubrious Lord's Prayer.

Forgive us our trespasses, as we forgive those that trespass against us. And lead us not into temptation...

Lili felt a pang of guilt.

She'd wanted to go and explain to Max why she'd left so abruptly on that winter's afternoon. But her mother had expressly forbidden her from visiting the house by the lake.

'It's not right, Otto. What does he want? He's old enough to be her father,' she argued with no regard to Lili's presence.

Her father was in his usual armchair reading the newspaper. Lili, seated to his right hand, observed with amusement as he rolled his eyes as if to say 'here we go again' – a gesture hidden from her mother by the Sport's headlines.

'People will start to talk. She's reached that age ... For goodness sake. Stop sticking your head in the sand all the time. It's got to stop ... Otto!'

His name was uttered with a force which startled Lili and made her father drop his cover. It was as though he'd been reminded of some binding oath.

Lili saw the look of defeat now appearing on her father's face. A flash of hatred filled her eyes. How could she ever think of this dowdy woman – undoing her apron strings and smoothing her starched blouse in anticipation of imminent triumph – as her mother?

The stolen photograph flashed into her consciousness.

'Otto,' the voice had lost its harsh edge, but her expression retained its severity.

Lili felt her cheeks flush with resolution. She'd kept silent for too long; something in her snapped.

'You've got no right to tell me what to do … You're not –'

'Lili!'

The look on her father's face stopped her in her tracks. In that instant she knew the penny had dropped.

He must have discovered the photograph was missing from its secret hiding-place but until now had assumed Anna found and destroyed the last memento of his first love. Lili's insolence had now awoken him to the possibility of another explanation.

His eyes were daring her to utter another word.

In her fury Anna had failed to recognise the implications of Lili's outburst. She issued commandment upon commandment, prohibition after prohibition designed to break the spirit of rebellion Lili had been unwise enough to exhibit. Following every new restriction she sought her stunned husband's assent. She was not going to allow him to get away with playing the indulgent father any longer.

Her father was powerless to do other than acquiesce to the stringent demands. Lili's tearful eyes begged her natural ally to intervene.

'Papa, please…'

'You will do as your mother tells you,' he said pointedly.

She bowed her head in dismay. They had closed ranks against her. But there was worse to come.

'Now get out of my sight.'

Lili's heart sank like lead.

Never before had he banished her in such an implacable tone of voice.

'Yes, Papa.'

*   *   *

Her presence in church this morning was one of the many ways her mother had chosen to curb her restless spirit. Lili watched motes of dust circling in the shafts of light coming through the window announcing a bright, sunlit day and couldn't wait to get outside and away from her mother's triumphant power.

The pastor was moving towards the lectern.

'Brothers and sisters,' he began. 'Let us consider this morning a story from the Holy Scriptures. It is most appropriate for our harvest celebrations.'

The village pastor was elderly and was not without his critics among the congregation. He placed his spectacles carefully on the bridge of his nose and found his place in the large bible on the lectern in front of him.

Lili knew the story the pastor had begun to tell; they had been taught it at Sunday school. It was the story of Ruth, a young widow who left her own country to accompany her mother-in-law, Naomi, to Bethlehem.

She was already starting to lose interest, what with all those strange-sounding biblical names. Lili quickly stifled a yawn on catching her mother's censorious look.

The pastor continued the story. His words washed over Lili as she added up the numbers on the hymn-board by way of distraction.

'…Now Naomi begged Ruth to stay in Moab with her own family. What did she have to seek in a foreign land? There was much weeping and kissing, pleading and sadness; Naomi insisted that there was no future for a widowed stranger in her own land.'

The pastor looked up from the text. He removed his glasses as he addressed his congregation directly. Lili stirred slightly from her reverie.

'Can we imagine the pain of this separation – a separation which would last forever? But the story tells us that Ruth clave to Naomi and said…'

The pastor turned back to the page open on the lectern but appeared to have lost his place. Lili saw two of his harshest critics exchange a glance.

'Eureka! Here we are … And Ruth said: Do not ask me to leave you. Do not stop me from following you. For wherever you go, I will go; and wherever you live, I will live: your people shall be my people; and your God my God.'

The simple beauty of the words assailed Lili with the force of an as yet shapeless emotion. How could something written thousands of years ago have such power to move her? The unremarkable village church was suddenly transfigured by Ruth's expression of unconditional devotion.

Every word the pastor spoke increased the intensity of this raw feeling.

'Let us pause at this moment, brothers and sisters, and try and imagine what Ruth felt. She'd left everything behind her. Family, home, fatherland. What was she to do in this strange country she was about to enter? How did she feel as she crossed that frontier, leaving behind Moab, her homeland, never to return again? How was she ever going to provide for herself and her mother-in-law?'

The shapeless took on a shape and became compassion; what was without form entered a human body. That body was sitting behind her.

She looked down hard at her feet, resisting the force of those dark eyes willing her to meet his.

The pastor took up the story once more.

'Now Naomi had a wealthy relative, a man called Boaz. Boaz had many fields. So Ruth, the Moabitess, said to Naomi, 'Let me now go to the field and glean ears of corn.''

The preacher hesitated before asking: 'What was this she was minded to do?'

He peered over his glasses at his parishioners. To Lili's surprise they were all looking up at him in rapt attention. He answered his own question.

'Ruth was hoping that if she trailed the harvesters as they worked, she might be able to pick up the odd ear of corn here and there, particularly if the harvest workers were kind and did not force her away … Or worse. For she was a despised foreigner, a Moabitess, after all … Let us read on.'

To the relief of some of his listeners his penetrating gaze returned to the sacred text.

'And so she gleaned, from morning till evening, gathering the ears left behind by the harvesters. From his house Boaz saw all this, watching with growing admiration as the maiden patiently gathered a few ears of corn. He went and asked his foreman who the girl was.'

The pastor stopped. Lili was deaf to the shuffling and throat-clearing which marked this further interruption.

'What might he have done at this point? She was, you might say, from a legal point of view, trespassing on his land. She was, according to the letter of the law, stealing his property. But Boaz was a just man. He did not act merely by the letter of the law. He was not, if our brethren down the road will excuse the saying, more catholic than the pope himself.'

Well-meaning laughter greeted his joke. Lili too profited from the opportunity to clear the lump in her throat. She even dared a quick glance round.

Their eyes met.

Lili's heart thumped alarmingly at the desire in his eyes. She struggled to compose herself.

The pastor continued.

'Boaz spoke to Ruth, telling her that she was not to glean in any other field but his. She was to take refreshment from the water drawn by his workers, and he would protect her. Hearing these words, Ruth fell on her face and said ... 'Why have I found mercy in your sight that you would pay any heed to me, seeing I am a stranger.'

Waiting for the words to sink in, he appeared to be singling out individual members of his flock with his gaze.

Lili looked round again. The young man, a shock of black hair covering his eyes, was bowed in private prayer. She felt the sharp jab of her mother's elbow in her ribs.

'... seeing I am a stranger.'

The pastor's voice had fallen to a whisper and trembled as he moved towards the end of the story.

'And Boaz answered: I have seen everything you have done for your mother-in-law, and how you have left your father and mother, and the land of your birth, and you have come to a people you knew not before … May the Lord reward your works, the Lord God of Israel, under whose wings you have come to take refuge … And when Ruth rose again to glean, Boaz commanded his young men to let her glean among the sheaves also. And he told them to let handfuls fall for her and leave them, so she could glean these also.'

The conclusion followed quickly. The preacher had lost interest; the end of the story was a mere afterthought.

Instead of the customary shuffle of relief that it was all over, a hush descended on the congregation.

The concluding hymn played out. Lili hazarded one more backward glance.

But he had gone.

*   *   *

Weeks passed. Lili learnt the stranger's name.

In free moments she walked the path to the jetty passing the house by the lake and peered over the garden wall. There was no sign of life.

The days lost their heat, and the nights got longer. Occasionally a light burned in a room, and Lili would see Max taking a book off a shelf or sitting at his desk writing. The young stranger seemed to have disappeared like all the other guests.

Winter came and went. The house was deserted. It was as though its inhabitants had left for good.

* * *

Then she saw him again by the lake.

A warm late April day brought cyclists and hikers to seek refreshment in the shade of the restaurant garden. Lili was helping some of the lads she had known since childhood with the rowing boats, greatly in demand among the day-trippers.

At a long wooden table under a chestnut tree sat a group of uniformed Hitler youths. They had come across by ferry to cycle along the shoreline path or into the surrounding countryside. The local lads had seen them coming from a distance and heard them singing their marching songs as they rode along. They raised their eyes in silence to the skies. Gone were the days when they would openly taunt their neighbours from the north with their own rendition, before scattering in all directions:

Hail! Hail! Hail!

Hang the Führer on a nail.

Let him dangle for a bit,

Adolf Hitler's full of shit.

Now the warning was pressed through gritted teeth.

'Here come the 'roaches.'

The other guests in the garden got up one by one to leave as the singing and shouting became more raucous with the passing of the afternoon. The dark haired stranger was reading from a book at a table as he sipped occasionally from a glass.

The Hitler youths soon turned their attention to the village lads busying themselves at the side of the lake with the rowing boats. They started taunting.

'How are our Swiss cows today? Fucked any cows today?'

One went down on all fours.

'Moo … moo! Mooo! I'll take it up me! Moo!'

'Tell you what … We'll have your women, the good-looking ones, and you can keep the cows for yourselves.'

Coarse laughter filled the air.

'Nazi pigs,' uttered one of the lads under his breath.

'But seriously. Don't you cider-guzzlers want to be proper Germans?'

Lili looked at Freddi, who glanced up from his book at this last exchange. He'd turned pale with fright.

'Let's go rowing,' shouted one of the brown shirts.

'D'you want me to row you out?' asked Ueli, the son of farmer Ursprung, who tended the boats.

'I didn't know cows could row.'

Ueli smiled to himself.

Meanwhile the clouds had darkened in the west. The wind had picked up and was driving waves towards the shore. The lake was divided between an area of blackish green where the storm had broken, and an area of translucent turquoise still bathed in sunlight.

After some debate two of the Hitler youths decided to row out on the lake. The others, sleepy from cider and sun, lay in the grass or wandered off into the nearby bushes to relieve themselves. Lili saw two of the village lads wink at each other and then gesture to her as the Hitler youths got in the boat and started to row drunkenly away from the shoreline.

Stillness descended on the scene.

The impending storm had stuttered on its march across the lake. Only an occasional clink of a glass and a desultory snatch of conversation interrupted the oppressive silence.

Lili looked over to Freddi and smiled. Catching his eye, she invited him to observe the scene about to be played out before them. Intrigued he put down his book on his knee and squinted at the rowing boat swiftly putting distance between itself and land.

One of the rowers shouted back to the lads watching from the shore.

'This is how real Germans row, Swiss cows!'

The wind picked up again. The storm was gathering a head of steam. It would not be long before rain cascaded onto the lake.

In their drunken stupor the two Hitler youths in the boat had failed to notice the leak.

They were slowly sinking.

As the water started to rise above their ankles they panicked. They stood up unsteadily in the sinking boat, shouting and gesticulating and crying for help.

'What's that they're shouting?' asked Ueli. 'Sounds like hell? … hill? … hail? I know! It's Heil … Heil Hitler!'

The village lads wandered down to the side of the lake.

'Look! They're giving us the Hitler salute.'

In the distance the arms of the unfortunate rowers were outstretched, waving for help.

'Let's salute back.'

And the village lads stood in line, arms outstretched in the Hitler salute.

'Heil Hitler to you too,' they cried.

Every time there was a cry for help, it was echoed with a 'Heil to you, too' from the bank.

Lili looked over at Freddi. In his curiosity he had wandered down towards the edge of the lake to get a closer view of the scene. She saw tears of joy running down his cheeks and joined in with his laughter.

'Hey, you lot,' cried one of the village lads to the Hitler youths dozing under the chestnut tree.

'Your friends are saluting. Aren't you supposed to salute back?'

By this point the rowing boat was half-submerged. The cries for help became more desperate; the 'Heil Hitlers' more hilarious.

Realising what was happening, the other Hitler youths rushed to grab a boat and row out to their sinking comrades.

The storm broke.

Lili, Freddi and the village lads dived for cover.

They stood drenched in a barn. In the chaos and excitement her hand brushed his. As in a parched summer a mere spark ignites a flame which sweeps across the dry fields turning them bright orange, so the slightest of touches had set their hearts alight with the fire of passion.

That was the last they were to see of brown-shirted visitors.

* * *

From that drenched afternoon and the first accidental brush of hands grew a frivolous game of glances and touches.

Lili waited with a pounding heart for Freddi to come to the Bellevue for his cup of coffee. Some days he stayed away, and she felt an exquisite pain.

And he for his part sat reading his book; but the words were a jumble of crazy characters dancing around the page. How much longer before he dared raise his head above his book to see those wonderful green eyes? Who would believe a mere glance could wreak such havoc?

She came to take his order, standing so close he could breathe in her sweet scent. His forearm touched her black skirt and he held it there. She didn't withdraw; indeed, she seemed to shift slightly to maintain that fleeting contact.

And when Lili came to take his empty cup, a cup from which he had drained every drop over the last hour, she leant across him, and her crisp, white blouse brushed against his shoulder.

'Would you like anything else?'

'No, thank you. I must be going,' he answered with a lump in his throat.

Lili plucked up the courage to continue the conversation.

'Do you have to go to work?'

Freddi took a moment to consider his answer.

'No. I don't work.'

'Are you a student?' Lili glanced at the book in his hand.

'This? Oh, it's just something I found lying around on Max's desk – do you know Max, the writer? He lives in the big house ...'

Lili nodded quickly. She took a step back, afraid that he might hear her heart pounding in her chest.

'What is it?'

'Just some old love story ... and there's a cat called –'

'Hiddigeigei,' Lili exclaimed in delight.

Freddi's brow furrowed; he appeared to be working out a riddle. Then he smiled.

'So you were the little girl Max told me about who used to bring milk for his cat and who ... You're Lili, aren't you?'

Lili's heart skipped on hearing her name on his lips for the first time.

'I'm Freddi, by the way.'

I know your name, Lili thought. How often have I spoken it in my dreams?

'How is he?' she asked.

'Who? Max or Hiddigeigei?'

'Hiddigei ... Max, I mean.'

'As mischievous as ever and catching lots of mice. Hiddigeigei, that is.'

They both laughed.

'And Max?'

Freddi became pensive.

'I owe a lot to Max. He takes good care of me. You see, as a foreigner I'm only allowed to stay here under sufferance. Max has to pay the authorities a surety for me to stay and vouches for my good behaviour. I have to keep my head down. If I get into any sort of trouble, I'll be kicked out. Every three months I have to go to the county police to have my permit extended. They expect me to move on ... You wouldn't believe the countries I've made enquiries about.'

'Why can't you stay?' Lili asked, her voice failing to mask her disappointment.

'They can't stand the likes of us. You see, I too am ... well ... descended, you might say, from Ruth and Boaz...'

Lili blushed at the memory of the harvest service.

'... though my parents converted and worshipped in a Christian church like you. I was there that Sunday as a way of remembering them.'

'You have no family, then?'

Freddi shook his head sadly.

'Where will you go?'

'Who knows? Somewhere exotic. San Domingo, Australia, Shanghai. Or perhaps to South America ... Argentina, Ecuador or Brazil.'

'Rio de Janeiro is very beautiful,' Lili said with the conviction of one who had been there.

'In reality, I doubt I'll be going to any of those places. No one really wants us.'

Despite the melancholic look on his face, Lili struggled to suppress a sigh of relief at this unfortunate obstacle to Freddi's onward journey.

'So between you and me,' he said leaning towards her to betray the closely guarded secret, 'when I have to fill in the form saying where I'm going, I choose the most beautiful place I can think of, knowing I'll never get there.'

'Where's that?'

'Cuba.'

He stood up slowly to leave.

'You know, Lili, I'm sure he'd appreciate you bringing some fresh milk again.'

'Who? Max or Hiddigeigei,' Lili joked.

'All three of us.'

Freddi was looking into Lili's eyes with such intensity she thought she was going to faint.

* * *

A few days later Hiddigeigei rediscovered the forgotten delight of milk straight from the cow's udders. Lili stood at the door of the villa with the kettle held firmly between both hands.

'Ah, Lili. Grüß dich … How are you? I haven't seen you for ages.'

Max was wiping his hands on an inky rag. He greeted her like a long-lost friend.

'I know. I'm sorry. I've been busy …'

Lili felt her face burning. Max smiled.

'Yes, of course.'

Max stood awkwardly at the door. 'I'm sorry … Are you going to come in?'

She held out the kettle with the fresh milk. 'I've brought some milk for Hiddigeigei.'

'Yes, of course. He will be pleased.'

1938

XIII

SEEK OUT CAPTAIN REITLINGER SANKT
GALLEN STOP
SOLIDARITY! STOP

Max folded away the telegram and watched the
countryside flash past the window. An elderly lady sat
opposite had been observing him closely throughout
the journey. She seemed to read his thoughts.

'We're very fortunate where we live, don't you
think? Given what is happening elsewhere in the
world.'

Max smiled. What did she know? Did any of these
good citizens going about their daily business know
what he knew? Perhaps there was something in the air
causing unease.

*   *   *

Freddi returned from his last trip in March with dreadful tales to tell. He'd found himself in Vienna on the day the Germans entered Austria.

'It was like the dregs of humanity had been let out of the underworld,' he told Max, his eyes burning with anger.

'On every street corner you'd hear them like angry hornets shouting their 'Sssieg Heil! Sssieg Heil!' and singing their stupid 'Horst Wessel' song. Jews were being beaten up in every street. I saw elderly men and women being forced to scrub the pavements clean of anti-Nazi slogans. The SA gave them toothbrushes for the job ... They're expelling all their Jews.'

'All of them? How is that possible?'

Scrutinizing his friend with barely contained impatience Freddi asked: 'Ever heard of an SS officer called Eichmann?'

'Eichmann? I can't say I have.'

'Well, he's been put in charge of the forcible expulsion of Jews from what they're now calling the Ostmark. He's made his head office the Baron Rothschild Palais from where he's plundering our people of everything they have. Do you know that everything that's happened to the Jews over the last five years in Germany has taken a matter of weeks in Austria? Jews enter the building by one door, pass from one office to another, along one corridor after another, waiting, returning, waiting again. When they come out at the other end they've been stripped of everything. Their hard-won rights, their possessions. Their bank accounts have been plundered. Others are arrested, thrown into jail, mistreated appallingly and forced to sign a declaration that they'll leave the country and never return. If they dare disobey they're told they'll end up in a concentration camp.'

'Where are they all going?' asked Max, still struggling to take in the scale of events.

'Most are heading for the Swiss border. I came back on a train packed with hundreds of them. They were travelling with next to nothing. Even when leaving the country they aren't free from beatings and humiliation. I saw how some were forced into a compartment and told to sit upright with their hands on their knees looking into a light bulb. If they flinched, they got beaten. If they closed their eyes, they were whipped across the face. They had to say they were filthy Jewish pigs. If they refused, they were beaten until they did say it. Even if they said it, they were still beaten.'

Freddi paused. He was biting his lip so hard he was on the point of drawing blood.

'Do you believe in hell, Max?'

Heaven, hell. Max stopped believing in such things a long, long time before. He gave a slight shrug of his shoulders.

'Well, this was hell on earth. And it didn't stop when we reached the border. The Gestapo are dumping their Jews across the border, often secretly and by night, with the threat of death if they dare to return. The Swiss border guards catch them and force them back over.'

Max listened with a grave expression. Freddi's voice had sunk to a barely audible whisper.

'We were told about a woman who was forced at gunpoint by the Gestapo to wade in the dark through a river. She was petrified she would drown if she carried on, but would be shot if she stopped or turned back. Eventually she reached the Swiss side, shaking uncontrollably. The Gestapo officers were laughing. They knew very well that the water would only cover her knees. As soon as she arrived, a Swiss border guard grabbed her by the arm. 'Heil Hitler!' he shouted at her, 'Back you go!' He forced her screaming and kicking over the border, delivering her back into the hands of the Gestapo.'

'What happened to her?' asked Max, visibly shocked by what he was hearing.

'We don't know. Nothing good ... Another refugee, part of a small group which made it across, was threatened with expulsion. He pleaded with the border guard saying it would be better if they hanged themselves there and then since there was no future back in Germany. Do you know what he was told by the guard?'

Tears of rage filled Freddi's eyes.

"What a waste of rope that would be!"

The words of unimaginable cynicism echoed through the study. Freddi fell silent; his gaze fell to the floor. He was emotionally exhausted by the events he'd witnessed.

Max felt the need to say something to break the painful silence.

'We need to get a leaflet across.'

'A leaflet?'

Freddi glanced up. He was giving Max a searching look.

'It's got well beyond that.'

Max realised what was going through his young friend's mind.

'It looks like we'll have to expand our activities then,' he said, with a deep sense of foreboding.

* * *

Max quickened his step though the busy station of the pretty county town and walked down the Bahnhofstrasse. They'd sought Harry Haller's advice, and he came up with police captain Reitlinger as a man they might be able to do business with.

Oskar's transport column already had an extensive network. There were couriers who could provide refugees with detailed itineraries, sketches and photographs of quiet border crossings, and telephone numbers in case of emergency. There were guides who knew the steep mountain paths in the east. Smuggling was a traditional way of life for many in this poor region. Instead of smuggling coffee, sugar and alcohol, they'd be smuggling people.

Safe houses already existed for those who made it across – in recent years Harry's socialist friends had made extensive use of them when travelling illegally through Switzerland to reach Spain to fight for the Republic. And members of the wealthy Jewish community could be relied on to dig deep into their pockets to provide funds.

But there was a missing link in the chain – at the border itself. Without guards who were prepared to ignore the regulations and officials to provide legitimate documentation they knew there were few prospects of success. Reitlinger looked like being their one hope.

Max turned past the twin towers of the monastic church and walked through a cobbled market square. Contacts in the transport column spoke of Reitlinger's unconventional approach to policing, but some suspected he was corrupt and playing a double game with the Gestapo. The general feeling was that it was worth testing the water, given his connections on both sides of the border.

Reitlinger's first floor office was besieged by people when Max walked up the stairs. Some were standing; others, having grown weary, had slumped to the floor. He stepped carefully over their extended legs.

Eyes full of expectation looked up when he knocked.

'Fucking go away!' came the gruff reply from within.

Somewhat taken aback, Max knocked again and slowly opened the door. Whoever had uttered the unwelcoming words was concealed behind the outspread sheets of a newspaper. Its reader folded it noisily and cast it aside.

'Bloody shambles.'

A uniformed officer lifted himself out of his seat at an untidy desk; his hair was grey and precisely parted. Max noticed bits of a pistol lying on an oily rag.

'I thought I told you to –'

'Grüezi, Captain Reitlinger,' Max said quickly. 'My name is Maximilian Meyer. We have an appointment.'

'Oh. Well, come in and close the fucking door. Or they'll all try and get in.'

He waved his hand vaguely towards the stairs behind Max.

'It's a pleasure to meet you, Captain Reitlinger. I've heard so much about you.'

'Have you indeed?'

The phone on his desk burst into life. Reitlinger gestured his visitor to sit down. Max now identified the shrewd grey eyes of a man in his mid-forties; his thin lips were half-stretched in a grimace.

'Why can't you deal with it?' Reitlinger was shouting angrily into the black mouthpiece.

He looked across to Max.

'Will you excuse me briefly, Herr ... What was your name again?'

'Meyer. Maximilian Meyer.'

Captain Reitlinger left the office to a chorus of pleas from the waiting throng and shut the door behind him.

The office was sparse. There were the obligatory photograph of a plain looking woman on his desk, whom Max took to be his wife, and another of two even plainer looking young girls – no doubt his daughters.

One wall was covered with photographs of serious looking sportsmen lined up in two rows: one seated, one standing. The dates spanned at least a decade. He read through the names identifying the footballers. A thinner, serious looking Paul Reitlinger was never absent from his central position in the seated row. In one of the photographs he was holding a trophy.

'That was the 28-29 season when we won the title.'

Reitlinger was standing behind him.

'That's me. I was captain,' he added, proudly pointing at the player Max had already identified. 'We had a good team in those days. Not like now. I was just reading the report of the weekend's match when you knocked. They were an absolute shambles.'

Max studied the photograph once more, out of politeness.

'Is that why you're wearing a different jersey?' he asked naively.

Reitlinger failed to disguise a look of astonishment.

'You don't know a great deal about football, do you?' he smiled thinly. 'I was the goalkeeper. A goalkeeper is different from the other players. You have the freedom to use your hands. It's a strange position, really. You spend most of the match alone in your penalty area watching, waiting for the forwards to attack your goal. It's your job to keep them out. Everyone else can get away with making a mistake, but not the goalkeeper. If he fucks up, that's it. You can't relax for a moment, even if the play is in the other half of the field. To relax is fatal ... Some say you've got to be mad to play in goal.'

He pushed his dismembered pistol to one side and uncovered a small, silver case under a scattering of papers.

'Cigarette?'

Max declined.

'You don't mind if I...'

Reitlinger tapped his cigarette on the case before having second thoughts and putting it to one side.

'Anyway, I'm sure you didn't come here to talk about football – alas. So, what can I do for you, Herr Meyer?'

'I've come on behalf of Oskar's Transport Column. We specialise in transportation. Imports, exports.'

Reitlinger had picked up two bits of his pistol and was examining them carefully. He looked up briefly.

'And what do you transport exactly?'

'Stationery.'

The short-lived flicker of interest quickly faded. He put down his pistol and lit the cigarette, firmly pinched between his lips.

'So, what is it you want from me?'

He exhaled the first, invigorating cloud of smoke into the space between them.

'We're looking to expand our activities.' Max coughed. 'We need to diversify.'

'Away from stationery?' His interest flickered back into life. 'Go on.'

A thin wisp of smoke caught Reitlinger's eye; Max had the impression he was winking at him.

'We need someone we can rely on who has ... certain resources.'

'Resources?'

'Men on the ground, secure routes, safe storage, help with the documentation. In particular we need help getting the goods across the border.'

Max paused for a reaction.

'Tell me, Herr Meyer. What 'goods' are we talking about exactly?'

Max swallowed.

'People.'

'People?' echoed Reitlinger with raised eyebrows. 'What makes you think that I can be of assistance?'

Max decided it was time to stop beating around the bush.

'We have contacts in the transport column who've told us how helpful you were to them when they were trying to make their way to Spain. They spoke with gratitude of your leniency.'

Reitlinger's face darkened.

'Leniency? If the stupid fools wanted to get themselves maimed or killed fighting for some hopeless cause, who was I to stop them? I did nothing more than turn a blind eye.'

Nettled by the police captain's cynicism Max couldn't stop himself objecting: 'They thought it a cause worth fighting for,' he said firmly.

Reitlinger took another drag on his cigarette. He appeared mildly chastened.

'I couldn't care less about politics. Red, brown – it's all the same to me ... You know, we called them Spanish travellers. They entered illegally, and I was supposed to find their safe houses, close them down and send them back over the border. It was a futile task. They kept on coming. We worked closely with the Austrian and German authorities but it got to be like a triangular passing game we used to practise on the training ground: one country would pass its undesirables to the other, they kicked them on to the next, who booted them back to the first. But still they came. I could've arrested them, but what was the point? Why should we pay to keep them in prison at our expense? That was probably what some of the vagabonds wanted in any case – free board and lodging. So I let them go. Oh, I tried to dissuade them, the young idiots ... Spanish travellers, ha! It was far from a holiday. They'd go out as young men, strong, fit and with the world at their feet. And I'd see them return – if they returned – broken in mind and body, having lost limbs, shattered and fit for nothing.'

He paused before adding pointedly: 'So much for good causes.'

Max was just starting to think that Harry had played one of his pranks on him by suggesting that this cynical police captain could be of use when Reitlinger suddenly asked:

'How many are we talking about?'

Taken aback by the question Max fumbled nervously with the straps of his leather briefcase and took out two closely typed sheets of paper.

'You know, it's chaos on the borders,' Reitlinger said as he gestured for him to hand them over.

'So I've heard,' said Max.

'There's hearing and there's seeing ... So who are all these people you want to transport? More political opponents of the regime seeking asylum, I imagine.'

'Not exactly.'

Reitlinger looked up.

'No?'

'No. They're Jews.'

There was a pause.

'Jews? You want to transport Jews?'

The phone on Reitlinger's desk shattered the silence. He stubbed out his unfinished cigarette.

'You'll have to excuse me, Herr Meyer. I have to go. There's been an incident at the border.' And as an afterthought he added: 'Why don't you come along for the ride? See with your own eyes what we're having to deal with?'

*   *   *

Shortly into the journey Max wished he'd not been so willing to agree to the invitation. The Captain was putting his rusty old official car through its paces. At every bump in the road it would leap alarmingly into the air.

'Don't worry. It'll get us there,' he assured his nervous passenger. 'Might not get us back, though.'

Max clung on for dear life as Reitlinger swung the car round another hairpin bend. The warning of the skull-and-crossbones by the roadside clearly didn't apply to this policeman.

'It's tragic what's happening,' the Captain was saying.

Max assumed that he was talking about the awful refugee problem.

'There's just no creativity in the game anymore. It's all about 'struggle' and 'willpower'. It's sickening. Football has become the expression of national dominance and power. That's not sport ... Not as I know it... You ok there, Meyer?'

With the rest of his body paralysed in fear, Max could only respond with a jerk of his head.

'On my last trip over the border I went to see a match. You know, players in the Reich now greet each other with 'Heil Hitler' and shout 'Sieg Heil'. I saw kids in the park standing with outstretched arms. What's happened to the artistry? It's tragic.'

To Max's relief the road straightened.

'Vienna Sporting Club once had a coach. His name was Geyer. He said that in football the head comes first, then strength and stamina. It probably had to do with all that art and music they have there. Now, there was a team with flair.'

Although fully aware of his complete ignorance on the subject, Max felt it would be churlish not to make some contribution to the conversation.

'Tell me, Captain Reitlinger, what was the most memorable moment in your sporting career?'

'I thought you were never going to ask.'

Max sensed he was about to hear a well-worn anecdote. At least it might take his mind off being shaken within an inch of his life.

'It was in the season we won the title. It all came down to the last match and we needed a win to take the title from Grasshoppers. You were looking at the photograph of the team, remember?'

Max nodded.

'We scored an early goal, but Grasshoppers equalised before half-time. With just fifteen minutes to go we got back in front and it looked as though the title was ours. They won a corner. A high ball was not cleared properly by the defence and they equalised. Not only that – in the confusion I injured my shoulder badly and had to leave the field. Someone had to take my place in goal. It was Nemes, the outside-right.'

'Outside-right?' asked Max.

'An attacker. Plays on the right-hand side of the field... We thought he was the only one capable of taking over in goal. The last ten minutes looked hopeless – down a striker, with an inexperienced 'keeper, it looked like we'd had it.'

Reitlinger paused, as though to register any sign of enthusiasm in his passenger.

'Anyway, I managed to recover somewhat and came back on with my arm in a sling. My shoulder was still killing me, but at least I could make up the numbers. I took up a position on the right wing and made a couple of lumbering runs. Their defence decided that a 'keeper playing up front, with his arm in a sling, and one who didn't look as though he could run anyway, was not worth bothering about. What was the point in marking a half-invalid? They pressed forward in greater numbers looking to finish us off. Nemes managed to hold on to a cross, sent a swift kick over to me on the right where I threw off the sling and found myself in open space. A sprint, a shot and it was three-two. The title was ours. Their players and fans were beside themselves.'

Reitlinger was grinning.

'Is that what's meant by 'head first'?' asked Max with genuine amusement.

To his relief the car was drawing up at the border.

*   *   *

Any relief was short-lived. Two border policemen were carrying away a body wrapped in a canvas bag.

'Another?' Reitlinger asked casually of the border guard reporting to him.

'I'm afraid so Captain. When he was refused entry, he just pulled out a gun. It was over before we could do anything.'

In a guest house at the border, acting as a temporary holding room for recent arrivals, the two men sat and listened to the stories of terrified, desperate men and women. Freddi hadn't been exaggerating. They'd been through a living hell.

They were about to leave the scene when two children rushed up to them.

'Please help us,' pleaded a girl, aged about eleven. She was holding her younger brother by her hand, but he broke free, ran up to Reitlinger and clasped his arms firmly around his legs, refusing to be budged.

'You must help us. Please let us in!'

The two children had got separated from their parents during their attempt to flee. The children had no idea where they were. They had no possessions and no documents.

Brother and sister begged and begged to be let in; they were crying and screaming hysterically. Reitlinger was trying in vain to detach himself from the boy.

The regulations were clear. They had to be sent back.

Max looked across to the police captain and was surprised to see him close to tears.

* * *

In the car on the way back to Sankt Gallen Max broke the paralysing silence. The little boy and his sister had fallen asleep on top of each other on the back seat.

'Is there anything we can do to get these people to safety, Captain Reitlinger?'

This was a different Reitlinger sitting beside him. All trace of his earlier cynicism had gone.

'You can't imagine the stories I've been hearing on this drive back to town in recent weeks. I couldn't believe they were telling the truth. I convinced myself it was a ruse to get in. After all, their stories were more or less the same. I couldn't help suspecting that word had got round: if you say this, say that, they'll let you in. Then there was one. I can still remember his face.

He only spoke once during the whole journey. 'Tell me sir,' he said. 'How can you hit someone you don't even know with such unrestrained hatred and violence?' After that I had no more doubts.'

'Our contacts in the transport column have been telling us the same,' said Max, wondering whether he should repeat his request.

Reitlinger was silent. He seemed to be struggling with his thoughts as they drove along the deserted country road. Then he spoke.

'I've been thinking about what you said in my office earlier. You know, that bit about 'diversifying'.'

'Can you help us?' asked Max eagerly.

Reitlinger hesitated. 'Do you have any children, Meyer?'

'No,' answered Max.

Max was struggling to figure out what was going through Reitlinger's head at that moment. Had his slumbering conscience at last awoken, reinvigorated from a deep sleep?

'I'd like to help...'

'But?'

'There's a big problem with what you're asking. The refugees we saw today, these kids in the back, don't qualify as *political* refugees. They're Jews.'

He waited for the implication to sink in.

'Don't you see? There's a difference. Officially, they're fleeing for racial not political reasons. Whereas we've been able to allow in those claiming they were being politically persecuted, we're under orders to send back anyone entering on grounds of race. They've no right to asylum here. All Jews now have a J stamped in their passport. Anyone arriving with it has no chance.

Others haven't got any documents; they usually leave in such a rush. No passport means no entry.'

'But they've nowhere else to go,' Max urged. 'Every other escape route has been closed to them. No one wants them. We have to get them in. You heard what they've been through, and what awaits them if they're turned away.'

He knew he was making enormous demands on the Captain who was, after all, responsible for security at the border. It would no longer be a case of turning a blind eye as he'd done in the past; now he'd be taking an active role in breaching that very security. The inevitable discovery of his role would mean the end of his career and reputation.

Reitlinger stopped the car. He turned to face Max.

'You haven't got much time,' he said.

'Why, what's happening?'

'A few weeks ago I was called to a secret conference of police captains by our chief-of-police, Doctor Hardenschild. I'm sure you know of him.'

Ruthless and with National Socialist sympathies, Hardenschild's was a name Max had heard uttered with fear and loathing within the transport column. He had connections with powerful men in the press and the corridors of power and was proving himself to be the man with credentials when it came to getting rid of undesirables.

'He represents the official position, and that position is hardening,' Reitlinger continued.

'In what way?'

'In short, he wants to close the borders. To seal them hermetically.'

'How long have we got?'

'Weeks. Maybe a couple of months. Given our geographical situation it's not going to be that easy to seal all our borders quickly.'

'You mentioned documents. I assume we'll have to get forgeries.'

Reitlinger gave a dismissive wave of his hand.

'It'll take too long. There's a quicker way. There are plenty of long-term prisoners sitting in our jails who aren't about to be embarking on any foreign travel for the foreseeable future. Their passports could easily become available ... But there's a much more serious problem ...'

'Go on.'

'Personnel.'

'Personnel?'

'Hardenschild's going to increase the size of the border protection force and replace those he suspects of collaborating in human smuggling with men acting under his direct command who are fiercely loyal to him.'

'Hardenschild's hounds,' said Max.

'I see their reputation has spread ... Any of my men caught assisting refugees will be severely punished.'

Max hesitated. The question he was about to ask left behind a bitter taste in his mouth.

'How much do you need?'

A dark cloud passed across Reitlinger's grey eyes.

'How much? Are you suggesting I bribe my own border guards to let in refugees?' he said angrily.

'There are reports that some are doing it for financial gain. Twenty francs a head is the going rate,' Max defended himself weakly.

'I will not bribe my men or allow them to be bribed.'

Max had misjudged Reitlinger. He felt ashamed. 'I'm sorry. I'd never expect you to compromise your position.'

'Look, I'm their captain. I'm responsible for them. I know there are a few rotten apples in my corps; those who are doing it for money or who delight in tormenting the weak. But rest assured: I will stamp that out. Most of my men follow my orders in the way they've been trained. They're good, honest souls. Are they to blame for the cruelty of the times? Are they the ones deciding who gets let in and who is sent back? They have families to feed. Why should they risk their jobs? And am I any different from them? Who's going to feed me and my family if I lose my job?'

Max could find no words to say in response. He had underestimated Reitlinger. He'd expected to find a venal and lazy official who could be bought. He realised now that the mask he was wearing – and which on this afternoon's excursion he'd seen slip – was deliberate and necessary in allowing him to carry out his unofficial activities. Reitlinger wasn't going to work for them. He would carry on doing what he'd done in the past – extending help where he could to those who needed it: unaided, alone and, hopefully, undetected. Max had to respect his position.

'I'm sorry. I can see we're asking too much. If you could drop me at the station as soon as we get back to town, I'll be on my way.'

They passed the rest of the journey in silence. The children on the back seat slept on soundly.

'Thank you for your time, Captain Reitlinger,' said Max on opening his door to get out.

'Wait, Meyer. I've been thinking. Perhaps there is a way we could make this work. Hardenschild doesn't have any jurisdiction on my patch yet. I'll use my name and reputation to guarantee the security of the border in person. We'll keep his hounds at bay as long as we can so that my own men are sure they're not being spied on. I'll speak to those I trust the most, a select few. I'll tell them that I'm taking full responsibility for allowing the refugees in. All the paperwork will be in order. That should help them sleep more easily in their beds.'

He pressed his forefinger and thumb to his eyes. Some detail was still concerning him.

'We'll have to make it look like what's happening is the exception to the rule.'

'How are you going to do that?' asked Max.

'Don't you worry about that; I'll work something out. You just make sure your guides get them to the border crossings I give you.'

Reitlinger reached out his hand. 'It's been good doing business with you, Meyer.'

'Thank you for your help, Captain. And good luck.'

*　*　*

Captain Reitlinger was true to his word. The missing link in the chain was in place. Freddi was away for weeks at a time as a courier operating between Vienna, Innsbruck and various crossings on the Swiss border, providing desperate refugees with the details they needed and often escorting them to the border. On his return Max was curious to know in detail the part Reitlinger was playing.

'It's very strange, Max,' explained Freddi, clearly puzzled by the drama he'd seen played out at various theatres along the frontier. 'The first time it happened I couldn't quite believe what I was seeing. I arrived at a quiet crossing with a small group of refugees where we were met by a border guard who'd clearly been instructed to show no leniency.

'The regulations allow no exceptions,' he told us, quoting the letter of the law. 'Anyone not in possession of a visa is to be refused entry. He or she is to be returned forthwith to the German authorities.'

On hearing this, the refugees I was escorting naturally protested. They pleaded, they begged, they implored him to let them in. But the official wouldn't budge. The women and children in the group were weeping uncontrollably until eventually the guard began to relent.

'There is one possibility,' he told us. 'I have to make a telephone call to a certain Captain Reitlinger – he's the one in charge.'

We sat around and waited anxiously for him to arrive, refugees and border guard together. And here's the thing, Max. Whilst we're waiting, the guard says something very strange.

'Listen carefully to what I'm about to tell you,' he says. 'Don't be afraid if the captain draws his gun. He's not going to shoot you.'

Well, you can imagine how we looked at each other in utter panic and incomprehension.

'He might threaten you. But be ready. You need to say the right thing when he does."

Freddi paused.

'And what was the right thing to say?' asked Max, increasingly intrigued by what he was hearing.

'We had no idea.'

'Didn't the guard tell you, or at least give you a clue?'

'Absolutely not. He wouldn't say another word... Anyway, Reitlinger arrived in this old wreck of a car which is practically falling to pieces. He looked fed up and impatient and started haranguing the refugees.

'What the fuck's going on here,' he yelled at the border guard. 'Why have you pulled me away from important police work back in town?'

The border guard replied sheepishly: 'Captain, these refugees insist on staying. They say they can't go back.'

'Can't go back? Can't go back?' Reitlinger barked back at him. 'They have to. There's no way they can stay.'

I watched in horror as he took his gun out of its holster and started waving it angrily at the clouds. 'If you don't go back we'll have to shoot you.'

Well, at this point we're looking at each other in utter astonishment. And then we see the guard gesturing towards us. What in God's name are we supposed to say?

Finally one of the refugees speaks up: 'We'd rather stay here and be shot. Whether we die here or back there is all the same to us.'

Reitlinger stands there motionless. He slowly puts his gun back in its holster. 'In that case, you give me no choice. I suppose we'd better let you in.'

Upon which he signs the forms and drives away.'

Freddi stood shaking his head. He seemed at a loss to make sense of what he'd witnessed.

'You said that was what happened the first time you took refugees to the border. Was Reitlinger always there?' Max asked.

'Every time, without fail. And every time it was the same charade ... Well, once I'd been through it a few times, I realised that we just needed to get the refugees to act along. Since then it's gone like clockwork. By my reckoning he's let in close to a hundred.'

Max was smiling to himself.

'What do you make of him, Max? You've had dealings with him. What game's he playing?'

'Game? I'm not sure, Freddi. He used to be a good footballer – apparently he played in goal. And you know what they say: you've got to be a bit mad to be a 'keeper. Perhaps what you saw was just a bit of madness.'

Freddi was looking at Max with a mixture of astonishment and disbelief.

'Since when have you been interested in football?'

XIV

'What's happening? What's the latest?'

Vogelsang was breathless as he burst through the door of the restaurant. All the regulars were huddled around a large table in fixed concentration and appeared irritated by his noisy entrance.

'The Face is clear again, Otto,' announced Riemenschneider, the blacksmith.

Cigarettes lay half-smoked in ashtrays, glasses of beer stood untouched on mats, sausages part-gnawed on plates as all ears strained to hear the words crackling from the loudspeaker high up on the wall.

'There's been a break in the weather. The cloud's lifted,' added Müller.

'They're still alive then?' asked Otto.

'Yes, but for how long?' commented Ursprung, an incarnation of the prophet Jeremiah.

Gruber stood by the bar. He had been rotating the same glass in his towel for half an hour.

'Heckmair's leading. They've got (wheeze) as far as the Spider.'

'The Spider? In that case there's a good chance they'll make it this time,' said Otto.

'Not a hope!' scoffed Ursprung. 'Look what happened to all the others. To Sedlmayer and Mehringer. To Hinterstoisser and Kurz and all the other mad foreigners who think that they can conquer our mountain. The ogre's invincible.'

'You've got to admire their pluck,' argued Riemenschneider.

'Pluck? Stupidity more like. They must be mad.' And turning to the new arrival he said: 'What do you think, Otto? You're a man of the mountains.'

Otto shrugged his shoulders. He'd followed the reports of every recent attempt in the *Sport*. He knew all there was to know about the climb those young men were attempting, all the difficulties and potential dangers. His brother, a mountain guide, sighed at the sight of these impetuous young men trying to overcome the last great unconquered peak in the Alps. 'More work for the local gravediggers, I fear, Otto,' had been his laconic comment the last time they'd met.

'Why do they (wheeze) do it?' asked Gruber, still drying the same glass.

Looking at Gruber's flabby belly Otto was tempted to suggest that they had an intuition of the emasculated comfort and domestic drudgery awaiting them in later life.

'The Nazis will have a field day if they make it … Just imagine. Germans and Austrians climbing together; the New Reich conquering our mountain. What a triumph for the Anschluss. And where are our mountaineers? How come they always climb under fascist banners?' said Müller.

'Give it a rest, Karl. What's that got to do with it?' retorted Riemenschneider, always the first to weary of the councillor's politics.

'They're a long way from getting there yet,' Otto muttered to himself.

Cloud obscured the Face once more. The voice on the radio fell silent. Normal drinking, smoking and chatter resumed. Cigarettes and pipes were relit, glasses emptied and Gruber resumed his customary activities. Supplies were brought from the kitchen for the exhausted, hungry followers of the historical moment.

Lili popped her head out of the kitchen to ask her father how things were going. His gestured response suggested all was in the balance.

Then the weather cleared once more. They were reconnected to the outside world. The voice of the commentator returned.

Heckmair has reached a rocky outcrop in the higher snow field. The second party is moving more slowly, but with the same steadiness and caution as the first. Heckmair and Vörg are now at a height of eleven thousand eight hundred feet, by my reckoning. It is ten minutes past four … Alas, mist has descended again. We are left abandoned here with our fears and hopes …

'For God's sake, they'll never get to the top.'

'How much further have they got to go, Otto?'

'More than a thousand feet … Sounds like the weather's closing in on –'

An almighty crash exploded through the loudspeaker.

The listeners leaped from their seats.

'What the fuck was that?'

They looked at each other in horror.

The thunderous noise subsided.

Dear listeners! I am sure you heard that infernal sound. It is as though the clouds have been torn apart. It must be hitting the Face and the four climbers on it like a tidal wave. I am surrounded by confused cries of alarm. The whole breadth of the North Face has become one fearsome torrent. Water is pouring down the rocks in ten, twelve, fifteen feet wide columns of seething foam … Dear listeners, you have to be here to appreciate what I am seeing now. Over the Alpiglen I am beholding a marvellous rainbow – but who has eyes for its miraculous play of colour? Up there, two of the men must be on the snow slopes exposed to the full force of the flood pouring down upon them. How can they possibly hang on?

'That's it then,' said Ursprung, seeing his prophecy of doom fulfilled. 'Defeated by conditions once more… When will they ever learn? I just pray they get their bodies down more quickly this time.'

'I'm off,' Müller declared with resignation. 'We won't see the North Face conquered in our lifetime.'

'Hold on, Karl. I'm coming too. How much do I owe you, Erich?'

'Otto, are you staying for another and a game of cards?'

Otto nodded; he was never one to turn down beer and cards. The gloom quickly dissipated as Saturday evening habits eclipsed extraordinary events elsewhere. An accordion played folk music in the background.

Coins lay scattered on the table. Regular customers came in and ordered their evening meal.

Lili and her mother rushed around the tables serving food and drink.

Suddenly the accordion fell silent.

'Wait a minute … turn it up, Erich, will you?' Otto called out to the landlord, sensing something was about to happen.

The voice was back. Cards were left exposed to cheating eyes on the table.

The cloud has lifted. My telescope is clear at last. I can see the great snow slopes …and, yes! There they are! They are alive! I can see the climbers moving calmly ahead. Ladies and gentlemen, dear listeners, the assault continues. They have survived that awful deluge.

'Hurrah! Good for you lads!'

Jubilation filled the restaurant. The feat of survival against such odds had banished territorial pride. These were four mountaineers, four young men, giving every ounce of their strength, courage and skill to defeat the Eiger's unconquered face. Whose flag they climbed under was now irrelevant.

News spread quickly that they were on their way again. The restaurant filled with anxious listeners, hanging on every word. The clock ticked by. The four heroes were now reunited as one party. Six o'clock came and went. Seven o'clock. Eight o'clock.

They were still moving. Twelve thousand feet and still they climbed.

'Will they make it tonight, Otto?'

'Impossible. They'll have to bivouac somewhere and hang on till the morning. What an amazing climb!'

News became more intermittent. They sat and listened to longer periods of silence, interrupted by terser reports.

Nine o'clock and the climb continued.

The voice crackled and faded, becoming more and more erratic.

'How can they (wheeze) see anything? It must be pitch black,' said Gruber, re-emerging from the kitchen.

'They'll be preparing a perch for the night. That'll be an ordeal, in wet clothes and at an inadequate resting place most likely,' Otto commented, more to himself than to the small crowd still lingering in the warm, brightly-lit restaurant.

They'll not get much sleep. They'll be crouching over their stove making hot tea and warming food. There's no retreat now … This has to be the most dramatic day's climbing ever. Who knows what tomorrow will bring, he thought.

* * *

The evening had stretched into the small hours when Otto left the Bellevue to stagger homewards. He had indeed endured the long hours of darkness. He had found no sleep, crouched over his beer and schnapps. There was, indeed, no retreat.

The cards had fallen favourably. But though success had come, the winnings in his pocket made a familiar thin jingle. Most of what he had won had passed from his hands to Gruber in payment for the generous refreshments regularly received through the many hours of play. Having settled the bill, swollen by the countless beers and schnapps enjoyed by the players and, it must be said, by Gruber's dishonesty, he was the last to leave and was somewhat surprised to see the sky already flaked with approaching day. He would have to forgo the pleasure of bed once more. Damn cards!

The morning's cold and slippery air slapped his face like a fresh fish. Otto walked briskly along the lakeside path thinking about the four young men on the mountain.

In his mind's eye he saw the two of them climbing together, bound together by a strong rope and absolute trust, just like those young men on the Eiger. She was intrepid and adventurous; no challenge seemed too great for her. Safe in the knowledge he couldn't be heard, he spoke her name into the morning air: Leni.

He still thought about her every day, several times a day. He'd imagined the pangs of loss would fade with time, and the gaping void she had left in his heart would be filled over the years. Seventeen years. How he still missed her.

Lili reminded him so much of the beautiful woman he had lost. She was so like her. The thick brown hair which refused to be constrained by the ribbon she tied around it; the delicate, slightly upturned nose; the way she blushed, and those stunning green eyes. And she could be as pig-headed as her mother too.

He loved Lili so much, but the way she unwittingly reminded him of his pain was sometimes too hard for him to bear. What a dreadful state of affairs! Since she'd grown into a woman, he could hardly remain in the same room with her. Occasionally he would catch that questioning look in her eyes. He couldn't bear it; he had to get away.

Otto sighed.

He thought about the photograph he'd kept of the two of them returning from a climb; he thought about Leni's life-affirming smile. He'd been utterly distraught when he found it was missing. At first he assumed Anna must have found it and he lived in fear of the full force of her wrath. Nothing was said. Perhaps she'd simply destroyed it out of spite, knowing it to be the very last relic of Leni he possessed.

Then there was that row. At that moment he realised: Lili knew.

He wanted so much to tell her about Leni. But he couldn't. That was the agreement he'd made with Anna when she moved into his bed. He didn't blame her at the time. Anna had cared for Leni in those last days; she'd done her best to help him fill the aching void. She'd borne him another daughter, worked hard to bring in extra money as a waitress and seamstress, and was always willing to satisfy his needs as a man – even after that episode with the barmaid.

He'd accepted her conditions: Leni's name was never to pass his lips. Lili was to be Anna's daughter. He'd kept his word, but the lie was eating away at him.

Otto raised his eyes to look out onto the lake.

In most other respects he could count his blessings. As one of nine children he remembered only constant beatings and hunger from his own childhood. He'd done well to get the position he now held. In these days of high unemployment any job would do, particularly if you had mouths to feed. But working for the state, with a uniform, small but regular pay and normal hours – that was like gold.

Even the rumblings carried across the lake on a northern wind did little to disrupt the satisfaction he felt in his comfortable routine. Instructions issued more regularly now by the chief of police had little relevance for him. The refugees – alien elements, as they were called – were getting across elsewhere. He had the good fortune to be guarding one of the widest parts of the lake. The would-be fugitives came across the mountains, waded across streams or simply jumped over barbed wire fences. It was a long swim to reach the shores he protected. So far they'd stayed away. 'And long may it remain so.'

Whatever time span he had just wished for himself proved to be too short.

An object was bobbing about on the water in the distance. Otto rubbed his eyes. Perhaps it was an illusion induced by a combination of excessive alcohol and his train of thought. A trick his befuddled brain was playing on him. Were the fishermen out already? The boat – if indeed it was a boat – looked too small.

He squinted into the sluggish dawn.

'Jesus Christ, there's someone out there.'

Otto quickened his step home, dashed into his office and grabbed his binoculars off his desk. Returning to the lakeside he looked out once more. The vague distant shape was brought into clearer relief, revealing, as he had suspected, a solitary figure in a small rubber dinghy making scarcely perceptible progress towards the shore.

'Damned idiot!' he said, not primarily out of any concern for the safety of whoever was in the boat.

'Why the hell couldn't you just wade across the Rhine like the rest?'

Choices flashed through his clouded head. Should he just ignore him? Someone else might pick him up and turn him in. He could let him land and make his way to wherever he was going. But then if he was captured questions would be asked. Why hadn't he detected the interloper? Was he up to the job? There were plenty snapping at his heels for a sleepy little posting by a lake with some good fishing. Otto recited to himself the most recent orders he had received, double-underlined. He really had no choice.

He strode to his boat. The fresh morning air was instilling in him a sense of purpose. He winced at the sudden roar of the motor after two brisk pulls on the cord. Spray splashed refreshingly on to his grey face as he moved across the deserted water. He tried again to recall the procedures he had to follow. In essence it came down to this: illegal entrants were to be sent back to the place they had come from.

'That could prove a bit difficult,' he said to himself.

He recited the questions he was supposed to ask. Where have you come from? How did you get across? Who helped you? What money or possessions have you got? He reached the dinghy. Instinctively he groped for the gun holstered on his right hip. Just in case. But nearing the boat, a pathetic sight on such a vast expanse of water, and seeing the wretched creature before him, he knew at once it would not be needed.

The man was in his thirties, unshaven and with a sunken expression. It looked like he hadn't slept for days on end. He was dressed like an office worker, quite inappropriate for a night out on the lake. He was soaked through. Otto was surprised he had made it this far. The dinghy was old, patched up and losing air. Whatever possessed him to attempt such a trip? A single oar lay redundant at his side. The poor wretch had exhausted every ounce of strength in him. Some smuggler had taken him for a ride. How much had he paid for this pleasure trip, he wondered.

'Stop right where you are,' he ordered, before realising the absurdity of the command. The man hardly had the strength to raise his head. 'Swiss border control!'

He was about to ask for documents, but this too seemed ridiculous in the present circumstances.

'I want you to come with me. We'll get you to the shore where you can warm up and get into some dry clothes.'

Otto stretched out his arm and had to practically heave his wet catch aboard his lurching boat. Should he bother with the dinghy? It was evidence, after all. What the hell. It'll wash up sooner or later. The kids might get some fun out of it.

Otto seated the wet and frightened man at the back of his boat, turned around and made for home. Not a single word was exchanged on the journey.

It was dawning. On the shore fishermen were about to set off for a morning on the lake. Farm workers were on their way to help with the cattle. He could see Lili on the way to get fresh milk, kettles in her hands. He waved, but she didn't see him.

A small group had gathered on the shoreline when he landed. Their interest was aroused by the huddled shape in his boat.

'Not like you to be out quite this early, Otto,' said one with a laugh.

'My goodness, what have you caught today?' added another, not to be outdone in pulling the policeman's leg about his talent for fishing.

But the fishermen stopped preparing their nets and studied the man with a mixture of incomprehension and pity as he stepped weakly out of Otto's boat.

'He's surely not been out on the lake all night?'

'Aren't you supposed to (wheeze) throw those fish back?'

The words came from behind the fishermen.

Otto saw his catch recoil as if hit by a bullet.

It was Gruber.

'Have some pity, Erich,' said one of the fishermen. 'Can't you see the state he's in?'

'Follow me,' Otto ordered.

He led the man to the police house where he lived with his family on the ground floor; the top floor had been vacant for some time. The authorities decided that it wasn't necessary to have two border guards in such a backwater, sound asleep rather than merely sleepy. Captive and captor climbed up the few steps to the green wooden door he'd left wide open in the earlier confusion. Although Otto knew he was supposed to keep a watch on the arrested man, he didn't bother checking. He wasn't going anywhere. Only when they entered his office did he turn around.

The man had lifted a hand to wipe tears from his eyes. The sight of this roused the border guard's sympathy for his prisoner.

'Please, sit down. You must be exhausted.'

He sat down at the other side of the desk shivering. Otto's weary eyes scanned the bare austerity of his office: the grey rows of files on the shelves; the faded brown maps of the region on the walls. He put down the pen he'd just picked up without writing a word.

'Come with me.'

They went into the kitchen where his longsuffering wife was preparing breakfast and brewing coffee.

'Anna,' he greeted his wife with a kiss on the cheek and stole her thunder. She had prepared a sullen breakfast for him, customary following his long nights drinking and gambling. Otto shrugged his shoulders by way of an apology.

'Could you make coffee for our friend here? Oh, and something to eat. He needs to get out of his wet clothes and warm up. He can wear some of mine for the time being. They'll be a bit big for him but ... We can talk later.'

Lili returned home from her early chores on the farm.

'Who is that man?' she whispered to her mother.

'Your father found him on the lake last night. The poor wretch was probably trying to escape .... Let's leave him in peace.'

It took no time for news of the arrival to spread. The children took a great interest in the man on the lake and crowded round the kitchen window to peer at him. The stranger had now washed and changed and sat with a blanket around his shoulders warming by the stove. Colour had returned to his face. The younger children started pulling faces and squeezing their noses and lips up against the window panes. The man smiled; soon he entered the game and started distorting his own exhausted features. After a while Otto returned to shoo the children away.

Lili went about her household chores. She listened with great attention and increasing astonishment to the story the fugitive had to tell.

His name was Felix Busch. He came from Vienna.

'When they marched in I knew I had to get out,' he said; his teeth had at last stopped chattering.

'Many of my friends went the same night. I didn't. I felt paralysed. I don't know why I didn't leave straight away. The borders were still open. But Vienna was where my family and friends were. I thought I could stick it out.'

Felix looked at Otto with pleading eyes.

'Tell me, sir. Will I be sent back?'

'I'm sure that won't happen,' Otto replied, trying – not entirely successfully – to reassure Felix who appeared resigned to his fate.

'Someone I knew had some sort of contact. He helped people who, like me, were desperate to get out. I had to run a gauntlet of SS and SA to find him. They were beating people up openly in the streets. He told me exactly what to do and I left on the next train out of Vienna bound for Zurich.'

Felix accepted another cup of coffee from Anna. She too had been listening with astonishment whilst paying scant attention to her chores.

'Thank you. Thank you so very much for your kindness.'

'It's a pleasure. Are you feeling better now?' asked Anna, wiping her hands on her apron.

'Much. Thank you. Thank you again for your hospitality.'

Lili failed to suppress a cough. Her mother became aware of her presence, kneeling on the floor.

'Lili, get a move on and finish that.'

'Yes, Mama. I'm nearly done.'

She was determined to make as good a job as possible with the cleaning while Felix continued his story.

'We travelled to Innsbruck where we were ordered off the train and questioned. We had to wait for hours before being marched back to the station. It was dark. The next train to the border was packed full of refugees and guards in brown and black uniforms. I made sure I squeezed into the last compartment which was already full. It was very hot. I took off my overcoat. My contact had told me to make sure I wasn't wearing a swastika badge on my lapel. All my fellow travellers had one. They were on sale at every newspaper kiosk for ten groschen. Everyone made sure they wore one. It was a way of avoiding getting beaten up in the streets. If you didn't have one you immediately attracted attention.'

Lili slowed the movement of the rag on the tiled kitchen floor. She was hanging on every word.

'Another passenger I hadn't noticed before stood up and offered me his seat. He must have boarded the train after Innsbruck. He was a young man, about twenty. He was carrying a book for identification – Schiller's *Wilhelm Tell*. As instructed, I said I didn't want to take his seat, but he insisted. He wanted to stretch his legs for a bit in any case. During the journey he stood reading his book. Every so often he would sweep his thick black hair from his eyes.'

Lili looked up in surprise. Surely it was a coincidence, she thought. She had no time to dwell on it.

'It was the middle of the night. We still had a couple of hours to go. As we got nearer to the border the atmosphere in the compartment became stranger. Patrols passed along the corridors outside and entered the compartment. They wanted to know names, destinations and how much money we had. You weren't allowed to take more than ten Reichsmarks or twenty Schillings – that was all I had – even the smallest amount above this would get you into serious trouble.'

At this point Felix stopped and laughed to himself. He looked up at Otto. His fear had gone, and he had begun to show more trust in the clearly hung-over border guard seated opposite him.

'I must tell you something that happened. There was a middle-aged man sitting opposite me. We started talking. After a while he took out a hip flask and offered me a small cup of schnapps. He himself drank straight out of the flask. He was sweating and looked red in the face. He was clearly nervous. When the control came round he told the official he only had the permitted ten Reichsmarks. Five minutes before the train reached the border, as it was slowing down, he suddenly turned green as though he was about to throw up. He jumped out of his seat, pulled down the window, took a thick bundle of banknotes out of an inside pocket and threw them into the night.'

Otto smiled a thin smile. His head was hurting and he was getting impatient. How were the four climbers getting on? They must have been on their way again by now. He needed to get back to the Bellevue to find out what was happening

'Herr Busch. Please be good enough to tell me how you came to be on the lake this morning.'

The impatience he detected in the policeman's voice reminded Felix of the desperate situation he was in. He decided that the best course of action was to tell the truth.

'We stopped again. The order came to leave the train with our luggage. As I was leaving, the man who had given me his seat offered me his hand and wished me a good journey. As we shook hands I could feel he was pressing a piece of paper into the palm of my hand. I folded my hand around it. He pressed my hand once more and smiled in reassurance. I stuffed the piece of paper into my pocket and forgot about it.'

The circular movement of Lili's cloth slowed to a standstill.

'We hadn't arrived yet in Switzerland. The platform was full of Hitler troops and passengers milling around. All along the platform were long wooden tables. Everyone had to empty out their suitcases and bags. Carefully folded shirts were flung open, socks were searched, inside soles of shoes removed and emptied cases checked for false bottoms. Every so often a cry went up from an SA man that a smuggler, some Jewish swine, had been caught. The inspections extended to physical examinations of the most –'

Felix stopped abruptly. He'd become aware of Lili's presence and immediately broke off from his description of the indignities suffered by the female refugees. Lili dropped her head in embarrassment.

'Lili, go and help your mother in the garden,' her father ordered brusquely.

Lili got up off her aching knees and walked out of the kitchen only half-closing the door behind her. There she stayed hidden and continued listening through the jamb.

'Carry on, Herr Busch,' her father said.

'It was dawn by the time we were allowed back on the train to Switzerland. I remember the cloudless sky as we passed the border. Salvation at last, we all thought ...'

The refugee's face darkened; his voice was barely audible.

'When we arrived there were awful scenes. Women were screaming. I had to go and be interrogated by the border police.'

Otto shifted uncomfortably in his chair.

'They took my passport and asked me all sorts of questions. Why did I want to enter the country? Why didn't I stay where I was? What crime had I committed? How much money did I have? ... I could see which way the wind was blowing ... If we let you in, they said, we'll have to let them all in. Entrance denied.'

'Lili! Lili! Where are you?'

Her mother was calling from garden.

'What happened next?' her father asked.

'They took me back to the border. What was I to do? For a while I wandered aimlessly. Around midday I found an isolated guesthouse in the countryside. I had no appetite, though I hadn't eaten properly for a couple of days. I wasn't tired, although I hadn't slept for three nights. When I wanted to pay for my drink I reached into my pocket and found the scrap of paper the stranger had pressed into my hand. I'd forgotten all about it. I read it for the first time.'

Lili almost blurted out the question: what was on it?

'It had the initials O.T.C followed by a number. I recognised it at once as a telephone number. I was desperate. I found the nearest telephone and rang the number.'

'Lili! Come at once. I won't tell you again.'

She had no choice. Reluctantly she tore herself away to do her mother's bidding.

*   *   *

Later that morning Lili set off to the bakery to run another errand for her mother.

It had been five days since she'd seen Freddi.

Over the last months she'd been trying to decipher a pattern in his frequent absences, without success. When she asked him where he'd been, Freddi became very evasive

At first he claimed he was in the capital visiting various embassies in the forlorn hope of obtaining a visa. On seeing the look of horror on her face he quickly abandoned this version. Then he said he was visiting university friends, but that story quickly ran out of legs.

'Freddi, please tell me,' she implored as he sat drinking his coffee in the Bellevue.

'Okay, Lili,' he answered, leaning close to her. 'But you must promise you'll tell nobody.'

'I swear Freddi. Cross my heart and –'

'Seriously, Lili. If any one finds out...'

She blushed, suitably chastened.

'You remember I once told you that I wasn't allowed to work, as a condition of staying here?'

'Yes.'

'Well. Max has got me a job.'

'A job? Doing what?'

'Shh.'

Lili looked around. The restaurant was empty apart from a few old ladies.

'I'm a travelling rep. That's why I'm away days at a time.'

'What do you sell?'

'Oh, erm ... textiles.'

'Textiles? That's good, isn't it Freddi?'

'Yes. It's not bad. I get to see different places travelling around... But you mustn't breathe a word to anyone.'

*　*　*

When Lili left the bakery with a large, warm loaf under her arm, she was surprised to see Freddi walking quickly towards her. She struggled to contain herself.

'Freddi, you're back!'

He fired a stern glance at her. She looked around; fortunately, there was no one to notice the warmth of her enthusiasm.

'When did you get back?' she said, as they walked together.

'Late last night.'

Freddi seemed distracted. She thought she'd tell him about Felix.

'You'll never guess what happened early this morning,' she began.

As she breathlessly and incoherently recounted what she'd seen and heard, Lili could see the colour draining from his face.

'...and then he remembered he had this scrap of paper the man on the train had given him with a telephone number ... What is it, Freddi? You look as though you've seen a ghost.'

He swallowed hard. In barely a whisper he said: 'Listen, Lili. The telephone number probably belonged to a smuggler. He would have picked him up from where he'd been sent back and brought him to the lake where it is much quieter and not so well guarded. The smuggler wouldn't have risked taking him all the way across. He obviously left him to his own devices.'

'But that's awful. He could've drowned if my father hadn't spotted him.'

'Where is he now? Felix, I mean,' Freddi asked urgently.

'At home.'

'With your father?'

'I think he's gone to the Bellevue. He's desperate to find out what's happening on the mountain.'

Lili became pensive.

'Freddi, how do you know all this stuff about smugglers?'

'I ... I overheard Max discussing it ... It ... It seems we've both been guilty of eavesdropping,' Freddi stammered.

They approached Lili's house.

'What will happen to Felix?' Lili asked suddenly.

Freddi shook his head. 'Your father will have to hand him over.'

'And what then?'

'He'll be sent back. They'll take him to the border and hand him over to the Gestapo.'

'Surely they can't do that to the poor man? He nearly drowned getting across.'

Freddi turned to face her. Lili had never seen him looking so serious. He placed his hands on her shoulders.

'Lili, can you do something for me? We need to win a bit of time – just an hour or so. Can you try and delay things? Tell your father Felix has to eat and rest … I don't know … anything you can think of. I'll go and find Max – he'll know what can be done for the best.'

Lili watched Freddi dash off, confused by what he'd told her and the earnestness with which he pleaded for her help. What was Felix to him?

* * *

Freddi knew there had been problems with last night's delivery. For some reason the usual telephone call hadn't come through warning them of 'grandmother's visit'. Poor Felix was only meant to be on the lake for a while, but they hadn't got out to him. What a complete balls up!

Max was sure to have contacts in the transport column able to sort out the mess.

Within moments a telephone call was received at police headquarters in Sankt Gallen. An official car, accustomed to such journeys, was on its way to the border.

Freddi needn't have worried about Lili's father being prompt in dealing with the matter. Otto had decided he was going to check on the form later in the afternoon. For now, it was back to the Bellevue to catch up on the progress of the four men on the mountain. Felix was left sound asleep in his armchair under Anna's watchful eye.

By mid-afternoon the Face had been conquered. Otto returned home, unsure whether Felix would be happy at the news that two of his compatriots had helped conquer the North Face of the mighty Eiger.

He entered his office with a bounce in his step and with the good news on his lips. There he was shocked to find a senior ranking police officer waiting for him.

Fuck, he thought. He'd left his prisoner unguarded and stank of beer. He was for it.

Otto struggled visibly to regain his composure before the police captain who, fortunately, seemed unconcerned by the border guard's appearance.

He gave his name as Captain Reitlinger. In his hand he held all the necessary papers: permission to cross the border and a residence permit. It would have been close to insubordination for Otto to inspect the documents. As far as he was concerned everything was in order. Anyway, it saved him all that tedious paperwork he hated. The car drove off, taking Felix to safety.

Otto breathed again. One way or another it had been quite a day.

*   *   *

What exactly are they up to? Lili wondered, as she reflected on Freddi's bizarre behaviour earlier and the coincidence of the stranger on the train.

Something in her brain was trying to connect Felix Busch with the time she and Eva had broken into Max's house as children, and the strange things they'd seen in his cellar. But at present the two ends weren't meeting.

XV

'… Elisabeth … Eva … Heidi … Hildegard …. Lili …Lili?'

The call of her name jolted Lili from her reverie.

When she and her classmates returned to school after the long summer break they were surprised to find a new teacher sitting in the high-backed wooden chair from which Huggenberg used to tyrannise them. The girls had never been able to tell which one of them was being fixed by the old fart's glass eye and sat in horror as globules of spittle flew from his mouth, some – the ones they feared less – randomly nestling like insects in his beard. Huggenberg smacked his cane fiercely on his desk in time with the dates and events he dictated to them at a speed deliberately faster than what they could keep up with. The old sadist, warped by decades of sarcasm and reciprocal detestation – he for his charges and they for him – had succumbed to a stroke and was left a dribbling invalid incapable any longer of intimidating schoolchildren.

' ... Magdalena ...Margit ...Roessli ... Ruth ... Trudi....'

During the unaccustomed recital of their first names Lili gazed absentmindedly out of the classroom window at the wooden bathing huts suspended over the jade of the lake where, during the long summer holidays, the girls furtively admired the fullness of the curves each other's youthful bodies had assumed.

The summer had been strange.

Dark forebodings interrupted the eagerly anticipated days of carefree joy whenever activity ceased and her mind came to rest. Lili had walked through the garden gate of her childhood and forgotten the way back.

Herr Grünbaum taught the girls history.

The past, once fettered and incarcerated under ice and snow, now revealed itself in the fractured remnants the thaw ejected to the surface of the present. Lili found herself concentrating more than ever before on her teacher's words.

'Refugees have always sought and found asylum in our country ...We should remember our traditions of humanity, hospitality and solidarity with those who are persecuted and threatened.'

Herr Grünbaum had left his chair and was walking slowly and deliberately around the room as he explained the situation of the Huguenots in France in the seventeenth century. Lili was sure many of her classmates had a crush on their new teacher.

'In this context it is worth recalling – is it not Jacqueline? – the massacre of Saint Bartholemew's eve.

Persecution on grounds of religion is nothing new, though we may be surprised at the levels of barbarity we have witnessed in recent times.'

Lili's thoughts wandered beyond the empty bathing huts across the lake to the distant shoreline.

'You are paying attention, aren't you, Lili?'

She felt the colour rising to her cheeks. She had been paying very close attention and was embarrassed that it might appear otherwise to her favourite teacher.

'Yes, Herr Grünbaum.'

He smiled at her and continued the lesson.

'Thousands of refugees once sought asylum in our country and were granted it. In one year, just to give you some idea of the numbers, some sixteen to seventeen hundred took refuge daily – daily, I repeat, in our country. During the course of the following years it is reckoned that some thirty thousand refugees, persecuted for their religious beliefs, sought salvation on our soil.'

A hand was raised.

'Yes, Heidi?'

'Sir, did the Hugu … Hugo …'

'Huguenots…'

'Did they all stay?'

'That's a very good question, Heidi.'

Bolts of envy shot across the room.

'No, many moved on. They travelled to Holland, Germany and England, making enormous contributions to those countries too. But it is important to remember that the regions here, though poor themselves, did not count the cost in helping the persecuted.'

Surety.

The word flashed into Lili's consciousness. She half raised her hand to ask about it, but Herr Grünbaum was well into his flow.

'It would be a mistake to think that they were simply a burden on us. The contribution made by these refugees was great. To quote from one account … Er, Trudi, will you read from the top of the page, please?'

There was a clearing of the throat, a reddening of cheeks and a leap of a teenage heart into sweet young breasts.

'From where it says 'science, art and economics'?' The eager pupil was looking at her teacher to confirm the place.

Herr Grünbaum nodded.

'Science, art and economics have been given a valuable impulse from their arrival. In my town they bring different trades. Many families have borne their new homeland excellent sons…'

'And daughters, we might add … Thank you, Trudi … Food for thought in our own dark times.'

The teacher let his pupils copy down what he had said in their books. Walking around the room, he would occasionally point with a long, delicate finger at a mistake.

*   *   *

During break Lili sat by the open window lost in her thoughts about events beyond the thin blue pencil line of the horizon. Fragments of what poor Felix had told her father violated the stillness of the late summer day.

On sudden impulse she tore a page from her maths book. Undeterred by the fact that the squared sheet in front of her was inappropriate for her intended purpose, she started to write, entering the date in the top left corner.

At this point she hesitated.

'Who shall I address it to?'

The idea now seemed stupid. She bit the top of her pen and thought hard.

'Dear Sir…'

That's no good, she thought. It has to be addressed to someone in person or it'll be ignored. Lili wracked her brains for a name, someone important with responsibility and authority.

She'd once overheard her father talk in awed tones of the chief of police. What was his name? Hart-something or – that was it!

She would write her letter to the head of the border police, Doctor Hardenschild. With stories of dawn arrests, false imprisonment, torture and flight swirling through her mind, she set about composing her letter.

Dear Dr. Hardenschild,

I feel I must write to you to express my outrage that refugees are being heartlessly thrust back from our borders into misery

Lili raised her pen to her lips. She became aware of three other girls hovering inquisitively.

'What's that you're writing, Lili? A love letter?' giggled Margit.

'Let's have a look,' teased Hildegard.

With some reticence Lili explained.

To her surprise her words were met with interest and sympathy. Soon a small crowd had gathered around her desk. She quickly redrafted the first lines. As she wrote others dictated ideas and argued about the sentences: Rosmarie reminded them of the power of rhetorical questions; Irma suggested adding biblical allusions. In this manner they wrote the letter to Hardenschild collectively. It read:

Dear Dr. Hardenschild,

We feel we must write to you to express our outrage that refugees are being heartlessly thrust back from our borders into misery. Have we completely forgotten that Jesus said, 'What you do unto the least of these, you do unto me'?

We could never have dreamt that this country, this island of peace with its traditions of friendship and hospitality towards those being persecuted, has thrown these freezing, trembling, miserable wretches back over the border like animals.

Surely we cannot behave like the rich man who ignored poor Lazarus?

Have not these people placed all their hope in our country, the country of the Red Cross?

What a dreadful disappointment it must be to be thrown back to the place they came from – there to meet a terrible fate!

If this continues, we can be sure that we will be punished. Perhaps others have commanded you not to accept any Jews, but it is certainly not the will of God, and we must obey Him above men.

For this reason we, humble schoolgirls, take the liberty of pleading for these poorest of the homeless.

With deepest respect,

After a momentary pause Lili was the first to sign her name. One by one the others followed suit.

Back at home she took an envelope from her father's desk. In her best script she addressed it to the chief of police. Her heart pounded against her ribcage like a frightened dove when Lili fed the letter through her fingertips into the mouth of the post box.

* * *

Nothing happened for several weeks. Summers by the lake were long. The water drank in heat during the sun-drenched months and now fed its gathered warmth into the surrounding land. Lili had forgotten about the letter until the afternoon she saw a large black car parked in the street outside her house.

She was met by a wall of grave expressions from her parents and three uniformed policemen. She looked to her mother; her head was bowed. Her father, agitated and nervous, stood by the window. No doubt he was asking himself what he had done to deserve this – another bloody high-ranking officer on his doorstep.

'Please come in and sit down, Fräulein.'

It was the most senior of the police officers who spoke, in not unfriendly tones.

'Allow me to introduce myself ... Doctor Ernst Hardenschild, chief of police. You at least know of me. It is now time you got to know me in person.'

She gulped when she heard the name.

'I have received this letter. I take it you recognise it?'

He held it lightly between his gloved fingers as though it were a soiled undergarment. She only had to glance at the squared paper and the script to know it was hers.

Lili nodded.

'Yours is the name which heads the list of signatures. Do I take it that you were the instigator of this ....this text?'

Hardenschild spat out the words. With his chin engorged by a black, pointed beard and his high-pitched voice, Lili couldn't help but think that he looked and sounded like a crow.

She nodded again.

'I see.'

The pause which followed only added to her discomfort.

'You have heaped recriminations upon me in this letter and made it abundantly clear that you do not agree with my conduct in respect of refugees. I don't know where your wisdom comes from and the source of your information. It is clear you did not have the respect owing to your parents, particularly your father as a servant of the state, to ask for their advice regarding this letter.'

Lili looked at her father. He was gawping like an idiot.

'Who advised you to write this letter? Has he made himself known to the right authorities? Is he someone who perhaps has no right to be here in the first place?'

The Crow was well into his interrogation.

'I ... I wrote the letter myself. I had no help apart from my classmates.' Her lips were trembling as she spoke.

'You had no help? Are you telling me that you, a sixteen year old schoolgirl, wrote this unaided?' Hardenschild snorted.

'I'm seventeen … and I wrote it with my friends.'

Momentarily derailed by the schoolgirl's impertinent correction, Hardenschild hesitated.

At that very moment a dagger of realisation struck her a piercing blow.

Freddi.

She remembered what he had told her about how careful he had to be about engaging in any sort of political activity. One word out of place and he was back over the border.

What had she done? She felt tears stinging her eyes.

Hardenschild, seeing this and misinterpreting the cause, changed tack.

'I am pleased your young heart is full of pity. It is rightly so. Your indignation is just. But when you got over your initial anger, you should have taken a moment – patience is not one of youth's virtues,' he interjected, smiling chivalrously at her mother who returned a thin smile of relief at this change of mood, '– to think a little. The first requirement in practising Christian love is patience.'

The grand inquisitor had turned into her father-confessor.

'Tell me. What grade are you in?' He was smiling coldly.

'The tenth, sir.'

'Then perhaps you should show some humility before you, a tenth grade schoolgirl, attempt to teach me – the head of the police in the whole country – my job.'

Lili reeled back from the unexpected assault.

'Sir, I wasn't –'

'Do you know that we spend millions on helping refugees? Can you imagine what that means? But even that is not going to solve the problem. Even twenty, thirty, forty million! Do you know that we have to cope with unemployment among our own young men? Do you know that if we take thousands and thousands of refugees, each one of them will need and want work?'

The flow of questions was gathering force. Hardenschild's rage was still restrained by a flimsy wooden dam like those they built as children by the river. It was beginning to creak under the pressure. It would not be long before cracks appeared.

For the moment the dam was holding firm. The voice softened. The Crow was biding his time.

'Think of your father. He has a job. He is employed by the state to serve the state. He can still provide for you...'

She winced. How could such a little word like 'still' make her feel like the traitor Judas?

'Do you know that every refugee wants to earn money here and that they would take away your father's job or jobs from the young men of this village? ... If we had no controls.'

The dam was groaning under the strain.

'Do you know that there are dubious elements insinuating themselves into the body of the nation? Do you know that there are foreign agents and spies among the so-called refugees? Are you, little schoolgirl, aware that a large department works day and night on these problems and does nothing other than deal with the question of the refugees? Did your adviser not tell you that our land is at the forefront of those countries helping to alleviate the pain and suffering of the refugees? Do you know we have little room for refugee camps, and that our communities want our own unemployed to be cared for? Have you been told all these things – or did your informer keep them from you?'

The Crow was screeching at her; angry blotches of red appeared on his face.

Lili's eyes implored her father: do something! Say something! Why wasn't he defending her, his own daughter? Why was he letting this ridiculous man humiliate her? Why was he just standing there quaking in his boots?

She was ashamed of him. Her fierce gaze conveyed that shame. Otto averted his eyes.

'Who told you that we were acting under orders from the Germans? I demand to know who it was. Who?'

'I never suggested –'

'Whoever it was is a pathetic wretch among men!'

Lili turned away to avoid the tidal wave of aggression crashing down on her.

The anger subsided.

The force of the torrent seemed spent. She had been smashed to the ground by its overwhelming power.

Hardenschild was silent for a moment and then smiled his cold, contemptuous smile.

'Just imagine for a moment, Fräulein Vogelsang, that you are married with many mouths to feed. Your husband doesn't earn much.'

He turned with a chivalrous half bow towards her mother, standing rigid in the corner with her hands clasped together as though in prayer.

'I imagine your mother knows all about how you have to think about every penny you spend. If a stranger comes along wanting food and a roof over his head, you'll think long and hard about who he is and where he's come from. Fine words butter no parsnips.'

Lili counted the ticks of the clock punctuating the intolerable silence which ensued. The Crow appeared to have regained both his composure and his hauteur.

'You will have noted that I did not throw your letter straight into the waste paper bin where it belongs. Have patience. I am sure you will be red with shame when you one day discover everything that has been done to help these people. You may also be sure that I shall answer to God for what I do. I have no fear of examination.'

At this Hardenschild's gaze lifted towards the ceiling giving him the air of a martyred saint. Lili felt an urge to laugh – an urge she immediately repressed when his eyes returned from their celestial heights to fix her with their beady look.

'Now I shall leave you to answer to your parents who have sacrificed much so that you may have the opportunities they did not enjoy. But before I go, I think I am owed an apology from you for what you have written. That is the very least you can do.'

Hardenschild waited, fully expecting a humble apology to come his way.

The clock ticked.

For a reason Lili could not exactly explain, and despite frantically gestured urging from her parents, she dug in her heels. What I have written, I have written. Although she fervently wished to be rid of his bullying presence, she was not going to be humiliated by a man so pompous he was fit to burst, whoever he was.

'Well, Fräulein?'

The stand-off continued.

Lili shook her head slightly from side to side. Seeing this, Hardenschild, slapping his leather gloves into his palm, stormed out of the house without another word.

On the same day Herr Grünbaum was interrogated by Hardenschild and accused of stirring up his pupils and insulting the authorities. The questioning went on for hours. In the end, there was no conclusive proof. Lili felt both relief that Freddi had been untouched by the affair and indignation over her teacher's humiliation.

* * *

A large flock of flamingos took to flight as one, colouring the Camargue sky pink and rose. The shadow of the approaching Zeppelin had alarmed them. From her viewpoint in the gondola Lili watched as the freshness of the green countryside gradually disappeared. Even in her dream she could feel the searing heat as the terrain became more barren. She wiped the sweat off her brow.

'You sure can feel how hot it is even up here, can't you?'

Lili turned to see a large gentleman standing at her table.

'May I?'

Smiling warmly, he gestured to an empty seat.

'Be my guest,' Lili responded.

'Are you travelling alone?'

'Yes, to Rio de Janeiro.'

'Very courageous, Fräulein…?'

'Vogelsang … Lili Vogelsang.'

'What a beautiful name. Flowers and birdsong … Allow me to introduce myself. Hans-Bruno Metternich. Bass. On my way to tour South America.'

'You're a singer?'

'Of opera, my dear.'

The Zeppelin sailed along the eastern coast of Spain. Herr Metternich, having made the journey before, pointed out the various wonders to Lili.

'Look, Fräulein Vogelsang. That's Gibraltar, where apes guard the entrance to the Mediterranean.'

'There's Tangiers.'

Lili looked down at the whitewashed flat-roofed houses, narrow streets and mosques. Soon the desert of the Sahara lay beneath them. Sweat began to drip from her temples. The heat rising from the endless expanse of sand snatched the air from her lungs. She only felt at ease again when the desert hurtled over a great precipice into the sea.

The sun went down. It was time for dinner. Sated by so many different sights the passengers were content to leave their seats by the windows to move to the dining room. A long table for over thirty guests dominated the room. It was laid as elegantly as in any luxury hotel. Blue-patterned china glistened under the lights.

The captain made his entrance and invited Lili to be his guest of honour and to listen to his wondrous tales.

'On one occasion,' he began, as the soup dishes were being cleared by waiters in white jackets, 'we were crossing Spanish West Africa …. May I serve you, gnädiges Fräulein?'

'Thank you.'

'We were flying low to avoid the blustery wind when we saw a camp of nomads in the distance…'

'More wine, madam?' a waiter inquired.

'For you too, sir?'

The captain nodded towards the waiter but held up his hand before the red line rose too far.

'We don't want to lose our way crossing the Atlantic, do we? … Anyway, as I was saying … We saw this tribe of nomads, and I thought it would be a real hoot to fly over them. Well, you should have seen them rushing hither and thither in their dark cloaks. When the ship cast its dark shadow over them, they ran inside their tents fearing the end of the world or the return of Allah, or some such thing. And their camels stamped in the sand in panic. It was quite a strange scene.'

'What has been the most exciting event you've ever witnessed, Captain?' asked an elderly lady to his left.

The captain stroked his chin as he pondered.

'Let me see … There've been many, of course. But it's particularly at night when most of the passengers and crew are asleep that you see magical sights; when the moon lights the surface of the ocean. Sometimes you see flying fish scared by the noise of the engines shoot out of the water in shoals, fly a hundred meters over the waves and re-enter the water like torpedoes.

And there are magnificent rays just under the surface of the water which look like enormous butterflies with coloured patterns on their fins.'

He took a sip of his cognac and lit up a cigar, paused to inhale and blew out the smoke before continuing.

'I remember one crossing. We were between Cape Verde and the Doldrums when we beheld a most amazing and cruel sight. I hope, ladies, you won't be too distressed if I relate it?'

A frisson of excitement passed along the table.

'A great whale lay in the ocean. It was being torn to shreds by a mass of sharks, biting with their fierce jaws into the whale's sides and thrashing the waters all around with their tail fins. The sea was frothing with the red blood of the whale.'

He paused. There was silence around the table. All private conversation ceased.

'But I told fishermen at a port what we'd seen. They said the attackers couldn't have been sharks. Sharks don't attack great whales. It had probably been killer whales.'

The meal ended. It was dark and late. Lili felt a lot cooler now that the north-east trade winds were taking the ship towards the equator. The night air chilled; she shivered at the drop in temperature. In bed she couldn't rid her mind of the violent image of the great whale thrashing about, blood pouring out of it.

Lili woke, tugged the blanket around her and pulled her knees tight into her stomach.

I'm cold.

'Mama, I'm cold.'

She felt a blanket being wrapped tightly around her, a hand feeling her forehead.

'Go back to sleep, Lili.'

She slept for many hours; hour after hour. It might have been days. They'd been in the doldrums. Nothing but sea upon sea, wave after wave, and the occasional tiny island poking up from the endless blue.

After the doldrums black clouds threatened. A menacing wall could be seen ahead of them. The crew moved quickly and purposefully to their positions. In moments the rain was covering the ship. Weighed down by the tropical downpour, the Zeppelin needed all the power of its engines to weather the storm.

Calm returned. The ship passed over freighters and great four-mast sailing ships, crossed over penal colonies and was greeted with enthusiastic waves by fishermen on large balsawood rafts.

In a small reading room Lili joined other passengers having a break from the unending ocean to read the newspaper or pen a letter home. Turning a post card with a scene of Sugar Loaf Mountain in her fingers Lili took up her pen and wrote:

My dearest Mama, my dearest Papa,

The journey has been quite wonderful. We are now steering a course along the Brazilian coast towards Rio. Everywhere there are endless bays with the powerful surf of the Atlantic crashing on to their white sandy beaches. We see shipwrecks, sinking into the sea, washed by the waves. Some have just their masts showing. Fishermen wave from their rafts. How I wish you could be with me now!

Your loving daughter,

Lili

The Zeppelin had turned hard west to enter the magical bay of Rio de Janeiro when she returned to her table near the window. She sat there stunned by the beauty of the moros covered with lush, verdant vegetation. The shadow of the airship glided over the precipitous face of Sugar Loaf Mountain and gave bathers on Copacabana beach some welcome shade from the sun's intensity. It rose towards Corcovado where the enormous statue of Christ opened his arms in welcome. Everything she saw exceeded her wildest imaginings in beauty and wonder.

The airship began to sink.

Delighted children in rags ran out in the favelas to wave at the Zeppelin. She could see their wide, white smiles across their dark faces and heard their whoops of delight.

Suddenly there was a loud crack, out of nowhere, like the single crack of a whip.

Lili jumped from her seat and looked around.

Nothing.

Then another sharp crack.

Fire spat from the gondola of the airship.

Lili couldn't believe what she was witnessing. The other passengers started to shout in panic and horror.

'No! No! Stop it! Stop it!'

'This can't be. What in God's name is going on?'

Beneath them, the happy children of moments before were writhing on the ground, clutching their stomachs. Some lay lifeless.

The first act in a pitiless war had been committed.

The poor people were running for cover in their shantytown shacks. Gun-fire and grenades sprayed them, clattering onto the tin roofs, blowing limb from limb.

'No! Stop it! Stop it!'

She ran to plead with the captain to halt this slaughter of the innocents. But as she moved towards the stairs which went down to the gondola, the airship suddenly jolted.

Screams filled the air.

A shout went up.

'We're on fire!'

'Fire! Fire!'

The heat was consuming her.

Passengers in panic searched vainly for an escape. The narrow stairways were blocked with bodies scrambling over each other.

Lili was choking.

The faces of those around her changed into hellish distortions of hatred, fear and cruelty, shouting and spitting at her. The Zeppelin's captain turned into Hardenschild. He was standing in front of her waving the postcard she had written to her parents under her nose. It had become the piece of squared paper with the fateful letter.

Her body was on fire. She was burning.

'No! Stop it! Don't let it happen. Please help me.'

Lili writhed around; her head was spinning.

There was no escape.

She was going down with the Zeppelin, now grotesquely angled and swallowed by flames.

'I'm so hot ...'

Something cooling and damp moved across her forehead.

'Shh, Lili. It's alright. Shh…You've got a fever.'

Lili half-opened her eyes.

She saw a face leaning over her, an indistinct blur of a shape.

'Go away! You're not my mother. I want my mother.'

She looked towards her father standing by the door in the same pathetic and helpless way he'd stood by during Hardenschild's visit.

'Papa, where's Mama?'

'What do you mean Lili? She's right there beside you,' he answered, full of concern.

'No, she isn't Papa … Where is she? Tell me.'

'The poor thing's delirious,' said Anna as she continued to mop Lili's brow. 'She doesn't know what she's saying.'

'Will she be alright?' asked Otto.

XVI

The corridor leading to Reitlinger's first-floor office was deserted. Max knocked gently on the door.

On a crisp October morning, Max had taken the first train to the county town and made his way directly through the sunlit streets to police headquarters. The telephone call from the Captain had given him cause for concern; he could tell from his voice that all was not well.

'It might be better if we went outside to talk.' Reitlinger gestured as though to suggest his office was being bugged.

Max was immediately struck by Reitlinger's careworn appearance and couldn't help wondering whether his paranoia was justified. Since his first visit back in the spring, he'd been in frequent contact with the Captain. Max understood how vital it was that Reitlinger's cover remained intact for as long as possible; not even Freddi knew precisely what he was up to. He also understood the lonely path the police captain had chosen – Max was the only person he could confide in when he was desperate. Those moments of desperation were becoming ever more frequent.

'Grüezi, Captain.' A call came from across the street where a scruffy looking man was selling newspapers on the street corner.

'Ah, Siggi. Sorry, I didn't see you there,' Reitlinger called back. He turned to Max: 'Excuse me a second. I need to have a quick word with an old friend from the club.'

Max joined them, nodding a greeting to the newspaper vendor.

'My God, Captain. You look out of sorts. A long session at the Golden Stag last night, was it?'

'If only,' Reitlinger replied.

'There's a report of Saturday's match in here. It doesn't make for very cheerful reading, I'm afraid.'

Reitlinger handed over a coin and folded his copy under his arm.

'Did you see the score? They were a right bloody shambles.'

'I'm afraid I didn't, Siggi. I've been a bit busy lately.'

Reitlinger seemed ashamed of his ignorance.

'Are you feeling alright, Captain?' his friend from the club asked with concern.

The two men walked on through the old town, crossed the market square and descended the street leading to the station. Over a coffee in the station buffet Reitlinger gave expression to what was troubling him.

'I'm not sure how much longer I can carry on with this, Max. Things are slipping from my grasp. I feel like I've dropped a simple cross and I'm on my knees, helpless to stop the ball bouncing across the line.'

Max smiled briefly at the football analogy but he could see that the situation was serious.

'What's the problem? Everything's been going so well.'

'It's become a deluge at the border. The numbers of refugees are too great to cope with. The phone's ringing incessantly, and I can't be in twenty places at once. I've reached the end of the road.'

Although Max had seen the Captain in this depressed mood before, there was something in the absent look in his eyes which alarmed him. He was afraid that his friend was about to enter a place he knew all too well himself.

'Keep going, Paul,' he urged. 'You've already helped so many desperate people. Your reputation has spread all over the region. There are hundreds still in danger who are holding on to the hope that they've only got to find you and they'll be safe. You can't take that hope away from them.'

'I'm in an impossible situation, Max,' Reitlinger sighed. 'As long as it was a trickle, it was fine. No one noticed a few here, a few there. It was all under control. Now, with the increased numbers, it's become impossible to let them all in. That means I have to decide. How do I choose who I let in and who I send back? Even if I only took women and children, there would be too many. I've been letting in more than is advisable, but even then I'm turning away ten times that number.'

'No one can reproach you for the decisions you've had to make.'

'You know what they call it, the refugees?' The Captain laughed bitterly as he stared into his coffee cup. 'Reitlinger's roulette.'

'And you're also known as the 'good captain',' Max countered gently.

Reitlinger looked up. He was close to tears.

'Am I? Am I good, Max? ... I had a dream the other night. A nightmare, more like. I was at the border but I was wearing the uniform of an ordinary guard. An endless column of refugees was wading through a river towards me.

I ordered them to stop where they were. I had to write down their details; I had to fill in the forms.

But still they came. From the faceless mass I began to make out their features. To a man and woman their eyes had been gouged out; their cheeks were sunken, their pallor grey. Nooses hung around their necks; blood spurted from head wounds.

I ordered them again to stop. In panic I reached for my gun. I pulled it from my holster. I waved it in the air and shouted.

They heeded my threats. The endless column halted a few steps in front of me. Silently, they followed my order and lined up two by two. Their eyeless sockets stared at me, waiting for a word – a decision.

The hand holding my revolver dangled limply at my side.

They waited. They stared.

And looking down on myself in my dream I saw in horror how I was pointing to one of the first pair to go to the right to safety; the next I ordered to the left, back across the border to where the hangman was waiting.

I had the power of life and death.

I was God.

You there, to the left! You, to the right!

Left! Right!

Right! Left!'

Reitlinger was pressing his palms hard into his eyes in an attempt to drive out the terrifying scene.

'I can't go on. My nerves are shredded.'

Max could only sit in silence and watch his friend's spirit disintegrate before his eyes.

Suddenly, Reitlinger threw his head back and laughed a hollow laugh.

'You think I'm good? Let me tell you what happened the other day.'

Max was pained at the sight of his friend torturing himself.

'Paul, please. You don't have to tell me anything.'

'Oh, but I do ... It was late in the evening. I'd been at the border all day when I arrived back at headquarters. On the stairs I found a young woman sitting and waiting. Judging by her weary demeanour she'd been there all day. As I stepped past her to enter my office she looked up, but quickly looked away again.

Not quite what you were expecting am I, I thought. A greying, forty-eight year-old melancholic hardly fits anyone's picture of a knight in shining armour.

When I turned the key in the door, the well-dressed young woman looked up again. She had large dark eyes, an oval, slightly Asiatic face and wavy, long black hair tied back with a green ribbon.

'Herr Reitlinger?' she asked in an accent I couldn't identify precisely.

'I'm Captain Reitlinger, yes. Was it me you were waiting for?'

I felt bitter resentment that this beautiful young woman was only interested in what I could do for her. She'd show no interest in me otherwise. As she stood up I couldn't stop my eyes wandering from her pretty face to the outline of her breasts, hips and legs under a thin dress.

I invited her in.'

Max shifted uncomfortably on his chair.

'Paul, I'm not your priest...'

'She gave her name as Klara Cervenka. She had come to plead for her parents to be allowed into the country. Their situation was desperate.

For one so young she spoke eloquently. She'd obviously thought long and hard about what to say to me. As she spoke of her parents' predicament, I found my attention wandering. I couldn't stop the dark thoughts returning. I couldn't stop thinking of the power I had in my hands; the power to save or damn – but not just others. That power was now being turned against myself.

I felt feverish. Occasional words were breaking free. They were unhooked and flying through my office randomly, rebounding off the floor, walls and ceiling. I tried to turn my thoughts to what she was saying, to grasp on to disconnected words. I recognised phrases I'd heard at the border or read in reports a thousand times before. Yet they'd lost all meaning.

Out of the cacophony suddenly came a sentence I understood. I seized it and its implications almost physically.

'I would do anything to get my parents back with me.'

I stared into those big black eyes. I imagined undoing the green ribbon restraining that luxurious mass of perfumed hair, kissing her parted lips, uncovering those sweet breasts ... The girl was mine to command.

Then I felt it: a sharp slap of remorse struck me across my face.

'I'm really very sorry, Fräulein Cervenka. There's absolutely nothing more I can do.'

Something about the tone of my words must have convinced the young woman that any further pleas were futile. What more could she do than offer herself to me?

She seemed relieved.

'I understand, Captain Reitlinger. Thank you, anyway. Thank you for what you have already done for so many of us. We will always be grateful,' she said.

After she left, I broke down in uncontrolled spasms of weeping. It was weeping the like of which I haven't experienced since I was a child. It was as though it washed the air clean of all impurities and brought back contours of the sharpest intensity. I could see things as they are.

It's over, Max.'

There was nothing Max could say. How much more could one man possibly do? He'd already saved over three hundred souls from certain death.

Reitlinger was reaching into his pocket. He took out two sheets of paper.

'In any case, Hardenschild's got his way,' he said as he unfolded them and pushed them across the table to Max. 'The borders are closed. He claimed he was only thinking of his men faced with carrying out such awful duties. I must admit I have sympathy for the argument. The lifeboat's full. He's not going to tolerate local commanders like me taking responsibility for their own sections of the border. His hounds are closing in.'

Max picked up the first of two official letters and read:

We have already asked you for detailed information concerning the means and authority by which emigrants have reached your city and have been allowed to stay. We still await an answer. We further request you to carry out the necessary investigation and let us have the answers we seek.

'He must've realised some time ago that there was a lone wolf operating against his wishes. It's just taken him a bit of time to work out it was me. No doubt one of his spies – or one of my own men I've misjudged.'

Max picked up the second communication.

As for the authority given by certain officials for such illegal entry, we issued strict instructions regarding conduct at the border. It appears from my sources that you have been acting on your own initiative in promoting or sanctioning illegal entry. This matter is to be thoroughly investigated and action taken. You should be under no illusion of the serious nature of your misdemeanours.

Max let the sheet of paper drop on to the table.

'But what can they get you for? You were acting from the very best of motives. Surely they'd recognise that?'

A faint smile flickered across Reitlinger's lips.

'You don't know Hardenschild. He'll stop at nothing to get rid of his enemies. He's got plenty of options.'

'Like what?'

'Taking bribes from refugees. Trafficking. Misuse of police property. Dereliction of duty – I've been away from headquarters rather a lot in recent months. If they're really feeling vindictive, they'll accuse me of having immoral relations with female refugees. It shouldn't be too difficult. They'll pull one in – a young, vulnerable girl – threaten her with expulsion unless they get a full confession. After she's signed they'll throw her out anyway for immoral behaviour.'

Max felt a wave of nausea rise in his throat.

'But in the end they'll probably go for something less dramatic. I've left a trail of evidence, Max. I had no choice ... They'll nail me for falsifying official documents. It's enough to finish me.'

He shrugged his shoulders; Max could see he was resigned to his fate.

'I'm sorry, Paul. I'm sorry I ever troubled you with all this in the first place,' Max said.

'Don't be. I'd do it all again, if I could. It was good while it lasted.'

His face brightened as though in memory of happier times.

'I certainly had it all to deal with: high balls crossed in by tricky wingers; long shots skidding treacherously off the grass in front of me; dribbling centre-forwards trying to pass me at close quarters; powerful headers flying towards the top corner of my goal. But my ninety minutes is up, and I don't think there's going to be any extra time.'

The burden had been lifted; light had returned to his eyes. He was smiling.

'You played a blinder, Captain,' Max said.

XVII

'Where is he, Max?'

Max was about to ask what had happened to Hiddigeigei's milk but thought better of it.

'Who? ... Freddi, you mean?' he said, unsettled by the determined look in Lili's eyes.

'Where is he? I need to speak to him.'

'He's just gone away for a few days. He'll be back soon,' he answered weakly, withdrawing his eyes from hers as though caught red-handed in a criminal act.

Lili was close to tears.

'I have to speak to him, Max. I need to know.'

'Know what, Lili?' There was barely disguised alarm in his voice.

'If he still cares for me.'

'You'd better come in.'

Max led Lili into his study. He gently moved Hiddigeigei from his favourite armchair and sat the troubled young woman down. He left her there momentarily to fetch a glass of water.

'Tell me what's happened,' he said on returning. Lili's face was buried in her hands.

'I don't know who to turn to, Max. You're the only person I can confide in.'

'What is it, Lili?'

Lili took a sip of water, barely enough to moisten her trembling lips.

'We had a row. The night before he went away.'

'A row?' Max sounded genuinely surprised.

'He's been very quiet the last week or so. Distant, almost cold towards me. It's as though he doesn't want to be in my company. He's been a different person, not the Freddi I know. I just don't understand it, Max.'

'Did you ask him why he was behaving like that?'

'Yes. That night. I couldn't bear it any more. I hadn't slept for a week. I just kept thinking that he didn't want to be with me. So I asked him: 'Freddi, are you tired of me?"

'And ... what did he say?'

'He wouldn't answer. He wouldn't even look me in the eye. I got angry and started crying. "Why are you being so cold to me? I thought you cared about me!" Then he muttered something about me being young and having my life ahead of me and that he didn't want to –'

'Didn't want to what, Lili?'

'He said he didn't want to ruin my life ... It all sounded like excuses to me, like he was scratching around for some reason to jilt me. I ran off in tears calling him every name under the sun... Oh, Max. What am I to do?'

Tears were rolling freely down Lili's cheeks. Max walked towards her and put his hand on her quivering shoulder.

'Freddi cares about you a lot, Lili,' he said gently.

'Then why is he treating me like this?'

Max didn't reply. He walked back to his desk and picked up a folded newspaper.

'About ten days ago Freddi came back in a terrible state,' he said. 'I asked him what the matter was and he showed me this.' He reached the newspaper across to Lili.

The Front

It meant nothing to her. Yet the shield bearing a thick cross next to the title did remind her of something. Then she recalled: the twinkling badges of those skittle-playing business men that night in the Bellevue; they all wore the same symbol on their lapels, as though they were latter-day crusaders.

'What am I looking at, Max?'

'The article in the left-hand column.'

Put an end to racial impurity!

Lili scanned the page with mounting incomprehension. Disjointed phrases leaped from the page: ...*proud and ancient Confederation ... once completely free of Jews ... proudly anti-Semitic ... the Jew is not the same as us ... Every school child knows that he is not and cannot be* ...

She was just about to discard the rabid drivel when a passage caught her eye. Lili studied the words with furious concentration.

Some women seem to have forgotten the debt they owe to their people and race. There are methods for teaching a lesson to those who throw themselves at Jews for Mammon's sake. One day we shall use them!

Lili raised her eyes from the page.

'Don't you see, Lili?' Max's face had assumed a grave expression. 'Freddi doesn't want to put you in danger.'

'Danger of what?'

Max began to feel uncomfortable with his explanation. He shifted from one foot to the other.

'What danger, Max?'

There was an insistence in Lili's voice he couldn't ignore.

'In the Reich any German woman having ... er ... relations with a Jewish man has her hair shorn in public and is paraded through the streets with a placard round her neck with the words ...'

He stopped in his tracks. This was the same girl who not many years before had sat in the same chair stroking Hiddigeigei while he read stories to her. He felt he was committing an impure act by allowing the barbaric insult to pass his lips. He shook his head in refusal.

'What words, Max? Tell me. I'm not a child.'

Her green eyes were flashing with anger.

'Jewish whore.'

The ugliness of the words resounded in the study before fading away.

'He's trying to protect you,' Max explained.

'Well, he doesn't need to,' Lili said firmly. 'We're Swiss not Germ...' She held her hand to her mouth but failed to check herself in time. Her cheeks reddened. The last thing she wanted was to offend her friend.

'I'm so sorry, Max. I didn't mean...' she said contritely.

'It's alright, Lili. You can't imagine how ashamed I am of what's being done in the name of the German people.' His sad gaze scanned the shelves of his beloved books. 'A nation of poets and thinkers,' he added bitterly to himself.

'Who are these people, anyway?' asked Lili.

'The Front?'

Lili nodded.

'They're Nazi sympathisers. Swiss.'

'Swiss?'

'I'm afraid so, Lili.' Max felt as though he was stripping Lili of all her cherished illusions.

'Like those men in the skittle alley,' she muttered to herself.

'Which men?'

'Oh, nothing... Are there many in this Front?'

'Not many. But they have influence. Some politicians, police –'

'Like that pompous prick Hardenschild?'

'Lili!'

It was Max's turn to feel his cheeks flush in embarrassment.

'Well he is... And they soon saw off that Gustloff, didn't they?'

Max laughed; Lili too was smiling.

'And there's the *Front* newspaper, too,' Max continued.

'That's not very much really, is it?'

Max turned serious again.

'It may not seem much to you, Lili, but they have quite a bit of influence on public opinion. There's a mood of hysteria in the country at the moment.'

'Surely, people aren't going to swallow this poison?'

She gave the newspaper on her lap an angry flick.

'Maybe not in such an extreme form ... But many see the refugees as a burden. They're afraid they will take jobs away from their own young people. They fear that some refugees will stop at nothing in their attempt to gain permission to stay here permanently.'

'I don't understand, Max.'

Max tried to swallow his discomfort.

'Some people suspect ... suspect that a refugee will enter into a relationship with a Swiss woman simply to be able to claim the right to stay. Particularly if,' Max hesitated, 'if certain circumstances were to arise.'

Lili felt her cheeks burning.

'Freddi's not like that.'

There was a force behind her words which left no doubt of their truth.

'I know Freddi has only honourable intentions towards you, Lili. You can't imagine how torn he is.'

Max changed tack.

'It doesn't help that you're the daughter of the village policeman. He's responsible for protecting the border and upholding the law. How would he react, if he were to find out? ... And what would your mother say?'

Lili bit her lip. She was fingering the oval-shaped locket hanging by a silver chain around her neck.

'My mother?' she said dreamily. 'My mother would say that I'm old enough to make up my own mind.'

Max appeared not to hear her answer. His thoughts were elsewhere as he gazed towards the far shore of the lake.

And if they march in here like they did in Austria, he asked himself, how long will it be before they introduce the same barbaric laws on 'racial purity'? He glanced across to Lili and those lovely waves of hair.

He thought about his young friend. All emigrants lived in fear of an invasion; Freddi was no exception.

These two young people who had barged into his life were falling for each other before his very eyes, and he was powerless to do anything to thwart love's perilous onslaught.

'Think carefully about what I've said, Lili.'

Lili recognised the earnestness with which he spoke.

'I will,' she said softly as she got up to leave. 'You'll let me know as soon as he's back, won't you?'

'I'll be sure to.'

*   *   *

Her father was just leaving the house when Lili arrived at the door. He was red in the face and flustered.

'What is it, Papa?'

'Ask your mother,' he barked back at her as he brushed past her. 'I'm off to the Bellevue.'

Lili had never seen him in such a temper.

'What's going on?' she asked her mother with trepidation.

'Someone's moved in.' Anna gestured with a nod of her head to the vacant first floor of their house.

Reinforcements had been sent by the authorities to help protect the border. Her father protested in vain that he needed no help. But the command to seal the border was a reality he could no longer resist. The envisaged flood of alien elements had to be repelled.

Rudolf Vischer was the new border guard assigned to the village.

Lili was immediately struck by his dashing appearance. He was as tall as a Swiss guard. His uniform was immaculate, and his boots glistened in the midday sun. On first setting eyes on Lili he doffed his police cap and displayed a head of blond hair.

'Grüezi, Fräulein Vogelsang. What a pleasure it is to meet you. No one thought to warn me that the daughter of the household would be so beautiful.'

Lili was flattered by his gallantry. 'It's nice to meet you, Herr Vischer. I hope you enjoy your stay here.'

'I'm sure I will,' he said with a smile.

Although much the younger man, it soon became apparent to Lili that Vischer saw himself as her father's superior. He constantly reminded her father of the procedures they were supposed to follow and corrected the poor grammar and inappropriate register in his written reports. Vischer had drawn up detailed charts for their border duties.

Otto cut a sullen and bitter figure in the village. To his horror, he now found his evenings taken up with extra patrols, curtailing his drinking and cards at the Bellevue. His life had been well and truly put out of joint. He sought compensation in heavier drinking. Lili would often hear him cursing Vischer's name. But in his dealings with her, the new arrival in the village was charm personified.

*　　*　　*

Not long into his stay they bumped into each other at the shared entrance to the house. Vischer had the knack of appearing the very moment Lili was about to leave the house. He greeted her cheerily.

'And where's the young lady going to now?'

'I'm just off to the baker's for my mother, Herr Vischer.'

He smiled. 'Please, call me Rudi.'

Lili restrained a laugh. The idea of calling this man she barely knew, and who was twice her age, by his first name struck her as absurd. Thereafter she tried to avoid addressing him at all.

'Might I perhaps accompany you, Lili? May I call you Lili?'

'Er ... yes, Herr Visch... But there's really no need. I'm only going to get some bread.'

'You would do me a great honour, Lili.'

They set off for the bakery together. Vischer offered to carry Lili's basket, even though it was empty. Lili was starting to feel uneasy in his company. Walking by her side with her basket hooked on his arm, Vischer made his move.

'Have you no sweetheart, Lili? Such a beautiful girl like you must have many admirers?'

Lili hesitated. The conversation was moving in a direction she hadn't anticipated.

'No, I haven't.'

'You do surprise me.'

'Well, it's true. I'm very busy training to become a nurse. I really don't have any time for that sort of thing.'

'A nurse? Good for you, Lili. We're certainly going to need nurses ... But haven't you any time for a nice walk by the lake this Sunday afternoon?'

Lili's mind raced for an excuse.

'Er, no, really I can't. I promised I'd go fishing with my father. I row the boat for him, you see.'

She glanced across at Vischer. He looked like a man who had momentarily forgotten where he was. She felt constrained to say something to soften the perceptible blow to his pride.

'But don't you have anyone ... anyone special?' she asked.

Vischer's eyes narrowed. 'Alas, I've had my heart broken, Lili. It is so difficult to find someone pure and innocent and completely trusting.'

*　　*　　*

Lili's heart leapt when she heard of Freddi's return. She ran all the way down the street to Max's door.

'Is he here? Is Freddi back?'

'What, no milk today, Lili? Hiddigeigei will be disappointed.' He smiled at his own disregarded joke. 'Come on in.'

Lili's eyes scanned the house for visible signs of Freddi. Max anticipated her question.

'I'm afraid he's rather unwell. He's returned with a high fever and is lying in bed sleeping it off. He should be on his feet again in a couple of days. If you'd like to come back then ...'

Come back in two days? How could Max be so cruel? She couldn't wait a moment longer.

Max read the distress written on Lili's face.

'Unless…' he said.

Lili stared at him, eyes wide in expectation.

'You're soon to be a nurse. The practice would do you good. You could care for him. I'm not very experienced when it comes to tending the sick. I've never had to look after anyone else but myself. What should I –?'

Lili shot out of the room and up the stairs to where Freddi had taken to his bed. There he lay in a deep sleep, his face as white as the sheets. For the next few days she sat by his bedside watching over her patient, mopping his brow, moistening his lips and straightening his pillows.

*   *   *

One evening she interrupted her vigil to join Max in his study. Freddi was sound asleep. He was clearly drained from his recent journey.

Lili curled up on the armchair and opened her book. Max was busy writing at his desk with his back to her. Hiddigeigei jumped up and sprawled out on her lap. But Lili couldn't concentrate on the story. She put her book to one side.

'Max, who's Oskar?'

'Oskar? … I don't know anyone called Oskar.'

'Yes you do, Max.'

'I don't think I do …'

'Does *Oskar's transport column* ring any bells?'

Max raised his eyes slowly from his text.

'It wouldn't have anything to do with that printing press in the cellar ... the messages in bottles ... those strange books, would it?' Lili perceived his discomfiture. She was exacting sweet revenge for the way he'd once teased her about Hiddigeigei's antics.

Max turned to face Lili. There was an ironic twinkle in her eye.

'How the hell? ... Oh, I see. You and your friend – I take it there were two of you? – you were evidently even more curious than I'd thought.' Max laughed in the forlorn hope this would deflect Lili from her line of questioning.

'C'mon, Max. I've got a pretty good idea about what's going on. I'm not that stupid.' The twinkle turned quickly into a schoolmistress's frown.

Far from it, thought Max. But you are the border guard's daughter.

'Don't worry. I'm not going to tell my father about any of this.'

How does she read my thoughts as though they were inscribed across my forehead, a bemused Max asked himself.

'I'd have to own up to breaking into your house, wouldn't I? Anyway, he's got enough on his plate with Vischer.'

Max's eyes darkened at the mention of the name.

'Vischer ... He's one of Hardenschild's spies. You watch out for him, Lili.'

Lili brushed aside the mention of her would-be suitor with a gesture of contempt.

'What are you two up to exactly? What are all these journeys Freddi goes on 'selling textiles?'

'Textiles? Oh –'

'He's not a travelling salesman, is he?' All irony had vanished from her eyes.

Max was in a corner. Lili and Freddi had grown too close. It wasn't fair to keep putting her through this torment every time Freddi went off for a few days.

He looked at her with an unexpected realisation. She was not the shy, wild girl he once invited into his home. She had lost that girlishness and become an assured and confident woman. The time for protecting her was over; it was time to come clean.

'Ok. You win, Lili ... It all started many years ago. It's all Harry Haller's fault really. You remember him? Hiddigeigei's friend in the tree. He persuaded me to get involved in smuggling propaganda across the lake for an organisation he was a part of –'

'Oskar's transport column?'

'What you and your accomplice saw in the cellar was work in progress ... I could've kicked myself for leaving the door unlocked.'

Max laughed. 'You obviously gave yourselves a bit of a fright down there, judging by your hasty exit. Whatever happened?'

'How did you work out it was me?' asked Lili.

'I'd never have guessed really. I imagined it was some of the boys in the village getting up to no good. But then I saw the way you climbed up the tree to rescue Hiddigeigei and the penny dropped. I'm sorry if I made you feel guilty, but I wanted to make sure you'd never tell anyone what you'd seen.'

'So how did Freddi get caught up in it all?'

'Believe me, Lili, it was far from my intention. There was no stopping him. There is no stopping him.'

'But you know how risky it is for him, Max. If the police find out about it he'll be deported and we'll never see him again.'

Her voice filled with tears.

Max moved towards her and took her in his arms to comfort her. As he held her tight, he felt a momentary sensation of pleasure. He'd forgotten what it was like to be this close to a woman.

Lili pulled away slightly and looked him in the eye.

'Tell me honestly, Max: what exactly is Freddi's part in all this?'

Max struggled to regain his composure.

'He ... he acts as a courier. He goes across the border – it's alright, he's on a forged Swiss passport – and makes contact with those we know are in greatest need, to help get them safely across.'

Lili thought for a moment.

'*Wilhelm Tell*,' she said enigmatically.

'Wilhelm Tell? No, he's not a part of the column, not as far as I know,' Max joked.

'Freddi *was* on that train from Vienna. He had a copy of *Wilhelm Tell* with him so that Felix could spot him. It was Freddi who slipped him the note with the telephone number. That's why he was so concerned about him.'

'Felix? Oh, yes. Felix ... Not one of the transport column's more glorious moments.'

Lili was sunk in thought. Then she said abruptly: 'What happens now, Max?'

A look of fear cast a shadow over her beautiful green eyes.

Max frowned. 'I'm afraid ... I think we've run out of options now the border's been sealed and the chain's been broken. And with the likes of Vischer around making life much more difficult for us ...'

'Do you mean that was his last trip?'

Max nodded. 'It's become far too dangerous. It's the end of the road for Oskar's transport column.'

Lili welcomed the news with a sigh of relief.

*   *   *

After days of intensive care by the heart, Freddi was well enough to sit in the garden and complete his recovery.

It was a beautiful late autumn day. There was freshness in the slight breeze ruffling the lake.

Hiddigeigei had caught a white mouse under his paw. He hadn't eaten it but was playing with his prey, guarding it closely like a captor his captive.

Lili and Freddi sat side by side on a bench under the same tree where she had rescued the injured cat many years before.

All was quiet. Golden leaves rained down on them. Freddi took Lili's hand gently in his. He looked at her with tenderness in his eyes.

'Lili, I've been meaning to tell you how much I...'

But in his emotion the thread of his words ran out.

Where words failed, their eyes spoke.

Where their eyes were silent, their hearts spoke.

Lili's cheeks reddened as though dawn itself had painted them. She wrapped her arms around his neck.

Their lips took over the words of their hearts. Impassioned, they placed upon each other their first sweet, heavy kiss.

Lili felt joy and sadness: joy at the first full kiss of love; sadness that it was now gone forever.

Hiddigeigei looked on from his favourite spot on the summerhouse roof where the sun warmed his coat and he could survey his garden.

And the eyes of the cat saw. And the soul of the cat laughed. Puzzled he asked himself why they were kissing. They were not biting each other in hatred. They were not eating each other in hunger. Why did humankind kiss? And why did the young ones always kiss as though they had invented it?

From his study window Max raised his eyes with a heavy heart from the familiar pages of the love story to look upon the scene unfolding before him.

'Kiss me again,' Lili said gently, placing Freddi's hand on her breast.

XVIII

The music of the violin, accordion and double-bass, accompanied by the rhythmical, regular stamping of feet, grew more distinct as Freddi walked the path leading to Ursprung's barn. It was a day of rejoicing and a night of celebration.

'Come along, Freddi. It'll be fun.'

He'd been reluctant, what with his two left feet, but Lili had insisted.

'I'll see you there at eight. I'll be waiting for you.'

The large doors of the barn opened to reveal a central area cleared of ploughs and presses, hoes, scythes, shears and pruning hooks. A red-orange glow of light escaped into the dusk. Inside, the barn was lit by coloured lanterns suspended from the beams; candles reflected in the rows of glasses on long wooden tables. The walls were decorated with garlands of flowers and grasses from the meadows. An improvised platform had been erected for the band: the violinist dressed from head to toe in black, with a sprig in his top hat, was leaping about as he frantically bowed his fiddle, putting in constant danger the glass of beer placed near his feet; the accordionist sat morosely on a stool, hardly looking up; the squat double-bass player was hunched over his giant instrument plucking its heavy strings and making the barn vibrate.

Freddi stood in the doorway. A row of couples promenaded the improvised dance floor with an occasional hop and a skip. His eyes searched for Lili amongst the swirling skirts and blouses embroidered with Alpine flowers. There were girls with beautiful eyes; girls with beautiful noses; girls with beautiful figures; girls with ribbons in their beautiful hair. But none was as lovely as the one now waving to him from the crowd as the last bars of the dance played out.

Lili was running towards him, delight shining on her face. He kissed her cheek, warm and dewed from the exertion.

'You came!'

'Did you think I wouldn't?'

The music changed to a sedate country waltz.

'Dance with me.'

'Lili, I told you I'm not very good.'

'Come on. I'll teach you.'

With other couples they took up a position opposite each other on the square. Seeing the other men bow to their partners, Freddi did the same. Lili took hold of her striped skirt in both hands and curtseyed in return.

'Hold me tighter.'

Freddi's right hand pressed into the small of Lili's back. He spread his fingers to enjoy the sensation.

'What do I do now?' he asked in panic.

'Walk forwards. It's very easy. Listen to the rhythm ... One-two-three, one-two-three ... That's it.'

As they walked Lili turned smoothly under his raised right arm. Her skirt swished from side to side revealing her shapely calves. She had her right hand on her hip and was smiling flirtatiously at him. With an occasional skip they walked around clockwise in a circle swinging their outstretched arms from side to side.

'Kneel!'

Freddi dropped to his right knee in instant obedience. He was starting to feel intoxicated by the sensuousness of it all. With her left hand on her hip and her right hand lifting her skirt, Lili danced her steps around him, swaying in perfect time to the music.

'Now it's your turn.'

Freddi tried to follow the other men. Stamp, stamp, leap. Stamp, stamp, leap. They danced their steps clapping their hands. Men and women circled each other, nodding and greeting as they executed a swing. As they passed each other, Lili stole a kiss. Not to be outdone Freddi was ready to steal it back the next time round.

Lili took his arms and twisted them between her own in a complicated hold. She peeked at him through the triangular shaped windows their contorted limbs had created:

'Look at me,' she said coquettishly.

'Now we waltz.' Lili placed her hand firmly on Freddi's shoulder. He felt at one with the music and his partner. As the dance came to its conclusion he took hold of Lili's waist and lifted her as high as he could before letting her slide slowly down his body.

They sat down for a rest and drank generous amounts of cider. The dance floor emptied. The violinist put down his fiddle and went and picked up a saw from among the tools at the end of the barn. Gripping its handle between his thighs he slowly moved his bow across the teeth as he bent and released its flexible, metal form with his other hand. The ghostly sound he made sent shivers down their spines.

After the interlude the music became more and more frenetic. In all the whirling and spinning, laughing and singing, the two lovers forgot themselves and the world. The sound of joyful celebration spilled out of the barn into the surrounding countryside where a full moon had risen. In all the chaos Freddi often found himself separated from Lili. When they came together again they greeted each other like long lost friends. At times Freddi needed to sit down and rest. His eyes watched sadly as Lili overflowed with joy as she danced with other partners. She deliberately avoided his mournful gaze.

'Are you jealous?'

'Not at all. Why should I be?' he lied.

'So why do you look so sad when I'm dancing with other men?'

'I'm not jealous. It's just that I can't stand dancing with other women. It's like I'm holding a block of wood in my arms.'

Lili gave him a vivacious glance.

'Let's go outside and get a breath of air,' she said quickly.

Lili led Freddi by the hand away from the noise of the barn. The velvety evening air fanned their flushed faces.

'Come with me,' she said. They walked a few steps into the darkness. 'You see this wall? This is where I used to sit with Eva when we were little. I had to practically pull her up, though.'

'Eva? Who's Eva?'

'She was the short girl in the green skirt, the one with blond plaits.'

'Oh, you mean the one who squeezed my hand suggestively during the round dance?' Freddi teased.

Lili looked at him with a faint pout. It hadn't escaped her keen eye how closely her childhood friend had danced with Freddi when given the opportunity.

'And no doubt you were introduced to her crotch, too.'

'Lili!'

'What? It's true. Ask any of the boys in the village.'

'Are you drunk, Lili?'

'I might be a bit tipsy ... Come on. I'll give you a leg-up,' she said, softening.

'What?'

'A leg-up. Help you get up on the wall.'

Freddi stepped tentatively into Lili's joined hands. He heaved himself up the wall, his knees and feet struggling for support. With an effort he hauled himself to the top, turned awkwardly into a sitting position and was astonished to see Lili already seated beside him.

'How the hell did you manage that?'

Lili grinned. They sat in silence on the wall which was still warm from the afternoon's sun.

'I remember once we sat here, Eva and me. We'd been in the barn drinking apple juice fresh from the press. We tried to out-drink each other. Then we got dreadful stomach cramps. In panic we jumped down off the wall and ... well, it was like an explosion. We laughed till we cried. Then we peed ourselves.'

Freddi was laughing.

'I like it when you laugh,' said Lili earnestly. She had one eye on the ground over the other side of the wall. How kind of Ursprung to provide plenty of loose straw for a soft landing – and a bed, she thought.

'Come on. After three. One ... two ...'

'I'm not jumping down there,' interrupted Freddi with a look of feigned horror on his face.

'Why ever not?' Lili's voice betrayed the disappointment of thwarted designs.

'After what you've just told me? I don't know what I'm going to land in.'

'Freddi, we were eight years old!'

They laughed together. Lili stroked his face.

'Don't be scared,' she said gently. 'I'll hold your hand if you want.'

They landed as one in the thick mattress of straw.

'Lili –'

She put her hand to his lips to silence his words.

'The music's stopped,' she whispered. 'They're leaving the barn to go down to the lake. Squeeze up close to me.'

Their hearts thumped in unison as a procession of decorated paper lanterns, held aloft on long poles like cheerfully decapitated heads, moved along the top of the wall as the revellers made their way to the lakeside. The two lovers stared into each other's eyes, flickering red, yellow and orange as each lantern passed by. They heard voices:

'Where's Lili? Has anyone seen her?'

'She must've set off already.'

'I saw her. She slipped out with that dark stranger. No prize for guessing what they're up to.'

Lili giggled on hearing Eva's voice. It was Freddi's turn to press a hand to her lips.

Raucous singing accompanied the parade of lanterns and torches as it descended to the shore of the lake. An armada of rowing boats awaited them. Shrieks of laughter faded in the distance.

There was silence. And then a nightingale broke out into a song of love.

'What are you thinking?' asked Lili.

'I'm just looking at the stars remembering the time I was being sent back. Konrad, my police escort, abandoned me close to the border. I was all alone, lying in a field, on an evening like this. I hadn't a clue where I was. I remember how desperate I felt.'

'Freddi,'

'Yes, Lili?'

'You're not alone. You're with me.'

Freddi turned to look at Lili. Her fingers were toying with the button of her blouse. Moonlight caught the mother-of-pearl as it slipped reluctantly through the tight slit of the button-hole. The fabric of Lili's blouse opened up like a flower. Freddi's eyes moved from the glint of a silver locket buried deep in her shadowy cleavage to the soft mounds of flesh constrained by curves of lace. Lili swiftly undid the other buttons and slipped off her blouse.

'Undo it,' she ordered.

Freddi reached awkwardly around her back and struggled with the clasp. Lili pulled his head towards her, ruffling his thick hair. He kissed her neck and shoulders. In the instant he lifted up to admire her, a high-pitched screech rent the evening air. The spangled light of the exploding firework shone on Lili's bare skin.

Interrupted by the explosion, they sat up on their elbows to look in awe at the fireflies now hovering over the inky lake. The lantern-bearers were rowing out to get a better view of the fireworks.

Freddi's hand moved chastely into the lovely valley of flesh between Lili's ribs and hips.

'Don't be shy,' she said. Encouraged, he drew his fingers gently across the slight rise of her stomach, over the pronounced jut of her hip-bone until they came to rest on the soft inside of her thigh. With one hand Lili yanked at his belt so hard he gasped audibly; with the other she freed herself of her skirt.

'Don't you want to?' she asked breathlessly.

'Of course I do!'

'Well then?'

'It's just ... It's the first time ...'

'That makes two of us.'

Flashes of exploding fireworks shone in their eyes and on their bodies.

He was clumsy and hasty. At one moment Lili let out an involuntary cry.

'Did I hurt you?' he asked.

'Don't be silly.'

She was smiling. A tear slipped from the corner of her bright green eyes.

They lay together for hours on their bed of straw. They watched the last man-made constellations fall from the sky and felt the night air cool their enflamed and trembling bodies.

XIX

A horseman was on the move.

It was not the horseman who rode over the frozen lake and died of fright.

A horseman was on the move.

He rode a horse that was the colour of blood.

To him was given power to take peace from the earth.

To him was given a great sword to slay all on the earth.

The unimaginable had occurred.

War had broken out.

Men had left the fields and become its serried henchmen. Jack-booted they roamed the streets with windows for eyes and great snouts for noses to protect against the death-bringing air.

The storm had been brewing for months. Black clouds amassed on the horizon in the north. The far shore receded ever more into the distance as friendship was traded for hostility.

No longer did fishermen meet in the middle of the lake to exchange a joke. No longer did day trippers come in their droves to eat fish from the lake at the restaurant. Throughout that spring and summer they were awaited. The tables were laid, and the waitresses stood ready to greet the guests. But only a handful arrived; they kept their heads down, spoke in hushed voices and left as quickly as they came.

In time the ferries stopped crisscrossing the lake. The hotels were empty, the restaurants deserted. Distant memories now were the honeymooners on their way eastwards to Vienna, Prague and Budapest; the families returning from holidays in the south in Venice, Florence, Rome and Naples; the businessmen en route to Berlin, Danzig and Warsaw; the tanned and optimistic climbers coming to challenge the mountains.

The ferries lay crippled in their harbours. Only fishermen ventured out on to the eerily deserted lake which echoed the sounds of shattered glass, tortured cries and marching boots.

In the village they were preparing for the end of the age of light. Starting in the early afternoon the most eager among the villagers pulled in their shutters, screwed in blue bulbs, locked their doors and covered every crack of daylight with black paper.

By six in the evening the whole of the region was plunged into a medieval darkness that deepened with the passing hours. Streets and squares were lost in the blackness; pale-bluish street lights at important crossroads were the last reminders that electricity had been invented. Children on bicycles swarmed like ghostly fireflies. Despite instructions to stay indoors, many wanted to witness the blackout for themselves.

Pedestrians could hardly see one foot ahead and walked constantly in fear of bumping into neighbours – unless a burning cigarette warned of their presence. Life-long friends passed each other without a word of recognition. Young lovers found plentiful opportunities for trysts and touches.

Small countries were disappearing off the map with the same haste with which they had once appeared. The machines of war were moving along the dusty streets, through the fields and across the skies. From the tops of trees and steeples you could see them amassed in readiness.

Uncertainty and fear polluted the dark water of the fountain in the square and infested the petals of the geraniums in the window boxes.

* * *

One Sunday afternoon the storm bells rang across the lake.

The square slowly filled; the villagers left their houses to share their fears. The fountain drank in their ominous words.

'So that's it then ... It's happened.'

'What'll become of us now?'

'There's no hope of peace ... So much for 'No more war!' What an illusion that was!'

'Peace? What's peace? It's just like our Emmentaler: if there's no war there's no peace – if there's no cheese there's no hole.'

'How's it come to this? I just don't understand it. Why can't they agree to differ?'

'It's their fault ... like it was last time. It's always those bloody Germans who start it.'

'That's one thing everyone agrees on – apart from the Germans.'

'But he claims he's only answering violence with violence.'

'What nonsense! What violence is he talking about?'

'How long is it all going to last?... Perhaps it'll all end in Poland.'

The early days of September saw much movement and activity. Soldiers came, were billeted in the stables and moved on. Sandbags were handed out, ration cards distributed.

Every evening the villagers would gather in the Bellevue to listen to the voice on the radio reporting on the progress war was making. After a few weeks of unbridled violence, peace returned. Or the war was pretending, keeping a watchful eye.

*   *   *

Some young boys were playing on the shoreline just outside the village. Deep in the thick undergrowth one of them noticed a small yellow object. The boys tugged hard at the brambles and branches to get at it. It was a package, the address could still be clearly read: *To Reich Chancellor Adolf Hitler.*

It must have fallen from the sky, dropped by one of the aeroplanes which flew over regularly. Astonished by their find and not knowing what to do with it, the boys took the square package to Lili's father. It sat on his desk, a menacing presence. Otto and the boys stood staring at it.

The border guard walked slowly round his desk looking at it closely from all angles while the boys speculated wildly.

'Perhaps it's a bomb ...'

'Or it's poison.'

'Maybe there are war secrets inside.'

Otto listened to each of their hypotheses in turn.

'Well lads, there's only one thing for it,' he announced with a grin.

'We'll just have to open it up and have a look.'

He took out his penknife and was just about to pick up the parcel to cut the taut string when Rudolf Vischer, alerted by the commotion in the recently tidied office, entered the room.

'Stop right there,' he barked.

Vischer inspected the package sitting in the middle of the table.

'That is the property of a neighbouring state ... Indeed, according to the regulations of the postal and telecommunications service, it is the property of the Führer of the German Reich. As such it must be returned forthwith.'

Lili's father closed his penknife with a loud click of disappointment. It was a disappointment matched if not exceeded by that felt by the boys.

'Aw, why can't we just see what's in it?' moaned one.

'We can always tie it up again.'

'Absolutely not ... It is forbidden by the regulations. I must make a report and telephone head office for instructions. Now, leave the office at once. This is not a playground.'

The boys filed out disgruntled that the mystery contained within the package had not been revealed to them.

Rudolf Vischer had already made enemies.

He closed the office door behind the last of the sulking boys.

'Vogelsang, how could you have even thought of opening it? It is addressed to Adolf Hitler.'

'Fuck Hitler,' Otto muttered to himself and left the room with a dismissive wave of his hand.

* * *

By the spring of the following year, war was back on its jack-booted march. It had caught its breath, refreshed itself and was ready to go. Countries fell one by one to its lightning attacks. Neutral countries, small countries like their own had been violated. It was just a matter of time and they would be surrounded from the north, the west, the east and the south.

The forests in the north were trembling.

Panic set in. Those wealthy enough to own a car set off from the border areas in search of safety in the interior. Without cars, the poor were left stranded and prepared for the worst.

The roads flowed with the escaping population; quickly they silted up.

Then, contrary to all their worst fears, the hostile armies moved off in a different direction, and the motorists returned home shame-faced.

*   *   *

The General appealed for calm.

But he had already drawn up his plan. The defending soldiers would retreat to a mountain redoubt, sacrificing the lower lying border areas to the invading forces. They would blow up all the bridges and passes and fight a war of attrition. The border population was to stay put. A part had to be sacrificed to save the whole.

The rumour of his visit spread like wildfire. His train would be stopping at their small station, and he was to address those about to be sacrificed.

The village hadn't witnessed such an illustrious arrival since the delivery by rail of three big bells for the church tower. Young and old congregated on that occasion around the platform as the train puffed in to the tiny station bearing the ornately carved bells. They watched them being hoisted on to a long platform and towed up the narrow street to the church, there to be pulled into the tower on thick ropes by strong young men. A long night of festivities followed the first peal of the new church bells.

The train pulled slowly in to the village station. Everyone strained to get a glimpse.

'The General!'

'Where?'

'There he is!'

'Where? I can't see him…'

From the midst of a cloud of billowing steam stepped a thin, frail looking man in a long leather coat, black riding boots and gloves. He was holding a walking stick. His peaked cap half concealed a thin face, long nose and grey moustache. A half-smoked cigarette was held precariously between his thin lips.

'It's the General!' a cry went up.

'Hooray for the General!'

'Long live the General!'

Those about to be sacrificed cheered in unison at the appearance of this little old man, the architect of their execution.

On the platform he turned towards the crowd and gave a short wave. His words were few and hard to catch in the chaos. Legend has it he simply said: 'Think as men and act as men.'

Then he disappeared as quickly as he'd appeared into the cloud.

1940

XX

There was something strange in the air that day. The fishermen kept looking nervously at the sky. The farmers were fretting over their fruit trees afraid that the hot dry blasts of the coming wind would leave them charred.

An unnatural stillness reigned. Man and beast laboured to breathe; all endeavour proved a strain.

It began with a gentle hush among the crowns of the trees. A light shore wind started to play upon the water's surface. Out on the lake the fishermen watched the patterns and interpreted the signs of things to come. They saw an unusual glow in the east and feared a hailstorm over the lake: whirring and crashing of icy stones turning the waters into a fury where pitiful souls cried out for mercy. Quickly they made for a safe haven.

The storm never formed over the lake itself. The mountains shrugged it off their mighty shoulders and left it to the mercy of the winds to haul it back and forth across the water. As one wind prevailed, the sky was turned into a pandemonium of black, grey, yellow and violet clouds. The lake beneath took off in a fury of greenish pitch as surf-covered waves hurled themselves after each other in a race to the shore. Where the other wind held sway and the sky was still a perfect blue, the lake was transformed into a mirror of the most wonderful turquoise. Yet anyone still basking in the sunlight knew that it was just a matter of time.

By evening the wait was over.

Flashes of lightning and rolls of thunder announced its arrival. In broad waves separated by wide valleys the water rose to three metres on the open lake. The storm grabbed hold of any boat that hadn't made it back to port in time, tossing it around mercilessly like a walnut. The spray shot over the harbour walls, threatening to consume the fertile land.

There is a great thrill in watching flashes of lightning illuminate the black depths of the water, thought Max as he observed the scene through his study window, a glass of wine in his hand.

The young lovers were in the kitchen preparing an evening meal. Wafts of fragrant steam made his mouth water in anticipation. He was enjoying their company.

The storm continued unabated. They ate together listening in silence to its raging. The lovers heard in it the unbound power of their own passions and were aroused; the older man listened to the storm of steel engulfing the continent and feared the worst. Only when they rose to clear the table and wash the dishes, late into the evening, were they aware of any diminishing of the violence outside.

Freddi wandered into the study and idly glanced through the telescope trained on the far shoreline. Thick clouds scudded across the sky concealing a pale moon. Every so often the still unpacified surface of the lake was revealed. He scanned the water out of habit.

During such an illuminated interval Freddi thought he saw an object rise and fall with the swell. He lifted his head to look with the naked eye.

Nothing. He must have imagined it.

Peering once more through the telescope he became convinced there was something on the lake, hidden and then uncovered with each lifting wave.

'Max, can you come here a minute?'

Max arrived drying his hands on a towel.

'What is it?'

'I think there's something on the lake ... Can you see it?'

Max put his eye to the telescope.

'No, I can't see anything ... Wait! There is something. It's some sort of raft ...and there's someone on it.'

'How could anyone be out there in this storm? We haven't had a call in ages,' said Freddi.

The sealing of the borders had brought an end to the telephone calls announcing grandma's visits.

'What are we going to do? We can't just leave him there? He must be clinging on for dear life in this storm.'

Max thought for a moment.

'He must've come from the camp at Friedrichshafen. He'll have been on the lake for hours.

We've got to fish him out, if he's still alive that is. Let's get the boat –'

'Can I come?'

Only then were the two of them aware that Lili had been standing at the door listening.

'Don't worry. I've been out on the lake with my father in far worse than this,' she lied nonchalantly.

Max looked at Freddi who shrugged his shoulders. There was no time to argue, and they both knew there was no holding her back.

The streets were deserted as the three of them walked quickly down to the small harbour where Max moored his boat. A torch guided their steps on the treacherous ladder as they clambered down. They set off quickly, a pale lamp illuminating a band of water which became more agitated as they motored out. Occasionally there was a break in the last remaining storm clouds allowing the moon to shine with greater intensity on the lake's surface. The boat bounced along covering them with spray. The noise of the boat thudding into the waves, and the spray of water splashing around them made any communication impossible. Max, Freddi and Lili all fixed their eyes intently on the narrow strip of water before them, searching for any sign of the raft.

'There! Look!' Lili cried out suddenly.

A raft-like object bobbed in the water. A dark shape sprawled motionless upon it. It was impossible to see if there was any sign of life.

Max cut the engine as they approached the raft. The lamp at the front of the boat struggled to hold the scene in its feeble beam.

'Hello! … Can you hear me?' Freddi tried to attract the attention of the figure clinging to a dark round shape.

At closer sight the raft was a pathetic structure of old boards strung to a couple of oil drums. It was amazing he'd made it this far. Whatever makeshift plank he'd used as an oar must have been wrenched from his tired grip by the storm.

The motor boat and raft were both lurching and heaving in the swell.

A head raised itself slightly from the boards.

'We're here to help you. We'll take you to land.'

The man uttered something in a language they didn't understand.

Max immediately confirmed his earlier supposition that he was a slave worker who had escaped from the concentration camp just outside Friedrichshafen. Most of the prisoners there were Slavs deported from their occupied homelands and forced to work under dreadful conditions for the German war effort. He'd heard of a few others who had managed to escape. More likely than not, the man on the raft was a Russian or Pole.

'Russki?' Max tried.

The man stirred.

Freddi leant towards the man, briefly given a more recognisable form by the moonlight. He stretched out his hand to grasp a slippery forearm.

'Come on … That's it …'

The exhausted fugitive half stood and half knelt precariously on his raft.

Suddenly there was a renewed gust of wind. The clouds obscured the moon. They were plunged into darkness.

There was a shriek, the sound of a thud against the side of the boat and a heavy splash.

'Shit!' cried Freddi. 'I've lost him. He's in the water.'

'Quick! The lamp ... Shine it over here,' shouted Max.

Paralysed by horror the three scanned the black water in vain.

'I can't see him anywhere ... We've lost him. Fuck!'

There was an awful pause.

'There he is!' cried Lili.

Before they could react, Lili had stripped off her jumper, kicked off her shoes and was over the side of the boat.

'Lili! What the –'

The poor wretch, knocked unconscious in his attempt to clamber off the raft, was drowning. Lili swam a few powerful strokes to where she had spotted him. She dived down.

Nothing.

'I'm over here! Shine the light over here,' she spluttered on re-emerging.

At that very moment the moon lit up the lake.

Calm was restored.

Lili glimpsed a darker mass appearing and disappearing.

She dived once more and caught hold of a limb.

She held tightly to the arm.

Come on! It's not far.

She stroked hard with her free arm.

'Come on! A bit further. Keep going,' she implored

She tugged the dead weight.

Voices were getting louder, showing her the way.

'Lili, where are you? Lili!'

One more push with her free arm.

She looked up and saw the shadow of the boat. She reached towards its wooden hull.

'There you are, Lili. Thank God!' Max cried out.

The two men hauled their heavy catch into the boat. Coughing and spluttering filled the cold night air as the fugitive came to, shaken and slapped by his rescuers.

'There you go … You're safe now…'

Lili sat shivering watching their efforts.

'Let's get him back as quickly as we can,' said Max.

The half-drowned man sat hunched opposite Lili. She could hear his teeth chattering with cold and terror. Never in all her life had she seen such abject misery. What indescribable torment must have driven him to attempt to cross on this of all nights?

Freddi wrapped his thin jacket around her and held her tight. Bitter tears rolled down her cheeks. The tears were not for herself, not even for the hapless refugee seated before her. They were an expression of pity for a cruel world.

They arrived back in the harbour. Chilled to the bone and exhausted, Lili was the first to climb up the treacherous ladder on to the jetty. As she reached the top a powerful light blinded her.

'Stop right there! Swiss border police!'

Lili raised her arm to shield her eyes from the beam.

She recognised the voice straightaway. It was Vischer.

Behind her stood the half-drowned man, frozen with fear. Max was just coming up the ladder and stopped on the topmost rung. Still in darkness, Freddi quickly hid himself against the side of the boat.

'What have we got here?' Vischer asked sarcastically. Then, shining his torch again in Lili's face, he changed his tone.

'Lili? What in God's name are you doing out on the lake at this time of night and in these conditions?'

He shone his torch at the two other shadowy figures.

'And you, Meyer?'

'We went to rescue this poor man from the storm. We must get him into the warm,' explained Lili.

'Just a moment ... You found him on the lake? I'm sorry. He must come with me for questioning.'

'But Herr Vischer ...'

Max spoke for the first time, moving away from the ladder in an attempt to distract the border guard from Freddi's hiding place.

'Herr Vischer, this man was on the point of drowning. Can't you see the condition he's in? We've got to get him inside, out of his soaking clothes, and give him some warm food.'

'Herr Meyer. I have my orders. He's entering illegally. As a suspect he is to be taken immediately into police custody, interrogated and then returned to the border.'

'Please ... Rudi,' Lili implored.

A sound of steps came from the direction of the village. Another beam of light flashed into their faces.

Vischer turned around.

'Ah, Vogelsang, reinforcements at last. We appear to have a refugee attempting to enter illegally.'

Otto looked at the assembled group.

'Lili? What the hell are you doing here? You're soaking…'

'Papa, we – I mean Herr Meyer and myself – went to rescue this poor man from the lake. I dived in to fish him out after he stumbled trying to get into Herr Meyer's boat.'

'For Christ's sake, Lili! How many times have I told you never to go out in a storm? You could have got yourself killed… And as for you,' he turned his anger on Max, 'What the fuck do you think you're playing at taking a young girl out in a boat on a night like this?'

'Otto –' Max attempted to respond.

'Vogelsang to you!'

Max held up a hand in apology.

'Please can we get this poor man into the warm? We can sort the rest out later.'

'Papa, please!' Lili begged.

Her tearful eyes softened her father's anger. Otto looked at the fugitive. He recalled the time he had to fish a refugee from the lake and heard the horrors that had driven him to such folly. Damn the regulations, he thought. He'd put up with Vischer pulling rank for too long. The conceited ass with his regulations and rotas! It was time to take charge of the situation.

'Come on! Let's get you into the warm, both of you.'

'Just a minute, Vogelsang. Aren't you forgetting something?'

'If I am, I'm sure you're about to tell me, Vischer.'

'How do you know he's not an agent sent over to carry out some act of sabotage. How can you be sure he's not a spy?'

Otto shone his torch over the quivering wretch.

'Does he look like a spy to you?'

Vischer hesitated momentarily.

'We have to follow the correct procedures.'

During this exchange their voices were becoming ever more animated as months of mutual distrust, resentment and suspicion finally found an outlet.

'To hell with your procedures.'

'Not mine. Those of the police department and the state. Where would we be –'

'I don't care whose they are or where we'd be … Damn them anyway.'

Lili's heart swelled with pride as she saw her father in a long forgotten light.

'This man is coming with me at once,' Vischer shouted, pulling the refugee roughly by the arm.

'I'll be damned if he is!'

Over the road a light went on in an upstairs window.

The window opened, and a drowsy head peered out.

'Hey, quiet. Some people are trying to sleep.'

'Mind your own business!' barked Vischer.

'Do you mean me?' The sleepy voice was stirring.

'Do I mean you?' was Vischer's sarcastic riposte.

'Don't you tell me my business, you puffed up little toad.'

'How dare you call me … that. I'll … I'll report you for insulting an officer of the state, whoever you are.'

A loud raspberry was blown from the window.

Another window opened.

'What's going on, neighbour? What's all the row about? Has someone had too much to drink?'

'The Sherriff's just threatened to arrest me.'

'The Sherriff? Pompous ass ... Hey, Vischer, what's all the noise about?'

'I'm arresting a fugitive who has tried to enter illegally.'

'What? This I've got to see.'

One by one, lights appeared in the upper storeys of the houses along the street. Windows opened and heads protruded, peering into the dark. Within a matter of minutes the whole street was awoken by the din. Villagers in nightshirts and holding torches came out to see what the fuss was about. Soon a small crowd had gathered around Lili, her father, Vischer and the fugitive.

'What's going on, Otto?'

'Herr Meyer and Lili saw this poor man out on the lake and went out to rescue him.'

There was a chorus of sympathy.

'For pity's sake.'

'Out on the lake in that storm ... what on earth was he thinking?'

'We must get him into the warm.'

Farmer Ursprung's wife took the blanket off her own shoulders and wrapped it maternally around the hunched shoulders of the fugitive. During the angry discussion he'd begun shaking uncontrollably with fright and incomprehension.

'Oh no you don't!' interjected Gruber, a latecomer on the scene.

'What do you want here, Gruber?'

'Yeah, what's it to you anyway?'

'If you let one in (wheeze), you'll have to let them all in. Where (wheeze) will it end?'

'Who's talking about letting them in? Just get him some warm food and clothes,' replied Ursprung's wife.

'And where's he going to stay?'

'So that's what you're worried about is it?'

'What d'you mean?'

'You know exactly what I mean.'

'We know your sort,' interjected Ursprung in support of his wife. 'It always comes down to money with you, doesn't it? You're afraid he'll be put up in one of your rooms for free, aren't you.'

The avarice of the innkeeper was legendary but never until this moment publicly challenged.

Others now joined in the argument.

'We can't keep taking these, these …'

'These what? People, you mean?'

'There's no room. Didn't you hear what they said on the radio? Well? … The lifeboat's full.'

'You and your clever sayings … We're not a lifeboat. We're a country.'

'Look at the poor man. What he must have suffered.'

'It's not our (wheeze) problem…'

'You're a selfish, greedy little man, Gruber.'

'Who are you calling greedy, you … you sharp-tongued hussy!'

'Hey, how dare you talk to my wife like that?'

'Been egging you on again, has she Ursprung?'

The burly farmer came to the defence of his wife for whom, after some forty years of married life, he still had a residual affection. The argument degenerated into a scuffle. The first punch was thrown.

'I've owed you that for a long time, Gruber.'

Long-held animosities between neighbours broke out into a scrum of pushing and shoving, with the occasional blows traded.

In the mêlée Lili, Max and Otto whisked the shivering fugitive away from the scene into the house where they were able to get him out of his soaking clothes and feed him hot soup. Freddi too had profited from the pandemonium to slip away from his hiding place and creep in darkness back to safety.

He had not gone unnoticed.

Vischer, seeing that the mood of the villagers had turned against him and recognising that he too was a target, had withdrawn from the fray. Hiding in the bushes by the path leading to the jetty he caught sight of Freddi making his escape.

'Him! I might have known he was involved.'

In that instant Vischer sensed an opportunity for avenging his spurned advances.

*　　*　　*

'You'd better take your charge back now, Otto.'

Max recognised the impossibility of doing anything more for the man they'd rescued. Too many people knew of his presence. Vischer was certainly not going to turn a blind eye. The rescue chain that operated so successfully for so long had been broken when Captain Reitlinger was suspended from his duties.

Where was the police captain with his old car and entry visas now he was so desperately needed? It was nigh on impossible to get any refugees who made it across the border to the city and a safe house.

They'd done what they could, provided temporary comfort and safety.

Lili sat, still shivering, dressed in a pair of Freddi's trousers and a shirt borrowed from Max. She looked at the poor wretch sitting opposite her.

His mood had changed. He'd stopped shaking and greedily ate the warm food they put in front of him. They'd given him hope; hope of an escape from his miserable existence in the camp where his only prospect was being worked to death. Hope of safety, food and warmth.

She knew from the way that Max and Freddi looked at each other that those hopes were about to be dashed. He was to be returned to his former existence. And what would happen to him when his captors realised he'd had the temerity to escape? Surely he would be made an example of to deter others. Tears scored her cheeks once more as she thought of his inevitable fate.

Otto was studying his daughter closely. In all the time he'd wasted in cards and drink, escaping the frustrations of his own existence, he'd missed something precious. The little child who once sat on his shoulders listening to stories had become a fine young woman of whom he could be proud.

How like her mother she was.

He caught Max's eye. It pained him to think that this stranger seemed to know his own daughter better than he did. And it didn't escape his notice that there was something between the young guest staying in

Meyer's home and Lili. His brow furrowed at the thought: there was trouble ahead.

How much has passed me by in recent years, he thought.

'Otto?'

'Yes, Max?'

His earlier anger had subsided. Max Meyer was a decent man. Otto felt ashamed that he'd allowed himself to be persuaded that he'd had anything other than honourable intentions towards his daughter.

Max was gesturing towards the fugitive.

'I'll take him to Vischer,' Otto said with barely concealed contempt.

The Russian stood up and, with a spring in his step and half a smile, shook their hands warmly in turn. Otto took him gently by the arm and led him up the street. Until this point he'd given no thought to any repercussions for himself. Vischer was bound to report him for breaching border police regulations.

To his surprise Vischer was sweetness and light. No mention was made of their earlier exchanges. After the formalities were completed Vischer turned to Otto with mock subservience.

'Do you think we should telephone now?'

Otto nodded.

He avoided the hopeful eyes of the fugitive.

The police car arrived shortly after to take the Russian prisoner back to the border. Otto struggled with the thought of what would happen when the Gestapo got their hands on him.

But the night's events had brought something else home to him. He had another battle to fight – with Anna.

XXI

Freddi looked out of the study into the dark autumn night. A strong wind was blowing. Branches scratched against the window panes.

They had scratched against the windows the previous night when he and Lili were alone in his room. She was lying on his bed half-reading a book and half-watching him as he paced around anxiously.

'Freddi, what is it?' she asked, putting down her book. 'You're like a cat on hot bricks.'

'It's nothing, Lili. I'm just thinking about something I was discussing with Max earlier.'

'Stop thinking for once and come here.'

Freddi turned to see Lili unbuttoning her blouse.

'Come and lie next to me.'

He took her warm body in his arms. He was shaking with fear and arousal. Their love-making had lost its innocence. It was as though he was trying to bury his existence deep inside her. For a brief, ecstatic moment he lost all sense of who he was.

He slept a carefree sleep in her arms. When he woke he found Lili had gone.

* * *

Freddi peered again out of the window.

Where has he got to?

He heard a key turning in the lock.

At last!

'Well?'

'It's all clear,' said a breathless Max. 'Vogelsang's at the Bellevue, and Vischer's just completed his evening patrol. You can set your watch by that man. I'd give it a little while before you go. Sit down for a moment, Freddi. There's no rush.'

Freddi put down his rucksack and did as he was told. Max took off his glasses and looked straight into the eyes of his young friend with deep concern.

'Please don't go,' he said.

'Max, don't start that again. We've been through it all.'

'What do you think you're going to achieve?' asked Max, rehearsing arguments from the day before. 'The work of the column is over. We don't even know if it still exists. The border's been sealed for months and is closely guarded. It's far too risky.'

Freddi sighed impatiently.

'You know why I'm going.'

'That doesn't mean I approve.'

'Approve? Max, please. I'd better be going. It's getting late.' Freddi stood up and slung his rucksack wearily over his shoulder.

'What do I tell Lili?' said Max suddenly.

Freddi stopped. The resolve he had been building during the day suddenly wavered.

'I don't know, Max. Tell her …Tell her …'

He collapsed back onto the chair, his head in his hands.

'Do you think I want to leave you – both of you?' There was despair in his voice. 'You're the only family I've got. Don't you think I'd rather stay here with you?'

'Don't go, Freddi. I beg you. It's too dangerous. If you fall into the hands of the Gestapo again –'

'Max, they're about to deport every Jew in Constance. We can't just stand by. Look at what happened to those poor people in Stettin – thousands deported to the East and simply abandoned in the middle of nowhere to starve to death.'

'But what can you do?'

'We've got to let the world know this is going on.' Freddi's dark eyes were burning with passion.

'Who's going to listen?' Max replied with equal force. 'Europe is at war. Any country not yet occupied by the Germans fears for its own survival.'

'There's still a free press here. Someone will bring it to the attention of the world. Once they know what's happening. Someone will help. They've got to.'

Max bit his lip.

'Anyway, it's all sorted. There are still contacts in town willing to help me. I've got to go now,' said Freddi.

'And Lili?'

'Tell her I'll be back.'

He moved towards the door. Max barred his path.

'Freddi … take care.'

'Of course. You know me.'

There was a hint of the old swagger in his voice. Max put his arms around Freddi's shoulders. He held him tightly as though still trying to hold him back.

'I'll be back tomorrow evening if all goes according to plan.'

Freddi gave a wave and strode off. The haggard autumn night quickly swallowed him up.

The wind had grown stronger during the evening and seemed, like Max, to be restraining him. As he approached Lili's house, all in darkness, he hesitated. He placed his hand on the wooden gate. What would he give for one more sweet embrace, he thought, and swiftly moved on.

Dry leaves rustled across the deserted path he took along the lake's edge. Freddi reached his hand back to check on the presence of the shoebox through the fabric of his rucksack. It hid the camera with which he intended to record the deportation. His contact on the German side would supply him with a bicycle.

In a sudden lull of the wind Freddi heard the crack of a branch behind him.

He span round to see fleeting shadows. It was too dark to make anything out amongst the grey willows. Some nocturnal creature, he thought. A deer perhaps? Or a wild boar?

He walked the few miles to the border town.

*   *   *

'It looks like it's about to take place sooner than we thought,' his contact from the column told him once they'd crossed safely to the other side. 'A comrade has been keeping an eye on the movement of rolling stock on the tracks by the harbour. He's seen a passenger train on the sidings. It's an old train, not of the sort that are any longer in use. We're puzzled as to why it should all of a sudden have turned up.'

At the safe house they waited for dawn without exchanging a word.

Freddi had been dozing for what seemed just a few seconds when he was awoken with a firm shake.

'It's happening! The Gestapo have been around the houses of our Jewish citizens and have issued orders. They are to be ready for departure within the hour. Everyone has been told to take one suitcase, clothing, a blanket, food and drink for several days, crockery and cutlery, one hundred marks in cash and a passport ... Where the hell are they all going?'

Freddi shuddered at the thought and the cold.

He got up straightaway, prepared his camera and rode into the streets of the pretty university town. People were already out and about. It looked like the deportation was going to take place in broad daylight. This surprised him, but at least it made the success of his venture more likely. Rumours had been circulating that the Jews would be dragged from their beds in the middle of the night and expelled under the cloak of darkness.

In the streets it was a day like any other, at least for Christians; religious Jews were celebrating the Feast of the Tabernacles. That was one way the authorities could make sure everyone was at home, Freddi supposed. Either that or the decision to carry out the action on this festival day showed a particular disregard for world opinion on the part of the authorities.

He was reassured to see others going about their business. Students were cycling to their lectures. Housewives were striding purposefully to the market to catch the early bargains. A small crowd was gathering in the square. Word must have got around that lifelong neighbours were leaving for good.

Freddi watched a Jewish family leave their home. As they walked away without even a backwards glance, SS men locked and sealed the door taking the key with them. He wondered whether they would ever see their home and possessions again.

Following the route taken by the family under police escort he soon found other small clusters of people with their suitcases joining them from the side streets. Like small streams running down from the hills and mountains they came together to form a wide river seeking the sea. A school building was being used as a collection point. Freddi watched them enter what looked like a gymnasium; all the time he was recording the event. There were grandmothers in their nineties, toddlers of two or three, pregnant mothers, and even the invalided borne on stretchers. Not one Jewish citizen was going to be left behind.

Freddi was astonished at the calmness of the scene. SS, Wehrmacht soldiers and police stood grouped around idly chatting or smoking. Occasionally one or two even exchanged a polite word with those about to be deported. No orders were being shouted. No dogs were barking. No hand was raised in violence.

He waited among a crowd of onlookers. It was the middle of the morning. About an hour had passed since the Jews had entered the collection point. He assumed they were being registered, checked against lists to make sure no one had been overlooked, and forced to hand over any valuables.

Trucks arrived and parked in a line outside the school.

With the formalities completed, people started to emerge from the gloom of the building into the brightness of a fresh autumn day. They squinted at the light streaming through yellow and golden leaves on the trees lining the street where the trucks waited.

Freddi photographed the deportees. They were indistinguishable from middle-class German citizens: the women were dressed as though for the opera in fur stoles and elegant hats; the men, in suits and carrying briefcases, looked like they were just leaving for the office. The number of onlookers increased. Some found a vantage point in upstairs windows, and children squeezed through the legs of the adults to get a better view. The Christian population of the town was adopting the Jewish festival for the day.

Freddi was struck by the absence of feeling. There were no tearful goodbyes, no words of encouragement or Godspeeds. These people must have lived side by side all their lives, attending the same schools, working in the same shops, giving birth in the same hospitals. Their children would have played together; they would have celebrated their joyful occasions with one another and shared their woes. Yet neither could he detect any expression of the hatred stirred up by relentless Nazi propaganda. An inexplicable indifference was all he could see and sense. It was as though the townsfolk were simply waiting for them to leave.

He edged as close as he could to the front of the crowd.

Two elderly ladies stood by the side of the road. As they turned to leave the scene, he heard one say to the other through a handkerchief pressed to her mouth: 'There will be a time of reckoning for this.'

The trucks departed one by one.

Without waves or cheers the convoy drove the few hundred yards to the railway station where the old but comfortable looking train was waiting. Freddi watched the SS, soldiers and police help the last hundred or so remaining Jewish citizens of Constance on to the train.

He walked back towards the town.

To his surprise the townsfolk were all rushing towards what looked like a large warehouse. All of a sudden there was real excitement in the air. People were laughing and shouting as they jostled each other in a good-natured way. The large crowd outside the building was slowly funnelling through a narrow doorway.

Out of curiosity Freddi joined the end of the queue.

'What's going on?' he asked his neighbour, one of the many housewives out doing the day's shopping.

'Haven't you heard?' she replied with a smile. 'They're auctioning off their possessions.'

'You mean the property of those who've just left?' Freddi asked in astonishment.

'Who else's? There are some real bargains to be had.' And she pushed forward another few feet towards the Aladdin's cave.

Freddi had seen enough.

Now he understood the indifference he had witnessed earlier. The Christian population of the town had been bought off. The chance to own what their wealthier neighbours had once enjoyed successfully disarmed any qualms they might have had about what was befalling them. He doubted whether they'd even asked themselves where their fellow citizens were going.

With a bitter taste in his mouth he made his way back to the border on foot.

There was a small queue waiting patiently at the German checkpoint. He waited his turn; in his right hand he held his Swiss passport. The guard scrutinised the photograph. He looked at Freddi. Without a word he waved him through.

Freddi breathed a sigh of relief. His hand reached back once more to feel the presence of the shoebox in his rucksack.

The Swiss checkpoint had quickly cleared. He was the last. He imagined he would be through in a matter of seconds, and then back to Max and Lili. But the border guard was taking his time.

'Wait here a moment,' he said.

'Is there something wrong?' Freddi asked, trying to hide his fear.

'Wait.'

The guard disappeared into a small, half-lit room. Freddi looked around him. Thoughts of making a run for it crossed his mind, but the checkpoint was too heavily manned.

The guard returned. Freddi noticed he wasn't holding his passport. His hand was firmly placed on his rifle.

'Come with me.'

'Why? What is it?'

The barrel of the rifle lifted towards him. He obeyed. Walking through the corridor of the customs building he looked to his left into an office. A number of Swiss border guards were sitting around a table smoking and laughing. He recognised one of them, half-concealed in shadows.

It was Rudolf Vischer.

Freddi was searched. The camera was found in his rucksack. Handcuffed and bundled into a car between two guards he was driven back over the border to Gestapo headquarters.

* * *

'One more time, what exactly was your purpose in taking these photographs?'

Freddi looked at his Gestapo interrogator then down at the large desk between them on which the incriminating evidence lay displayed.

'Why are you so interested in our Jewish citizens leaving to take up a better existence elsewhere?' his interrogator insisted.

The photographs in front of him seemed to Freddi to come from a bygone age.

'You must be aware how difficult, shall we say, things have been for them here of late. Do you not agree that it's better to make a fresh start somewhere they can live amongst their own kind in peace? There has only ever been trouble when Germans and Jews have lived together, don't you think?'

Freddi remained silent.

'So was it just idle curiosity? You should know: this sort of curiosity is dangerous nowadays.' His interrogator's words turned threatening. 'It is strictly forbidden to photograph army and police actions.'

He stood up and walked across to a window.

'However, I do not think you were carrying out an act of espionage. Fortunately for you...'

There was a knock at the door. A subordinate entered carrying a file in his hand. The Gestapo officer scanned its pages, glancing up at Freddi from time to time.

'So then, what have you been doing with yourself these last few years, Herr Engeler? It is Herr Engeler, isn't it?'

In an apathetic tone he read out details from the papers on the desk: 'Friedrich Engeler. Born twenty-eighth May nineteen-eighteen in Freiburg. Parents: Jews. Member of a communist youth organisation. Arrested March thirty-five for illegal political activities. Released three months later. Since when: whereabouts unknown, assumed emigrated.'

He paused to let the information sink in.

'It seems you haven't learnt from your earlier re-education programme at our expense ... So you are a Jew?'

'Yes.'

His interrogator tapped his fingers on his desk.

'It appears you have a deep concern for your people's wanderings. Am I right in thinking that?'

Freddi saw little point in maintaining his silence. They had enough on him to throw him into jail at the very least.

'Where are all these people going?' He pointed at the confused and terrified faces staring out of the photographs.

'Jews have been leaving Germany for years and years. There's nothing new about that. We're just assisting, if you will, those who perhaps lack the means or the determination to follow their example. After all, you too made a sensible decision to leave ... It's just a pity you decided to return.'

'Where are they going?'

'I see you are a very inquisitive young man. Well, I'll tell you what. Why don't I let you find out for yourself? You seem very curious to know, and I have been charged with the agreeable responsibility of helping the Gauleiter clear the area of Jews for the Führer – so why don't we kill two birds with one stone?'

Freddi felt the blood seep from his face.

'Oh, don't look so worried. It was just a figure of speech. I told you – they'll be starting a new life.'

Freddi couldn't decide if his interrogator really believed in what he was saying or was giving free rein to his cynicism.

'Elser!'

The underling returned.

'Herr Engeler needs to be escorted at once to Singen. If you get a move on he should be able to catch this morning's train. Gute Reise, Herr Engeler. And adieu. I somehow doubt we'll see each other again.'

* * *

At Singen station Freddi was herded onto the platform with hundreds of other anxious passengers rounded up from the surrounding countryside. He recognised similar faces to those he had seen in Constance: solid, middle-class Germans, no different from those still walking through the streets of the town going about their daily business. They were carrying suitcases and bundles, anything they could retrieve in those few minutes between receiving the order to leave and closing the doors of their homes for the last time.

They boarded the train under the supervision of SS officers and police. Freddi was perplexed to see that the wagons transporting them were French. He slipped through the confusion and noise of those looking for seats with their families, and those busy storing their luggage in the nets above them, and sat in the corner by the window where he could observe the last passengers embarking.

The train moved slowly out of the station.

An awful silence filled the carriages. Women and men wiped tears from their eyes as the countryside they had known all their lives passed out of sight for the last time.

Nerves had been shredded by the experiences of the past twenty-four hours. Rumours had been circulating for weeks, but no one really believed it would come to this. Thoughts turned to their likely destination. One dreadful word remained unspoken, although it was on everyone's mind.

The train slowed once more. Freddi turned away from the desperate people around him and saw the town of Donaueschingen coming into view. Brakes squealed, drowning all conversation.

How many years ago was it that he'd visited the pretty cobbled streets with their half-timbered houses? He recalled how the streets and houses had been decorated that day in swastikas. So this was what it had come to.

On the platform men and women were weeping and screaming. It was clear they had suffered brutal treatment. Compassion spread among those already on the train who at least had been accorded some measure of humanity by the officials supervising their departure.

The train departed once more, rolling through the peaceful south German countryside. Freddi observed the large families all around him; there were grandparents, fathers, mothers, children, uncles and aunts. He suddenly felt very alone. If their journey was to end in oblivion, who would be left to remember them? He thanked a God whose existence he seriously doubted that his own parents had escaped these cruel times. As far as he was aware he had no living relatives. Only Max and Lili could confirm that he had walked upon this earth. The memory of the house by the lake brought him some comfort. So too did the thought that he was now part of this extended family.

Freddi smiled at the grandmother seated opposite him.

At their next stop two SS men went through the train yelling instructions. 'Hand in all valuables and jewellery. Surrender money over the sum of one hundred Reichsmarks. Anyone found with more than one hundred Reichsmarks will be shot.'

Panic set in around him. Some had tried to conceal valuables in secret pockets or compartments. They turned pale, ripped open their hiding places and pulled out jewellery and bundles of money shaking in terror. Bank notes were torn into shreds and hurled with other precious items out of the train window. Others sat petrified and repeatedly counted every note for fear they were in accidental possession of more than the stipulated amount.

This flurry of activity was followed by another period of silence. Occasionally a passenger would get up and throw a letter out of the window: perhaps as a last desperate attempt to send word to any remaining relatives or friends who might have evaded the round-up; perhaps a warning to get out while it was still possible; perhaps a last farewell. Maybe they hoped a kindly farmer would find the envelope and post it on.

Freddi couldn't bear to watch.

Suddenly there was a shout from the far end of the carriage.

'We're going west!'

A middle-aged, balding man in a suit had been studying the names of the towns and villages as they flashed past.

'We're heading towards Mulhausen or Strasburg.'

There was a murmur of excitement.

So that's why we're travelling in French wagons, thought Freddi.

The mood changed.

A great oppressive weight had been lifted. Smiles and laughter were exchanged; the occasional black joke cracked about journeys to the East.

The carriage filled with chatter. Where do you come from? Do you know so-and-so? How long had you lived in …?

The elderly lady opposite Freddi looked into his eyes.

'Have you no one with you, young man?' she croaked as she put a wizened hand on his hand.

Shortly before reaching the French border another SS officer with a more civilised demeanour came through the train.

'Please take your money out. I have to make a list of who has what. When we get to Mulhausen you'll be told when and where to change money.'

It was just as he said it would be.

Their money was exchanged at a rate of twenty Francs to one Reichsmark. Optimism spread like wild fire through the clusters of passengers changing their one hundred Reichsmarks for the princely sum of two thousand Francs.

Freddi looked at his share. The crazy thought crossed his mind that his Gestapo interrogator had been speaking the truth: they actually were leaving Germany to start a new existence elsewhere. If that were so, should he not be pleased that the vast differences in wealth that had always angered him had been wiped away? Perhaps they really were going to have the chance to build a new society somewhere. But where? There had once been talk of the island of Madagascar, he recalled. Was that why they were on this French train?

Freddi slipped in and out of a deep sleep exhausted by the events of the past few days. His slumber was punctuated by regular warnings from the SS to surrender valuables and money. He could not help but smile to himself every time a cold draught hit his face.

A carriage window was being opened, and any remaining valuables jettisoned.

In Burgundy the train stopped for longer. Freddi peered sleepily out at the bustling scene on the platform. He saw that they were in a place called Mâcon. French Red Cross workers were handing out bowls of soup and chunks of bread. One was engaged in a conversation with a man reaching out of the window.

'Where are you from?'

'Baden.'

'Baden in the Reich?'

'Yes. Why?'

'We've only ever had transports from Alsace and Lorraine until now ... So they've started deporting from the Reich itself?'

'We're all Jews.'

The young woman's face betrayed shock as she handed the man soup and bread.

Day turned into night; night into day. Freddi slept fitfully, dreaming of Lili, Max and Hiddigeigei. As the train put ever more miles between him and the house by the lake he wondered if he would ever see any of them ever again.

By the time day had turned to night once more, he had lost all sense of where he was.

XXII

'Why did you let him go, Max?' Lili's eyes flashed in anger.

Max had no answer.

Three days had passed. Three days fraught with anguish. Three days pacing the room waiting for a knock at the door and Freddi's cheery greeting.

On the garden bench a young woman sat and wept.

Should he have tried harder?

'There was no stopping him, Lili. Once he made up his mind to do something … You know what he's –'

She wouldn't let him finish.

'You could have said something,' she said in accusation. 'Why didn't you tell me he was thinking of going? I might've been able –'

Doubt in her own success softened her rebuke.

Max took advantage of this abatement in her anger to move towards her. He opened his arms, and she fell crying into his embrace. He could have tried harder. He should have tried harder ... He hesitated a moment or two and raised his right hand to stroke Lili's hair.

How soft.

He began to feel intoxicated with the smell of her perfume; his face sank into the soft tresses of her thick brown hair.

Suddenly Lili pulled herself away from him. She took a couple of paces back. Max thought he saw a fleeting look of suspicion in her inflamed eyes. Had he betrayed his subterranean desires?

He turned aside.

'I'm going to find him.'

Tears obscured her eyes but her voice was steely in its determination. Max felt relief. But once this brief moment passed he had somehow to confront the impossibility of what she was saying.

'Where will you look, Lili? He could be anywhere.'

He stopped short of saying what he thought: that her lover was probably languishing in some Gestapo prison ... or worse.

'But you've got contacts. There's the transport column. You can find out what's happened to him.'

There was such pleading in her eyes, in her voice – in her whole being. He knew he had to do whatever she asked of him.

Later that day he was able to contact Freddi's liaison from the transport column. It transpired that grandma had arrived safely and enjoyed her trip. She had visited relatives in town and was bringing back some gifts from them. Grandma was dropped off at the border as arranged.

Something untoward had taken place at the border. Freddi must have fallen into the hands of the German border guards and – with the camera as evidence in his rucksack – was handed over to the Gestapo.

There was no hiding the bad news from Lili. She stood in stunned silence.

'That's it then. He'll be sent to one of those awful places.'

A mass of sad thoughts darkened her face. Tears streamed down from her eyes.

'We don't know that for sure, Lili.'

She shook her head to drive away the false consolation.

'Max, for goodness sake. Don't treat me like a child. Don't you think I've heard enough? All those terrible things Felix described.'

'Felix?'

'You know, that poor man my father picked up on the lake. You and Freddi were supposed to rescue him, but the call didn't come or something. In the end that police captain came to take him to safety. You must remember him. It was you who arranged it.'

'Police captain? ... Ah, you mean Captain Reitlinger.'

The mention of Reitlinger's name set off a chain of thought. Years had passed since he'd exited the stage, and Max had lost contact with the brave captain.

'Lili, your mentioning Reitlinger has got me thinking.'

He didn't want to raise her hopes too much.

'Yes, Max?' She dried her tears.

'Perhaps ... Perhaps he might be able and willing to make inquiries on our behalf. Oh, but then –'

'What Max?' Lili was looking at him with tear-washed eyes widened in expectation.

'It's no good. He's no longer a serving official. He'll have no authority to approach the German police.'

He felt as though every word was a stab to her young heart.

'Then he really is lost to us.'

She cast down her eyes, full of distress.

'Wait,' Max said, running his hand through his hair. 'I remember how some in the column were very suspicious of his relations with certain Gestapo officers. They thought he was playing a double-game. I'm pretty sure he wasn't, but he still may be able to exploit those contacts. That's if we can find him, of course. And if we can persuade –'

'No ifs and no buts, Max. We've got to find him.'

A look of sudden resolve lit up Lili's face.

* * *

Feelers were put out through Oskar's transport column. It didn't take long to come up with the information they sought. Former police captain Paul Reitlinger had, as Max strongly suspected, been suspended from his duties pending a full investigation of his activities on the border in the years prior to the outbreak of war.

His reputation took a battering. There were rumours doing the rounds that he'd made a lot of money smuggling in refugees. Some malicious tongues even suggested he'd also benefitted in more 'personal' ways.

The reality was he'd fallen on hard times and was trying to eke out a living from casual jobs and with the help of his mother's savings. He'd been evicted from his police apartment and had to move with his wife and daughters, and his one loyal friend – Tobias, his cocker spaniel – to cramped accommodation in the poorer quarter of town. Friends deserted him, he became persona non grata at his beloved football club, and the Jewish community who owed him so much was either ignorant of, or simply ignored his plight.

The investigation lasted many months. When his case came to court, Reitlinger was found guilty of dereliction of duty, specifically of falsifying official documents relating to the entry of refugees. On all other counts – bribery, corruption and immoral behaviour – he was cleared. In mitigation the court accepted he had done nothing for personal benefit or gain. It also conceded that he had acted out of an understandable, if misguided, sense of decency. Despite this, Captain Reitlinger was summarily dismissed from the police force, fined a considerable sum and required to pay court costs. He lost his police pension.

Some press reports of the case, reflecting a now less hysterical mood in the country, showed compassion and understanding for the captain's actions. Some in his corps, to whom he had shown unstinting loyalty, began to have second thoughts and rue the fact they'd previously ignored his calls. Others, who had been beneficiaries of his generosity when they'd fallen on hard times, rediscovered their consciences. And Reitlinger, never a man to bear any kind of a grudge, willingly accepted newly extended hands of friendship.

And so it was that much of his past life returned. His club made him honorary president and he could be seen standing behind the home 'keeper's goal on match days, dispensing good advice or stamping his feet in frustration when his successor let in a soft goal. And wealthy members of the Jewish community remembered their debt to him and arranged for Reitlinger to take up a modestly paid position as a travelling salesman in the textile industry.

*   *   *

It was a shortly before Christmas when Lili arrived at a door in a shabby apartment block in Dianastrasse. The days had shortened to mere episodes.

She'd wrapped herself up against the cold in a thick coat, and her face was partly concealed by a woollen hat and a thick scarf.

'Captain Reitlinger?' she asked.

'No longer.'

'Oh, I'm sorry.'

Lili felt all her hopes dashed in those two curtly spoken words. She'd persuaded Max that she should seek out Reitlinger and talk him into using his contacts to find out what had happened to Freddi.

Weeks had passed since his disappearance. She was missing him terribly. Today had been the first day in many she'd woken with a faint glimmer of optimism. On the journey to the county town, passing through the countryside she knew so well from childhood bike rides, hope had taken hold and flickered ever more intensely with every step she took through the snow covered streets.

'No longer captain, Fräulein ... But I am Reitlinger.'

He was smiling. Lili smiled back; she felt her cheeks glowing.

'So, what can I do for you?'

'Sir, my name is Lili Vogelsang. You don't know me, but I know you. Well, not directly ... My father ... You came to our house once and took a fugitive away with you. He'd come across the lake on a boat, well on a ...'

Everything she'd rehearsed on the way was coming out back-to-front. She ran out of words. Through a half-open door to a steam-filled kitchen she caught a glimpse of the broad back of a woman.

'Paul. Who is it?' she called out without taking her eye off the pot on the stove.

'I'm really very sorry ... I didn't want to disturb you. I should leave,' Lili stammered, aware of the impending failure of her mission.

Reitlinger looked back into his flat following the direction of Lili's crestfallen gaze.

'No. Wait a moment. I just need to get a coat. It's freezing outside. You can tell me what you want to tell me in a café round the corner. I'll treat you. Just give me a minute or two.'

He closed the door. Lili heard muted voices and barking coming from behind it.

The door opened again.

'Tobias wants to come too.'

The black cocker spaniel jumped up to greet Lili.

'I won't be long,' Reitlinger called back into the semi-obscurity of the apartment. He was carrying a dirty, somewhat deflated leather football.

They left the building.

'Tell me … Lili, is it? Who sent you here?'

The streets were almost deserted. They walked through the entrance to the park. Reitlinger bent down to let the straining Tobias off his leash.

'Max. Herr Meyer. He lives in the village where –'

'Max? Well I never! I haven't seen or heard from him in years. But then, there's been a lot going on. How is he?'

'He's well, thank you.'

'You make sure you give him my best regards when you go back. I owe him a great deal. He was a good friend to me.'

Reitlinger dropped the leather ball from his hands and kicked it on the half-volley into the park for Tobias to fetch. The cocker spaniel raced off, his black ears flopping as he ran.

'So what can I do for you?'

The emotion built up during the previous hours suddenly hit Lili. Tears started to well up in her eyes.

'Come on, young lady. I'll buy you a nice slice of cake and a coffee. You look as if you need cheering up … Tobias!'

The sight of the spaniel with an over-sized football in his mouth and the reassuring words from this kindly man revived Lili's hopes that something might come from the day.

*　　*　　*

In a quiet corner of a café in the market square Lili tucked into a flan under Reitlinger's sympathetic watch. Tobias lay obediently by his feet.

'Watch this, Lili ... Tobias. Here, boy! Good dog.'

Reitlinger patted him on the head; he took a dog biscuit from his coat pocket and held it out in his hand.

'This is from Adolf,' he said.

Tobias lay still, growling. His head tilted to one side looking at his master with his deep brown eyes. Reitlinger put the biscuit back in his pocket, waited and took out another.

'This is from Winston,' he said. The biscuit was on his open palm.

But not for long; Tobias jumped to his feet and gobbled it up.

'Good boy, Tobias.'

A refreshed Lili explained the reason for her visit. This time what she had to say made some sort of sense. Reitlinger listened intently. When she finished, he answered after a moment's pause.

'I'm not sure I can help you. You see Lili, I've no authority. I'm just an ordinary citizen now.'

He leaned across the table towards her.

'But I want to help you ... I think I have an idea what it's like to be separated from someone you love. It's just a question of how.'

He pinched the top of his nose with his forefinger and thumb.

'Where there's a will...'

Half-an-hour later Reitlinger was escorting Lili back to the railway station. On their way through the empty streets he explained how difficult it would normally be for a private individual to travel over the border in the current situation.

'But you know, Lili. There might be a way. My football club is due to play an important match in Stuttgart early in the New Year. There'd be nothing unusual about me, as honorary president, accompanying the team. Once there, I can try and make contact with my former Gestapo colleagues and see what I can discover about your Freddi's disappearance.'

Lili hugged the startled Reitlinger.

'Thank you. Thank you, so much.'

She set off to run for her train.

'Good luck, Lili,' he called out to her.

Lili stopped, turned round and called back: 'Good luck to you too, *Captain* Reitlinger.'

* * *

The weeks crawled through Christmas and the New Year. The darkest days of the year were behind them when Max announced Reitlinger's imminent visit.

His news brought a resurgence of hope. It appeared that Freddi hadn't been arrested by German guards but by border police on the Swiss side acting on a tip-off.

Vischer!

The Swiss police immediately handed him over to the Gestapo along with the camera. Once in their hands his fate was sealed. However, the Gestapo officer who interrogated Freddi was renowned for his capricious and erratic behaviour. Reitlinger had had many dealings with him. Freddi was put on a train leaving for the camps in unoccupied France. He was being deported along with all the Jews being evacuated at the time from throughout the region. The policy appeared to be to dump them well away from the territory of the Reich. Reitlinger had no precise information from his sources as to where the trains would have ended up. Somewhere near the Pyrenees, he thought. He was assured that although conditions were harsh, survival was more than a remote possibility.

Freddi was alive and far from the lion's den.

Lili wept tears of joy, while Max thanked Reitlinger effusively for what he had done.

'Once more we all have cause to be grateful to the good captain,' he said.

'Not at all. Not at all …'

Reitlinger became serious.

'Do you remember, Max. I told you about that time towards the end. There was a young woman, not much older than you, Lili. She came to my door pleading with me to save her parents. I didn't act. I've always regretted it. I could have saved them … I could have saved that girl's parents from –'

His voice broke with emotion.

'You did all you could, Paul. One day – when these dark times are over – the world will know of your deeds.'

Reitlinger dismissed the suggestion with a curt wave of his hand.

'I determined that if I ever found myself in the same position again, I would do everything in my power to help. I never thought such an opportunity would come. I can't tell you how pleased I am it has.'

He turned to Lili.

'I hope one day soon you'll be reunited.'

Lili's thoughts were moving down a single track.

How was she to get to southern France and find Freddi?

XXIII

With a jolt Freddi was awoken from his dreams. He'd
slept for hours wrapped warmly in a thick overcoat
generously donated by a fellow passenger who saw
him shivering in the cold.

'It's spare. Please take it.'

Freddi nodded in gratitude and felt his eyes close.

During the last night of the journey scenes from his
past life had populated his semi-conscious mind: his
childhood, his parents, his student days. One face kept
coming back again and again.

Lili.

She was smiling down at him lying beneath her on
the grass. The sun filtered through her thick hair
turning it into strands of gold.

A screech broke the spell. Steam hissed from the
engine. Whistles pierced the air, and doors banged
open.

'Sortez! Sortez! Out! Everyone out! Vite! Vite! Dépechez-vous!'

The strangely muted atmosphere of the last few hours, a sign of consideration for those who were asleep and dreaming last dreams of their lost homeland, was suddenly transformed into pandemonium. All the passengers struggled to their feet at once, reaching into the luggage nets for their baggage and trampling uneaten food into the floor.

With sleep still in his eyes Freddi peered through the window at the brightly illuminated station. French soldiers and policemen stood around in apathetic clusters on the platform. The sign told him they had arrived in Oloron. The name meant nothing to him. Days of travelling had confused all sense of direction. Speculation among his fellow passengers had dried up long ago. North, south, east, west. Who knew where they were?

Perhaps their journey had been a descent through the earth's core on a track leading to some inferno.

They were guided rather than ordered on to waiting trucks. Some of his fellow passengers took comfort from this.

An elegantly dressed lady accompanied by her daughter was speaking excitedly to a guard on the platform. She was asking, demanding to use a telephone. She insisted. She was not going to move from the spot. The soldier told her to wait. He went away for a few moments. On returning the guard told her that he would make the call on her behalf. Freddi overheard with disbelief the lady's instructions.

'Could you please reserve a double room with a bath in one of the better hotels in town? Mind you – a good one.'

She handed over a tip to the smirking guard and rejoined the convoy with her daughter.

They had to walk over a narrow bridge to reach the waiting trucks. Relief now turned to dismay. Peasant women dressed from head to toe in black cast hostile looks in their direction and spat out the words 'sales boches' as they passed.

It was dark and wet. The short lived chaos and confusion on arrival returned to subdued silence as they were driven through the blackness. Not a single contour or shape betrayed any clue as to where they were. Freddi felt dizzy and nauseous.

*   *   *

He was taken back to his time as a student skiing in the Alps with university friends during a winter vacation. The day started bright enough as they set off from their guest house. But within a couple of hours the weather took a decided turn for the worst. Clouds of thick mist enveloped them; visibility deteriorated by the minute. They decided to ski down to find a break in the clouds. As they descended they found themselves in even thicker fog.

He became detached from the rest of the group. There was no-one around him. He looked to his left and right. Nothing. He called out with increasing anxiety. No response. The poles marking the run were not even visible. He struggled to see the undulations in the slope beneath his feet. As his brain lost all contact with reality he was overcome with nausea. He felt as though he was skiing up the mountain. Panic set in. He stopped to try and get some bearing. It was useless. He set off again, breathing heavily, blindly racing. He thought at any moment that he would plunge into a crevasse or off the precipice. But he was beyond caring.

At last he heard voices. The mist evaporated and he could see the snow beneath his feet, feel his skis cutting into its crispness. He made out trees on the opposite mountainside and a welcome patch of blue sky. His breathing returned to normal.

'Where have you been? We've been waiting for you for ages.'

His friends laughed, and he joined in with a sense of deep relief.

* * *

The uncomfortable journey in the truck was soon over.

Freddi saw row after row of dim lights in what appeared to be a wide open plain covered with low dark buildings.

The trucks stopped.

'Seulement les hommes. Not women or children. Stay where you are. Men only. Out! Sortez!'

Panic spread through his truck. Fear and consternation were written on the faces of the women. What could be said in that moment? Nothing could stay the dagger of separation.

The men clambered awkwardly off the truck whilst holding onto the vision of their wives and children for just a few seconds longer. Bundles and bags were thrown into the night and burst open on the road, the one bit of hard ground around them.

'Just the men!'

They dropped down into a squelch of mud. There was mud everywhere. Those who started searching for their possessions were told to move on.

'Demain. Demain.'

Freddi trudged with a father and his teenage son through the clinging thick filth. On seeing what awaited them the father turned to him in shock and whispered.

'Buchenwald. This is just what it was like in Buchenwald. We're in a concentration camp.'

The path became even more difficult. They could hardly walk; their feet were swallowed up by the mud.

French soldiers counted off a number of them and ordered them forward.

'Où sommes-nous, monsieur?' asked one of his group.

The soldier answered with a word none of them understood. It was a single, half-strangled syllable.

They stood shivering in an empty barrack. It was more like a cattle shed. Under their feet was earth, above them a wooden roof, around them wooden walls. Two bulbs swinging in the draught dimly illuminated the misery. In the middle of the shed stood a small stove; it was unlit and there was no sign of wood or coal. There were no tables, no chairs, no beds, no food, no washrooms and no toilets.

Evening became night. One by one they decided all they could do was sleep. An elderly man called out to a guard in distress. He needed the toilet. In the end the guard relented, opened the door and pointed into the night. They lay down in their clothes on the bare earth. Those who had managed to retrieve suitcases and bundles used them as pillows. They were too exhausted from the journey to begin to wonder about what it all meant. Was this now to be their home or was it just a temporary resting point on their onward journey?

A milky dawn brought some relief from the discomfort of the night. Freddi rose early and found the door of the barrack open. Most of his fellow travellers still slept. He wandered through the mud. In the distance he thought he could make out the grey outline of mountains. Wherever he walked he came across barbed wire and ditches full of stagnant, stinking water. Everywhere he looked there were identical wooden barracks. There must have been as many as a couple of hundred. They were windowless. As their occupants awoke, wooden flaps in the barrack walls opened.

He had reached what appeared to be the entrance to his group of barracks. On a post was a large letter 'E'. Guarding it stood a French soldier, cupping a cigarette in the palm of his hand.

He decided to try his luck and walked up to the gate. As he approached, the sentry held up his rifle. He was not to go any further.

'Pass!'

He shook his head. Freddi stood for a moment, hands in his pockets.

'Où?' he asked.

The French sentry, dark in complexion, was obviously used to the question.

'Gurs.'

The same half-sound from the night before; it was barely recognisable as a human utterance.

Freddi raised his shoulders in puzzlement.

'Gurs …. Camp…'

'You're not going to get much out of him, I'm afraid.'

He turned round to see a bearded, middle-aged man in tattered, dirty clothing, smiling at him.

'Guten Tag. Allow me to introduce myself…'

He stretched a filthy hand towards Freddi.

'My name is Neter. Doctor Eugen Neter … originally from Mannheim where I worked as a paediatrician.'

'I'm Freddi. Freddi Engeler.'

'Pleased to meet you, Freddi. Although in these circumstances …'

He read the confusion writ large on Freddi's face.

'It's a shock for all the new arrivals. The most important thing is to forget the past and get through each day. Today is all that matters.'

'What is this place? Are we in a concentration camp? Somebody mentioned Buchenwald last night.'

Eugen held up a hand to stem the flow of questions.

'Not exactly. Look around you. What do you see?'

Freddi looked back blankly.

Eugen smiled.

'There are no Germans … No SS, no Wehrmacht, no Schupos. We're under French administration here.'

Freddi wondered what difference that made. Eugen read his thoughts.

'They're not interested in persecuting us. There are some here who suffered so badly back in Germany they actually prefer it here. They can at least see the sky and the mountains, walk around and play cards without any harassment.'

'So why the barbed wire and the guards? Where exactly are we?'

'Allow me to give you a guided tour, Freddi.'

He held out his arm to show the way.

'This is an internment camp built originally for refugees from Spain. Republicans fleeing Franco after the Civil War ... French Communists, the International Brigades, you know. It was meant as somewhere to keep them until it could be decided what to do with them all. Dreadful conditions, of course.'

They were standing beside one of the ditches which criss-crossed the camp.

'These ditches are always full of water. It's hardly surprising, really. They built it on the flood plains of the Gave d'Oloron river. On marsh land, essentially. And does it rain.'

They looked through the barbed wire fence to another cluster of barracks.

'They call each area an ilot. There are thirteen. Each ilot has twenty-five barracks. A barrack holds around fifty people. The women and children's camps are over there in a separate section.'

He looked with sudden concern at Freddi.

'Are you with someone?'

Freddi shook his head.

'Take it from me, you're better off that way,' he said.

'It's very difficult to visit. You can't leave your ilot without a pass, and they're hard to come by. Unless you're attending a funeral.'

'How long...?'

'How long are we here for? Who knows? Pour la durée de la guerre. However long that is. Essentially we've been dumped here like refuse by the Germans. They didn't want us. Neither do the French. But they have no choice. They've been defeated, after all, and although we're in the unoccupied part ...'

'Where are we exactly?'

Eugen pointed towards the mountains, sharper in outline now against the clearing sky.

'Over there are the Pyrenees. We're about fifty kilometres from the Spanish border.'

He turned around and pointed in the opposite direction.

'Pau.'

Turning again, he indicated towards the west.

'Bordeaux. Are you're lucky enough to have a visa for Great Britain or the United States?'

Freddi shook his head.

'No. I thought not. You see, safety is really not that far from reach.'

They looked towards the horizon. Freddi broke the silence.

'When did you arrive?'

'A couple of months ago. When we got here there were only a few hundred people scattered around the camp. Most were Spaniards; some political refugees, communists, prostitutes, gypsies. But numbers have been steadily increasing over recent weeks as each train load arrives from Germany. There are thousands now.'

The two men had completed a circuit of their ilot. Freddi told Eugen about himself and how he came to be on the transport. The older man listened intently. They arrived back at an open area where breakfast was being served. Long queues of men waited for a thin black liquid to be slopped into their waiting bowls.

The new arrivals from last night were desperately searching for the belongings which had been carelessly dropped by the side of the one proper road through the camp. Possessions lay strewn in the filth and rain. Photographs and other mementos of past lives were left abandoned in the mud, while the arrivals scoured the heaps for useful objects such as knives and mugs.

Or razor blades for the swiftest escape.

Outside the barracks Freddi saw small groups of older men with the same glazed look of shock in their eyes. They were sitting on sacks of straw, incapable of comprehending what had befallen them.

He wondered how these old men were going to learn to protect themselves from the elements. How were they going to dry their clothes or find a latrine in the dark?

Eugen was observing Freddi closely.

'Come and join our barrack,' he said.

'You'll find like-minded people. People intent on survival. It's important.'

In the barrack he was greeted with a straw sack to sleep on. He was quickly invited to join in the discussions of a group of around a dozen men, under the watchful eye of Eugen. Most were political refugees and had fought for the Republican side in the Spanish Civil War. There were some German communists and socialists among them.

All were willing to answer his questions in detail and to give good advice on surviving this new situation.

It emerged that they were essentially left to their own devices. The French weren't bothered with them. The gardes mobiles tolerated a certain amount of black market activity, conducted mainly with the long-term Spanish internees at Gurs. With the money each batch of new arrivals had been allowed to bring with them they were able to get hold of all sorts of useful objects. The commandant, a man named Gruel, was lazy and corrupt. A large part of the money he received for every internee from the authorities found its way into his pocket at their expense. Cuts were made in their provisions. As far as the distribution of the food was concerned the French couldn't give a damn.

Eugen explained.

'The food here is a major problem. There's too little to live on, too much to die on. You saw the distribution of what we jokingly refer to as coffee this morning. You won't have drunk coffee like it. The bread is a third the amount needed to live on. At midday there is a can of thin soup with some vegetables and a little meat –'

'Monkey meat! Count yourself lucky if you get a piece,' interrupted a thin, bald man. Freddi later discovered he was a leading German communist called Ludwig Mann.

'That's until you've tasted it. When you do, you'll find it so hard and tough you'll spit it out,' added another who spoke with a Spanish accent.

'You'll have tasted better dish water,' remarked a gangly Frenchman.

Eugen continued.

'It's always the same. Cabbage, turnips, pumpkins and one or two specialities of the region such as hard yellow peas –'

'Like eating bullets...'

'… and stuff they normally use for cattle feed thrown in for good measure.'

Ludwig Mann took up the account.

'Despite all this, at mealtimes everyone watches intently to make sure his neighbour does not get more than him. Hunger makes people spiteful. People who at home would have greeted each other respectfully in the street turn nasty over half a ladle of watery, inedible broth.'

*   *   *

At the end of October the rain which had greeted their arrival in Gurs stopped at last. The weather turned fine for a while. The distant mountains stood out clearly against the blue sky reminding Freddi of the home he'd left behind. But the nights had already turned cold. The wind blew mercilessly through the barracks, and they froze at night. Wherever they could, they tore wooden slats from the barrack walls to heat the utterly inadequate stove in the centre of the room. Then, quite unexpectedly, a supply of wood arrived. Everyone huddled around the fire to keep warm and cook.

Freddi volunteered for the task of keeping the stove lit at night and therefore enjoyed the privilege of sleeping beside it. This comfort was much diminished by the fact he had to get up every hour to feed the flames. When, at midnight, peace eventually descended and all were asleep, the rats arrived and circled around the stove for scraps of food. Finding none, they disappeared.

The straw sacks they slept on came alive at night with all manner of bugs, fleas and insects.

Relief from the rain was temporary. By mid-November winter had set in. The nights were damp and cold. Rain came down in thunderous storms which drummed on the wooden roofs of the barracks and clattered against the thin walls. The land flooded once more. Water gurgled in the drainage ditches, mingling with urine from the latrines. The stench was appalling. The barracks were not capable of holding out the rain. Bowls were placed all over the floor to catch the drips, and the thin straw-filled mattresses had to be piled up to avoid getting damp. There were days when walking outside meant wading up to one's calves in thick mud. On those days no-one ventured out of the barracks but remained inside in the unending gloom and stuffiness.

Arguments raged about whether the thin slats should be opened to let in air or left closed to keep out the bitter cold.

Condemned to doing nothing, lethargy took over.

It rained and rained.

The winter took its toll. Those with families suffered the pain of separation and yet knew their loved ones were just a few barbed wire fences away. There was little possibility of visiting wives, mothers and daughters in the women's camp. You couldn't leave your ilot without a pass, and they were extremely difficult to procure. Hardest hit were the elderly, the largest group in the camp. They felt helpless without their life-long partners and worried from dawn to dusk about what the other was doing, how they were coping and who was there to help them survive.

The poor food and sanitation brought disease. Dysentery, typhoid and tuberculosis took a grip on not just the elderly. Every day there were between ten and fifteen deaths. The elderly died lying in their own excrement. Funerals took place in the cemetery at one end of the camp. It too was always under water. Permission was granted to attend funerals. It often happened, when the list of the deceased was read out, that this was the first time relatives discovered they had lost their loved ones.

Within several weeks hundreds had died from the epidemic. The only medicines available were those brought by internees.

Eugen gave a stern warning to the group.

'Don't touch the camp food – even if it is cooked. Try and stick to onions, garlic and bread.'

'We're all going to die like animals if this goes on,' said Ludwig Mann.

The inevitable prospect of untimely death filled the circle around Eugen with brooding, silent melancholy.

'We've got to organise ourselves. Try and give ourselves something worth living for.'

'What were you thinking of?' asked Freddi.

'We need to create work, activity. We've been condemned to do nothing but die here, slowly, of disease and malnourishment. We need to try and recreate a sense of normal life, with work, play and entertainment.'

'We could convert one of the empty barracks into a carpentry shop...'

'Another could become the laundry room.'

'And in the evenings we could organise concerts, plays, readings ... There must be internees who have instruments with them. There are bound to be actors, musicians, artists among them. Let's find them.'

In the fever of enthusiasm a quiet voice made itself heard.

It came from a member of the group who usually kept his own counsel. A veteran of the International Brigades, he wore a patch over his right eye and had also lost three fingers on his left hand. He wore a long coat of the type handed out to French soldiers on demobilisation, and his face was always half-concealed by the shadow cast by his wide-brimmed hat. The others called him Wotan.

'I wish to propose another course of action.'

Everyone turned to look at him.

'Go ahead, Wotan. We're all equal here. Every one of us has a voice.'

'Let's get the fuck out of here.'

That night, as Freddi was feeding the stove in the middle of the barrack, listening to the snores, farts and crunching jaws dreaming of food, he became aware of a movement behind him.

'Mind if I join you?'

It was Wotan. He gestured to an area of bare earth next to the stove.

Wotan held his hands up, surrendering to the pale heat offered by the inadequate stove.

'It's not my real name ... Wotan,' he said after an embarrassing silence.

'I'd worked that one out,' Freddi answered with a smile. 'One eye, the coat, the hat ... So what's your real name, Wotan?'

'Josef. Josef Haček.'

Freddi held out his hand in greeting.

'Nice to meet you, Josef.'

They sat in silence, intent on contemplating the glow from the stove and listening to the chorus of strange noises from those asleep.

'You know, I was serious about getting out of here. We shouldn't lie around in this shit making things bearable with recitals and poetry classes.'

From his seated position he expertly caught an approaching rat with his right boot, kicking it half way across the barrack.

There was a loud squeal.

'So, how do you come to be here anyway, Josef?'

Josef recounted his adventures of the last five years. It was the most Freddi had ever heard him say. He told him about his wanderings through Europe, his struggle to get to Spain and the battles.

'How did you lose your eye?'

Josef seemed not to hear his question. If he did, he was ignoring it.

'I know many of the paths. The escape routes to and from Spain. I've got contacts over there. Safe houses in remote areas where we could hide out. We'll never be found. We could lie low until it's all over. It might only be a matter of months.'

'Do you really think so? And what about the Spanish Fascists?'

Josef's face darkened at their mention.

'In any case,' Josef continued, 'we've got to get out of here.'

'Aren't you forgetting something? We're fenced in and well-guarded. How do you propose to get out of Gurs?'

Freddi watched the light of the stove flicker in Josef's remaining good eye.

'There are work details for foreigners,' he said. 'GTE's they're called. Groupes de travailleurs étrangers. Slave labourers, really. Breaking up rocks, building roads – that sort of thing. You leave the camp by day, return at night. There are people outside the camp who can help. French communists. We join the work details. We watch. We wait. What do you think? You don't look the sort for poetry readings.'

'Condemned to wander then, Wotan?'

'Condemned to wander, Freddi.'

XXIV

Max gazed out absent-mindedly at the angry waves crashing against the wall at the bottom of his garden. In his hand he held a letter from Lili. It was the first he'd received since she left.

There was no stopping her. Just as there had been no stopping Freddi. They were both as impulsive as the waves, smashing themselves against an unyielding fate.

Now he was alone once more. The youthful laughter which once filled his house and his heart faded into memory. Hiddigeigei too noticed their absence. He spent much more time sleeping on his favourite chair in the study stirring only occasionally for food and to stretch his legs.

The only human voices he heard in the evenings travelled on airwaves from Beromünster. They brought news of further brutal onslaughts against the weak and innocent. When was it all going to end? Max had no intention of suffering the indignity of 're-education' at the hands of his enemies if, or rather when, the invasion came. Nor did he intend to flee to those few remaining parts of Europe, or indeed the world, still burning a flickering beacon for freedom. He had grown too weary for all that.

He kept close at hand a small brown phial for a gentle end in this violent age – when the time came.

Max looked at the words on the page. '*My dearest Max ...*'

He loved her contrary to every expectation.

Still at his time of life the instincts continued to play tricks. Still they made a fool of you when you thought you had suffered all the exquisite pain that life could dish out. And it wasn't the affection of a mentor or a guardian; it wasn't just the love of a friend. He was too honest with himself to hide behind such evasions.

In bed at night he dreamed of running his hands through her hair, of greedily kissing those full lips, of undressing her and lavishing his attentions on every inch of her body. On occasions, the lasciviousness of his own thoughts shocked him.

'*You are my only true friend,*' he read.

'*The only person on this earth I can share these feelings with ...*'

What could she possibly see in him, an ageing would-be lover, with failing eyesight and greying hair? How could he possibly compete with the vitality and freshness of youth? His rational being knew all this. In the harsh light of day he had no problem warding off the demons. But when night fell, he thought of every possible way in which he might seduce her in to his bed. When she embraced him in greeting or in gratitude he held on to her a little bit longer, a little bit tighter, feeling her breasts against him, and lust stirring within him.

At the same time Max had left no stone unturned to find a way for Lili to get to the South of France. He couldn't bring himself to tell her that she was searching for a needle in a haystack. And what if Freddi hadn't made it there in the first place? Since he'd gone, there had been no news. Contacts in Oskar's transport column across the border had fallen silent. There were dozens of places he could be. As far as the rest of humanity was concerned, the deported had disappeared off the face of the earth.

Pretending to share her youthful hope and optimism he had accompanied Lili to the capital.

'I'm going to find him,' she'd said with irresistible resolve.

He hadn't argued. Even if she did find out which camp Freddi was in, what then? Did she think she could just walk in, tell them she had come to pick up a friend and walk out again? A good thing the young are not debilitated by the habit, which comes with age, of thinking things through.

* * *

Holding her nursing testimonials firmly in her hand, Lili strode up to the door of Roberto Olmo's office. A brass plate announced him as the general secretary of the children's aid organisation.

'It's no bed of roses out there,' Roberto Olmo warned Lili as they sat in his cramped office. Newspaper cuttings and correspondence lay strewn across the floor.

'There are many internment camps scattered throughout the region; the Southern Zone, as we now call it. We've been involved in humanitarian work for several years now, originally in Spain and then, when that war ended, in southern France. That's where the Spanish refugees fled to. There are thousands of refugees who have flooded into what is already a poor, desolate region. Women and children among them.'

He stood up to point at a map hanging on the wall behind his desk.

'Here's the camp we'll send you to. It's at a place called Rivesaltes, near Perpignan, not far from the sea. It's become one of the dumping grounds the Vichy government is using for its 'undesirables'. Foreigners. Not only Spaniards, but Jews, Gypsies and the stateless. 'Apatrides', they call them.'

The word conjured up the vision of monstrous insects in Lili's mind.

Roberto Olmo looked out of his window towards the government offices. 'The French aren't the only ones to resort to such methods,' he said absent-mindedly.

With a kindly look in his eyes Olmo returned to Lili's testimonials.

'I see you've already had experience working with infants and mothers. Good. We've managed to set up a number of maternity homes in the area around the camp. There are never enough places, unfortunately.

You can stay at one, in Elne, for a night before going on to Rivesaltes. That's where you'll really be needed.'

He paused and looked up from the papers on his desk. His face had taken on a grave expression.

'I must warn you, Fräulein Vogelsang. The work is very hard. You will be faced with malnourished men, women and children living in dreadful conditions. The place is overrun with rats. Clothes and bedding are infested with bugs. The sanitation is catastrophic. Sickness is rife: diarrhoea, dysentery, starvation. There are few medicines. Internees steal and cheat to get a bit of bread. In short, it is hell on earth. Are you really sure this is what you want to do?'

Lili nodded fervently.

'I can see you're determined. You'll need all your strong resolve in the midst of all this misery. The French really don't want us there witnessing what is going on, but they can't cope with the countless problems. So they've let us in, along with other humanitarian organisations. But that's as far as their co-operation goes. This is not a normal world ... there are no rules. You will have to take responsibility and improvise from day to day. No-one will be there to give advice.'

Olmo waited for the impact of his words to sink in.

'Are you still sure this is what you want to do?'

Lili needed no time to reflect.

'When can I leave?'

Olmo laughed. 'We'll make all the arrangements and get you out there as soon as we can.'

*   *   *

Max held the letter in his hand. She'd kept the promise she made at the station.

At last I've arrived and I have a moment to write to you. You can't imagine how much I've been thinking of you and Hiddigeigei in your house by the lake. It's given me so much comfort to know that you will have been thinking of me too. Every time I thought about our parting at the station I wanted to burst into tears again. How much I wished you were there to hold me in your arms. Oh, Max, I feel so alone without you!

The journey here was wearing. It took twenty-eight hours. As Olmo promised, I spent my first night at Elne. It was beautiful there but deserted. There were only a few crumbling old farmhouses in the middle of nowhere. The maternité was clean but primitive. The only furniture they had was made from old crates.

Max, you wouldn't believe the conditions! There were twenty new-born babies lying in wicker baskets. The older children are desperately underweight. They arrive in rags, have no underwear, and are frozen and lice-infested. They have frost-bitten fingers and toes, bloated stomachs and eye infections. Their eyes lit up when I gave them the chocolate I packed in my bags. Please send more, if you can!

The next day was time for me to move on. Maurice, the director, drove me the hour or so to Rivesaltes. Well, I say 'drove'. We had to get out and push the old car since it refused to move whenever we came to a standstill at bridges or railway crossings. Maurice reminded me of the way you used to tease me: 'Come on, Lili! Can't you push any harder than that?' he shouted at me. I started to feel less lonely out in that desolate countryside. The camp at Rivesaltes is near to the sea, and the snow-capped mountains in the distance reminded me of home. But it is very grey. And the wind! I haven't known wind like it even in our fiercest storms. It drives mercilessly through the villages of flimsy wooden barracks. In winter, Maurice told me, it is icy cold, and in summer burning hot. If I thought conditions at the maternité were bad, the people here are living in a nightmare.

My spirits were lifted when I saw my barrack. The Red Cross nurses living there had painted a scene of a lake with a sailing boat on the outside wall. But then I felt sad again with longing for you and home. The other nurses, Rosli, Elsi and Friedel, were there to greet me and made me feel at home.

I have my own room. To be honest, it's more like a cell with whitewashed walls. The table is made of crates and my bed is a simple wooden frame with wires strung across it. The window is missing a pane of glass, and a dirty grey blanket hangs over it. I scarcely slept that first night. The wind whistled through every crack in the walls and the wires under my thin mattress cut into me.

Please don't think I'm complaining, Max, or that I'm unhappy. Olmo did warn me about conditions here. It'll take a little time to get used to it all. But I am happy knowing that I'm nearer to Freddi here. Do you know the words Ruth said to Naomi in the bible story? They are so beautiful. I remember the first time I heard them. 'Wherever you go, I will go; and where you live, I will live'. If I can't be at his side, at least I know he is not far from me. One day soon I will find him and the three of us will be together again!

I got up early as I felt excited about starting work. I helped hand out rice. Spanish women had already been cooking it in the kitchens. We put it into big pots and took it from one barrack to the next. The wind was so violent it nearly overturned our cart! I made my first visit to the sick barrack. Max, you wouldn't believe it. Patients were lying on filthy mattresses with no sheets. They stretched out their thin arms for the rice we poured into their bowls, their eyes following us greedily. Small children lie in cots. Their backs are red raw with abscesses and open sores. I just didn't know where to begin or how to help. Friedel said that the only hope for the children is to get one or two into Elne, but for that she has to do continuous battle with the French doctor. And then the children have to come back to the camp once they've recovered.

That night I cried myself to sleep. There seems a mountain to climb. Then I remembered what Olmo said about seizing the initiative. I decided we had to wash the children at least once a week. With some difficulty we managed to get hold of a tub, towel and soap from the French authorities. It would also help to have wood to heat the room but we had no luck there. I'm not going to give up!

Well, I must go now, Max. I'm falling asleep. I've only been here a matter of days, but it feels like weeks. Don't worry about me. Despite everything I'm happy. I'm so busy during the days I don't have much time to think about Freddi. The nights are hard, though. I've asked around about transports from Germany. None of the other nurses know of any.

Although I have little time to think of you and home, when I do it is with great affection.

May God keep you safe! Hug Hiddigeigei for me!
With all my love,
Lili

* * *

Seasons came and went in the sleepy fishermen's village on the lakeside. Nature was oblivious to the destruction being wreaked many hundreds of miles beyond her shores.

The leaves turned gold. The snow came. The lake froze.

The lake thawed, the snow melted and a shimmer of green appeared in the trees.

The wheel of the seasons turned its unending circle. At the same time the voice on the radio brought news of the relentless progress of jack-booted armies. Max had taken the precaution of placing the small, dark-brown bottle on the table beside his bed. Judging by earlier events, when it happened, it was going to be quick. They weren't going to wait politely for him to open the door. Of that much he was sure.

But then something strange happened. The threats and rumours fell silent. The forests across the lake trembled no more.

Stillness reigned.

The mighty military machine had turned on its heels. It marched off to the east, annihilating everything in its path. Precariously perched on the edge of oblivion the villagers sighed collectively in relief. There were expressions of subdued delight. Worry-worn faces smiled once more. The condemned had been reprieved.

Only Vischer seemed concerned at the turn events had taken. He found comfort in telling anyone who could bear to listen to him that at last the Bolsheviks were in for a hiding.

Max followed the campaign on a large map on his study desk. He listened intently to radio reports and looked for some chink in the apparently impregnable enemy armour. As the days shortened again and night and winter became masters of the earth, the mighty war machine seemed to stall. A cowardly attack carried out on a harbour in the Pacific had brought America into the war. This only seemed to stir up the lunatic prophet over the water into making yet more ominous threats.

Oskar's transport column had stirred into activity once more. Max received reports which made his heart freeze. Traumatised German soldiers returning on leave from the Eastern front were revealing to family and friends the horrific scenes they had witnessed or taken part in. There had been mass executions of innocent men, women and children on a scale unimaginable. Innocent civilians lined up in front of great ditches they had been forced to dig themselves had been brutally murdered at close quarters by squads of merciless executioners.

And in another house by another lake a decision was being made.

XXV

Winter had withdrawn to its glacier redoubt.

The plane trees, poplars and willows on the shoreline were slowly shrinking from his view as Max rowed out towards the middle of the lake. Soon they were merged into a single green brushstroke.

He stopped rowing, rested the oars and let the boat gently bob as it drifted away from land.

Max took out Lili's latest letter and started reading.

My dearest Max,

How long have I been wanting to write to you, to thank you for your letter and the parcel of chocolate you sent. You cannot imagine the delight on these poor children's faces when I handed it out to them.

There are days when I am filled with sadness and powerless to do anything. So you've heard nothing too? Oh, Max! What hope is there of ever finding him? I ask any new arrivals in the camp if they know of Freddi but all I get from them are blank stares and shrugs. With half of humanity on the move from one place to another, no wonder! They are now coming here from the other camps in the region, from Noe, Vernet, Gurs and Les Milles. We are at a loss to know what this means.

The winter was awful here. Rain like I've never experienced. The camp was flooded like a lake. You can imagine what misery it caused for the poor internees with inadequate shoes or no shoes at all. Now the warm weather is returning. We're making a little garden. Perhaps the sight of some green shoots will bring hope. But the warm weather brings problems of its own. Rats get into our storeroom and at the food. How we need a hunter like Hiddigeigei, but what with the shortage of meat…

Don't worry, Max. I'm alright. We eat twice a day. We try and look out for each other so that none of us gets too depressed by what we experience here. Rosli had to go to hospital in Perpignan with a bad case of diphtheria. Thank God the worst is over. It's amazing the rest of us didn't catch it.

It's the plight of the children which upsets me the most. We do our best for them. There are so many orphans or motherless children – that's as good as being orphaned, since the authorities forbid fathers from being with their children. We're getting parcels through the Red Cross, and Swiss schoolchildren write and tell the camp children about their lives. The delight on their faces makes you forget the misery. We push and push the camp authorities to allow sick mothers and infants to go to one of our maternity homes in the region. If we are insistent, they will give in. But it only means temporary respite, since they have to come back when they feel better.

The other day Elsi got into trouble with the commandant. She organised an evening procession for the children with hollowed out pumpkins lit by candles. It was quite a sight! But she hadn't asked permission and the guards were not amused. We thought she was going to end up in prison.

The authorities really are at their wits' end. They've now asked us to care for those starving to death. What good can we do? A daily ration of rice won't help them back to life.

When the doctor came round to see one of the poor creatures, a little girl of seven, I heard him mutter to himself: 'death has chosen her'...

A dog barked in the distance.

Max lifted his head and looked towards the shore. The memories he had resisted for so long were regrouping. His will to resist their attack was broken.

Death has chosen her.

Poor little Rosa.

His daughter had shared Lotte's frail constitution. She never played out with other children, never swam in the lake or climbed trees. She was most content to spend her time indoors, painting, practising the piano or playing with her dolls. And he and Lotte smiled on their child's contentment.

Winter that year refused to relinquish its frozen grip. The ice age had returned. The lake was sealed for months from shore to shore.

Its surface welcomed hundreds of pleasure-seekers with their sledges, skates and picnic baskets. They came to marvel and cast out the winter's gloom in play. Only in Easter week did the warm winds return. The ice began to thaw.

To complete their domestic happiness Max decided to give Rosa a little spaniel as a companion. For hours she cuddled and played with Chiara, the name they had chosen for the puppy, until both were worn out and fell asleep on top of each other.

The time for the first walk came. Rosa pleaded with them to let her take Chiara out.

'She'll be fine,' Max reassured a nervous Lotte as he fastened the new leash around the excitable puppy's neck.

Time passed.

The sun was going down. Lotte was becoming increasingly agitated.

And then the twilight stillness was shattered by the sound of furious barking.

Max raced out with neighbours to investigate.

They found a distraught Chiara, alone on the ice.

No one knew exactly what had happened. Rosa had last been seen setting off along the path skirting the lake. Chiara must have slipped her leash and run onto the treacherous ice.

Rosa had followed.

When Max returned home, Lotte was standing by the open door, her face contorted in a frozen scream.

The Easter bells were ringing.

Lotte was devastated. And he could find no words to console her. She accused him of all manner of cruelty.

'Why don't you say something?' she implored. 'You write all those fancy words but you can't even find a few scraps of comfort for me. Why am I the only one to shed any tears?'

On the day of the funeral the wind blew the black ribbons tied to the horse's mane as the village children dutifully filed past the carriage bearing Rosa's coffin.

Lotte began seeing and hearing things. She saw demons grinning at her from the infernal depths of the lake. And no power on earth could rid her of the sound of cracking ice.

One day Max came home to find her curled up like a child on their bed. Her hands were fixed over her ears in the vain attempt to block out the thundering noise. The time for him to say or do anything to save her had passed. Seeking reunion with their deceased daughter, her spirit had already descended into the black abyss.

*   *   *

'What misery I caused!' Max cried out to the surrounding shores.

Rosa would have been a grown woman like Lili now. He would have done anything to save her. He would have gladly traded places with her under the ice. What was his life, half-over, against a life scarcely begun?

His existence had been emptied of all meaning when Rosa died and Lotte's spirit abandoned him. He withdrew from life, from all its joys and woes, and sought to exchange the phantoms in his books for flesh and blood.

What vanity!

But real life had refused to let him be. First the little intruder and then Freddi reminded him what it was to be alive.

And now fate had dealt him a second blow. The healing wound was ripped open again. Once more, the two most precious things in his life had been taken from him. What was left?

His thoughts turned to the dark brown phial by his bed.

Max lifted the half-read letter he was still holding in his right hand. Lili's words ran with his tears.

Last Sunday I decided to go out on my bike into the countryside. Spring is here at last. The sun gilded the track which led down to the sea. Along the way the almond and peach trees were in full blossom. The meadows were green and there was such an intensely blue sky.

I sat on a rock looking down at the sea. The cliffs were covered with bright yellow gorse. Spain was not far away.

I spent hours there, watching and weeping. But the sun filled me with warmth again and I set off back to the camp.

As I write this letter to you, Max, there is a sprig of almond blossom in a glass vase on the desk in front of me.

You asked me when I'll return. How much I long to see you again and our little village by the lake!

Let me know if you receive any news. Keep a place warm for me in your heart.

God keep you well and safe. Is Hiddigeigei still catching mice?

All my love,
Lili

There was still hope: a sprig of almond blossom amongst all this despair.

Lili was keeping that hope alive. He couldn't let her down.

Max wiped away his tears, folded her letter and took up his oars.

XXVI

Lili's return came sooner than Max had anticipated. From his window he saw a woman walk through the gate and along the garden path to his door. Her uncovered head was bowed; her hair was closely cropped. Still he recognised her immediately.

He rushed to greet her.

'Lili! What are you doing back? I didn't expect you…'

He was shocked by her appearance. She looked exhausted and emaciated.

He embraced her warmly. 'Come in! Come in!'

'Hello, Max. I meant to bring some milk for Hiddigeigei. Where is he?'

'He's asleep on his armchair in my study. Since you left he hasn't shown a great zest for life … You look tired and hungry. I'm just cooking something. Come and eat. Tell me what's happened.'

Over a plate of steaming spaghetti, colour returned to Lili's pale face. Her journey from France had been slow and long. She'd only got back in the small hours of the morning.

Suddenly tears started streaming down her face.

'Max, it's hopeless,' she sobbed. 'He's gone.'

Max did not need to ask who or where. He put his arm around her shoulder and tried the best he could to comfort her. Such sadness in one so young.

'How do you know, Lili? Tell me what's happened.'

Lili wiped her eyes on the back of her hand.

'It all started back in the summer. More and more internees from other camps were coming to Rivesaltes. They were desperate, hungry people, Max. Crippled, young and old, abandoned – such a wretched mass. One night a large group of gypsies arrived – there must have been a thousand. We had no idea what was to become of them. A couple of days later we noticed the presence of black cars in the camp. It must have been around the middle of July. They were Germans. The first Germans we'd seen in the camp. It seemed that they were inspecting the camp for a reason that was not clear to us at the time. But in the part of the camp where the Jews were held, rumours started circulating about what was going to happen. Their numbers had increased rapidly since the arrival of hundreds from the occupied zone. They told us there had been a wave of raids and mass arrests of all foreign Jews in Paris and the rest of the zone. Many had tried to flee south but were caught at the border, stripped of their documents and dumped on us. They all kept asking me, 'Sister Lili, what's going on? What's going to happen to us?'

322

How did we know?'

Lili fumbled in her canvas bag by her feet. It still bore the sign of the Red Cross, though faded and dirty. She pulled out a packet of cigarettes and held one to her lips.

'Have you got a light, Max?'

'Sure.'

Max got up to get a box of matches.

'I didn't know you smoked.'

Lili squinted at the first curl of smoke.

'It's the best thing to quell pangs of hunger. I suppose I just got used to it.'

She removed a stray fibre of tobacco from her lip before continuing.

'I was writing my diary late one night. It was the second or third of August – I know because we had just had a muted celebration of our national day – it was about three-thirty in the morning. I hadn't been sleeping at all well for weeks. The heat had been unbearable through the summer months. I heard the arrival of trucks and went out of my barrack to see dozens of French soldiers, gardes mobiles, arriving. I rushed over to the section of the camp where the Jews were held. Everyone had been made to line up in front of their barracks. They were standing there while the soldiers went round with lists counting them off. Again they asked me what was happening. I answered as best I could.

'Be brave. Nothing worse can happen to you than has happened so far.' But I heard the dreaded word Poland whispered by many. There was no reaction. No uproar at the way they were being treated. I was astonished at the way they stood for hours lined up.

It was as though many knew what was coming. Some were swallowing whatever medicines they could get their hands on. Often it wasn't enough. Still more were arriving from Lyons and Paris. It seemed that the authorities were rounding up all the Jews forced out of Germany.

Then I thought – this must be happening everywhere.

I will never forget the weeping and screaming I witnessed that day. By the evening peace had returned. They were telling me that if it had to be, they would go in God's name.

In God's name!'

Max reached out his hand and placed it gently on Lili's.

'He might still have got away, Lili,' he whispered.

She looked into his eyes and shook her head.

'A group of new arrivals came from the camp at Gurs. I was doing the rounds of the barracks attending as best I could to the sick and the infants. There had been more suicide attempts during the night. A man came up to me. He was German. He'd been a doctor in Germany, a paediatrician, and wanted to help us. Of course, we needed all the help we could get. After we'd gone through the barracks dispensing what help and medicines we could, we sat down and got talking. He told me a bit about Gurs. For some reason, I don't know why, I thought I'd ask. I'd given up asking in recent months. What with all the new arrivals, I'd given up hope.

'Freddi?' he said. 'Why yes, he's alive. That is, he was when I last saw him.'

You can imagine the joy I felt, even at this awful time with all these poor people about to be sent to an unimaginable fate. My heart was leaping; I could hardly contain myself. The poor man was bombarded with questions which he answered with patience. Was he still in Gurs? He thought so. Some had been sent out of the camp to work for the Germans. Something called Operation Todt. He saw the shock on my face as he uttered the name. I'd understood 'Operation Tod', but he reassured me that although they had to carry out heavy labour, there was a good chance of survival. Recently he'd noticed that the labour gangs were returning to the camps worn out and no longer of any use to the Germans. But he hadn't seen Freddi return.

I knew I had to get to Gurs at the earliest possible opportunity. I had to find out whether he was there. But at that time it was impossible. There was so much to do.

Another six hundred arrived that night.

The mothers were pleading with us to intercede with the authorities to let the children stay. We were powerless to do anything. It was clear the French authorities were going to make no exceptions. The children had to travel, either with or without their mothers. The order came from Vichy.

We had a German woman who helped in our barracks, Frau Schwarzschild. She had three small children, and her husband was in the men's camp too. She was absolutely distraught, begging me on her knees to help. In her hand she held a photograph. It was of her first communion. Years before, during the persecution in Germany she'd converted to

Christianity hoping that this would give her some protection.

The commandant's car was parked in front of his office. Against all the regulations regarding our conduct issued by the Red Cross, I decided to plead for Frau Schwarzschild and her family.

I begged the commandant. I showed him the photograph. Look, I said, she is a Catholic mother with Catholic children.

'That is not an official document. Anyway, what difference does it make?'

'But you are a fellow Catholic, aren't you? Have you no conscience?'

He got angry with me.

'How dare you question me so impudently! You are here under sufferance as foreign nationals. As such, you are to follow implicitly and without question the rules and regulations for your conduct. In your own country you can do and speak as you like, but not here. Is this what you Swiss mean by neutrality? Your Red Cross is just an interfering busybody. The sooner we're rid of you, the better.'

I feigned humility and apologised profusely. I flattered him.

'I know you have a difficult job and you are running an excellent camp in such demanding circumstances ... but if I could just make this one request?'

'You have no right to ask anything of me. My orders come from Vichy not from some Swiss nurse!'

I wouldn't let go. I said that, in these circumstances, normal rules and regulations did not always apply. I could see he was a kind man with a heart. Could he really let a mother and her children undertake such a hazardous journey?

He threatened me.

'You have outlived your usefulness. The camp will soon be empty and you can go home. Be glad you have a safe home to go to.'

'So will you let this mother and her family go?'

He glared at me. I stared back straight into his eyes. He thumped his fist hard onto his desk.

'So be it.'

I thanked him profusely, praising his humanity and generosity to the skies. Then I remembered.

'And the father?'

'The father travels on the next transport. That is my final word.'

There was nothing more I could do. I turned to leave, but he hadn't finished.

'Know this, sister. We'll find replacements for all those you have just saved. The lists will be full.'

That is precisely what happened. Some who thought they had escaped the transport were dragged screaming onto the trucks.

What more could we do?

We did our best for those leaving the next day. We sang songs with the children and handed out provisions for the journey.

A convoy of trucks arrived next morning to take them to the station. I couldn't bear to watch.

I had to get away and set off for Gurs. My own search for happiness seemed obscene in all this misery. Everywhere there were soldiers and controls. I needed a special laissez-passer to get through. I pleaded – I was with the Red Cross, after all. It made no difference. Turned away from one checkpoint, I tried to work my way round. I slept in barns and fields. A friendly farmer took me in one night. I saw how impoverished the local people were. They hardly had anything to eat themselves. I wandered through the region trying to get through, but the net kept closing in on me.

Go home, I was told. There's nothing for you here now.

I returned to the camp.

When I arrived I found the other nurses in tears packing their bags. The commandant had demanded our removal from the camp for serious breaches of neutrality. We were being sent home.

I never got to Gurs.

But I knew that what was happening in Rivesaltes was happening in every camp. They even emptied our maternity homes of sick and dying infants. They were sending all the Jews to the East.

I don't need to spell out to you what that means, Max.'

XXVII

The last truck of the convoy carrying the detail had fallen behind the others. Its driver was forcing the vehicle, laden with a dozen exhausted labourers and two armed guards, along a rough track crossing densely forested terrain. Its frequent jolts shook the emaciated bodies of the camp prisoners, already shattered by weeks spent smashing rocks from dawn to dusk.

The truck came to a tight bend which the driver took at a greater speed than was advisable.

Suddenly there was a squeal of brakes.

'Verdammt nochmal!' The curse came from the driver's right-hand side.

'Was ist los?' one of the two unsighted guards called out from the rear.

'There's a tree in the road. Come and give us a hand.'

With a 'verdammte Scheiβe' one of the two guards stirred himself and clambered out of the back of the truck. His disgruntled muttering could be heard as he walked along the side to join his comrades.

'Why the fuck don't we get this lot –?'

His suggestion was cut short by a brief burst of machine gun fire and truncated screams.

In the rear of the truck Wotan caught the remaining guard unawares with a fierce punch to the stomach. He fell to his knees and was retching uncontrollably.

'Vite! Vite! Sortez!'

The prisoners clambered past the guard to get out. The last one gave him an uncompromising knee to the head sending him sprawling lifelessly into his own pool of vomit.

Freddi looked back at the scene as they fled. The windscreen of the cabin was covered in the driver's blood. The other two guards hung grotesquely in the branches of the fallen tree.

'This way. Vite!'

Freddi and Wotan raced after a bearded partisan. The dense undergrowth tore at their filthy camp clothes. They ran until their lungs were about to burst.

'Ok. We can stop and rest a moment here, mes amis. They won't find us now.'

Freddi and Wotan collapsed to the ground.

'Here, drink.' The partisan was smiling as he extended a metal flask towards them.

The two men hauled themselves up off the damp forest floor.

'Feeling better?'

'Thanks for saving us. Merci,' said Freddi passing the flask to Wotan.

'De rien. It was a pleasure, mes amis.' He offered them both a cigarette, before lighting up himself.

They sat in the cool forest recovering.

'So, where do you intend to go now you are free?' asked their liberator.

'We need to get out of France,' Wotan answered. 'Now the Germans are running things I can't see any future for us here.'

'Where?' repeated the partisan, blowing smoke from the corner of his mouth.

Freddi's first thoughts were of Lili and Max. How good it would be to return safely to them!

'What about getting to Switzerland?'

The partisan snorted derisively.

'Forget it. The borders are shut. No-one is getting through. And if they do, they're being handed back to the Gestapo. In any case, it won't be long before the boches invade. If our glorious army can't hold them back with our Maginot line, what chance have they got?'

Freddie and Wotan looked at each other in gloomy silence. How long would it be before they were back in a camp?

'We could try and get to Marseille. We might be able to get on a ship and get the fuck out of here.'

The partisan looked with increasing sympathy at Wotan. He was visibly struggling to find a way not to demolish their hopes.

'Perhaps that's not such a good idea,' he said after some thought. 'Everyone's going there. It's stuffed full of refugees looking for the last way out of the trap closing around them. There are hordes of German émigrés sitting around in cafes hanging on to the latest rumour. There's a ship in from … a ship going to … All illusions. They're living in a fantasy world with make-believe ships sailing to countries which don't exist on any map…Then the house of cards comes crashing down.'

He paused to allow his words to sink in.

'Most are like you. Apatrides. Stateless. No connections, no money, no papers … No chance. They wander from café to café, from this consulate to that one, in the hope of getting a passport or visa.'

The partisan stubbed out his cigarette on the boulder beside him and flicked the butt into the bushes. A mouthful of spit followed.

'Let me tell you something, mes amis. One day the rumour went round that you could buy a Chinese visa. You could get an official stamp for your passport which would allow you to travel. All you had to do was go to some bureau in some backstreet and hand over your hundred francs. Later on we found out that, translated, the stamp read: 'The owner of this passport is strictly forbidden, at any times and under any circumstance, from entering Chinese territory."

He laughed darkly.

'At least the average French border guard doesn't read Chinese.'

'Is there no way of getting the documents we need on the black market?' asked Freddi. He immediately knew from the askance look the partisan was giving him that his question had been ill advised.

'We live in the Age of Regulations, mes amis. You have to be 'en règle'. Say you want to get to a neutral country, Portugal, for example, so that you can then sail to safety in the New World – the USA, Mexico,

Cuba, San Domingo. You name it – the world's your oyster…'

He smiled briefly at his own inappropriate irony.

'You need a transit visa to go through Portugal. Ok?'

'How do you get one of those?' asked Wotan.

'To get a transit visa for Portugal, you need an entry permit for your final destination. Let's say that's Cuba.'

'And how—?'

'To get an entry permit you need a valid passport. To get a passport you could try trawling around the consulates.'

Wotan and Freddi looked at each other with increasing desperation. Both were stateless and without any papers. It was as though they didn't exist.

'It gets better.'

The partisan was into his flow.

'To get an entry permit you also need a ticket to your destination. Paid for.'

'Which presumably will cost thousands of francs,' said Wotan.

'Francs? No, no, mon ami. Not francs, dollars. Lots of dollars. The ticket must be paid for in dollars. Lots of dollars. To get dollars you need money –'

'Lots of it, presumably,' interrupted Freddi bitterly.

'A visa to Cuba costs two thousand dollars per head and another five hundred for the journey. Oh, and you'll need a permit to change your money.'

'Say you had the money …'

The partisan raised his eyebrows.

'Hypothetically … How easy is it to get a ticket?'

'Getting a ticket? Oh, you can get tickets. No problem. In the centre of Marseille there is a very elegant building with an English travel bureau by the name of Cook. If you go in there with your money, some snooty Englishman will sell you a ticket. They're selling dreams ... It will be a forged ticket for a mythical land.'

'What makes me think no-one wants us?' asked Freddi.

The Frenchman seemed to be running through a list in his head, like a shopper at the market.

'Oh, I nearly forgot. Obviously to get to Portugal you will need a transit visa for Spain. For which you need your Portuguese transit visa –'

'For which you will need ...'

'I'm sorry. It doesn't look good, I know. There is something else, too.'

'Go on,' the two fugitives spoke in unison.

'To leave France you will need a visa de sortie, an exit permit. You will have to go to Vichy to get one of those. To travel anywhere in France legally now you will need a sauf-conduit. Even with all these documents you are very likely to find yourself at the Spanish border with guards who will come up with all sorts of excuses not to let you in. Such and such a document isn't valid any longer; the stamp is incorrect. And even if you had a passport, they would see straight away that you are under forty-two years old and send you straight back – or intern you at their own concentration camp at Figueras.'

'Why?'

'The fascist authorities cannot allow passage to any men young enough to fight. You might get to England and end up fighting the Germans. They do it out of respect for Hitler – or because they're shitting themselves.'

'It's hopeless then,' sighed Freddi. 'We can't stay. We can't leave.'

'As I said, mes amis. The Age of Regulations … Cigarette?'

'What do you suggest?' asked Wotan.

'Go underground. Disappear. Become clochards.'

He saw the bewilderment written on their faces.

'As you can see, there is no legal way of getting out. Unless you are very rich, have excellent connections and are very lucky. The alternative is: disappear. Lie low for as long as it takes. This part of France is very remote. There are tiny villages in the hills and mountains that not even the French authorities bother about. We have safe houses scattered around. It works like –'

Wotan interrupted. 'You send us to one. They move us on the next, and so on. I know how it works. That's how I moved from Austria to Spain to fight in the war in the first place.'

'We've both had some experience of underground networks. Remember, we've been opposing the Fascists for many years, not just for the last few months,' Freddi added angrily.

'Yes, of course, mes amis.' The irony was dropped in place of respect for their credentials. The bearded partisan became more thoughtful.

'There is a way out of the country which has been successful so far. But you need to hurry up. The Vichy regime is ordering all foreigners out of the border areas. It will soon become very difficult, perhaps impossible. You need to get yourselves over to the

Mediterranean border with Spain. There is a route over the mountains where you can cross illegally. It's risky but…'

'We're used to risk.'

'Stay out of the towns. Avoid all buses and trains – you can only travel legally with a sauf-conduit, remember. Our friends will guide you from one house to the next. You will be safer on bicycles or on foot. The local farmers will also take you in when it's possible and feed you. Here, take these.'

He handed over paper coupons.

'Ration cards. Forged, of course. You'll need them for food. When you get to a small town called Banyuls go to the café in the main square. Ask for Azema. He'll see to the rest.'

*   *   *

In the days and weeks that followed they made their way through the remote countryside. On some days they walked miles and miles on circuitous paths through fields and forests to arrive not much nearer their destination than when they had set off. Always they remained wary of any other traveller, always ready to dive into a ditch if there was a rare passing car. Sometimes they starved all day and drank only water from village pumps. On other occasions the farmers fed them regally on their own produce.

Only once did they contravene the partisan's instruction to stay out of towns. That was in Lourdes where they reckoned they would be able to disappear among the crowds of pilgrims walking through the streets full of small shops crammed with souvenirs and religious artefacts. How much they would have loved to have stayed in one of the hotels and enjoyed a decent bed for one night!

But for that another piece of paper was required: a fiche d'hérbergement.

In the town there was a reception centre for refugees offering some food and a bed for the night. But they knew that, without papers, they would be arrested and sent straight back to the camps now in the process of being emptied. So they carried on through Lourdes out into the countryside and spent another night under a hayrick. They had indeed become clochards – vagabonds.

*   *   *

The small town near the Pyrenees was bathed in the last light of day when they arrived. They were quickly directed to Azema by the friendly patron of the café.

Azema was once the socialist mayor of Banyuls, the last town on the border. He'd helped many a refugee find a route over the mountains to Spain. Small in stature, like all the men in the region, he was broad-shouldered, with dark hair and sharp features. Intelligence shone in his eyes. He had been relieved of his post by the Vichy regime a few months before and retired to a secluded hamlet on the first slopes of the Pyrenees. From there he continued to help escaping emigrants as best he could.

He sat with them in the evening, going over the route.

'Unfortunately the path once used by many refugees, the one which ran along the ridge of the mountains and provided an easy walk, has become too dangerous. It's now regularly patrolled by the gardes mobiles acting under instructions from the Kundt Commission, the Gestapo in Marseille.'

'So how do we get across?' asked Wotan impatiently.

Azema, seeing his eye patch and the missing fingers on his left hand, knew he was talking to a veteran of the war.

'I'm sure you've heard of Lister.'

Wotan nodded.

'He was a general in the Republican Army during the civil war,' he said for Freddi's benefit.

'There's a smugglers' path named the Lister trail. Many of his troops fled fascist vengeance along it. It's a tougher climb. The path runs parallel to the 'official route' and beneath it. It's hidden by the overhanging rocks so you can't be seen by the patrolling douaniers. Be careful. At several points the two paths run close to each other. You must be very watchful.'

The mayor opened a bottle of wine.

'The danger's most acute when leaving the village at the start of the climb. That's where the douaniers will be keeping a close watch.'

He held out two glasses.

'Drink. It will help you sleep. The wine in these parts is very good ... I'll wake you well before dawn. You must set off early. Mingle with the vineyard workers and only carry a musette, a sack for your bread. Don't take a rucksack – it will give you away as Germans at once. Don't talk to anyone. In the darkness the guards won't be able to tell you apart from the vignerons.'

Azema got up and went to a drawer.

'Here, wear these.' He handed them berets and espadrilles. 'Fortunately you look as weather-beaten and tattered as the peasants around these parts.'

Azema laughed.

'You wouldn't believe how some try and cross with their suitcases, fur coats and city hats. You're young and strong. You should make it in four to five hours at most.'

'How do we know we've got there?' asked Freddi.

Azema pushed a scrap of paper with a pencil-drawn map towards them.

'Look here. When you cross a small stream and pass by an empty stable, you will see an opening ahead of you with a group of seven pine trees. That's where you must bear left; otherwise you will end up far too north. Keep the ridge to your right. The path at this point is harder to find. It is sometimes visible but sometimes disappears among the scrub and loose rocks. Once you've got to that point you should find your way to a steep vineyard. Climb up between the vines. You will see the peak.'

*   *   *

They set out before first light, struggling to make out the path winding through a group of cottages between the silhouettes of large trees. After twenty yards or so they joined the vignerons making their way with their spades and baskets to the vineyard. The bereted peasants showed no apparent surprise at the strangers' presence. They broke off from speaking Catalan to greet them briefly, but in a friendly manner, in French.

They had been climbing for several hours. The path was harder than anticipated. It was typical of mountain people to understate the difficulties, but they knew as they climbed that they were moving towards safety. The two friends sat down to rest. In silence they admired the view of the steep vineyard below them dripping with ripe, sweet Banyuls grapes. The vignerons who had shared their path were now toiling hard.

The sun warmed their backs. Wotan opened his knapsack and passed a chunk of bread and a tomato to his companion.

Freddi thought of Lili. With every passing day he found it harder to recall her features. The more he tried, the more she disappeared into a blur. But then at night she would suddenly appear, alive, lying beside him in the straw, and he imagined he could reach out and touch her as he did on the night they first made love.

He looked across at his friend.

Wotan was staring down in front of him at a sun-bleached skeleton. The skull looked like that of a goat, Freddi thought. Above them buzzards circled languidly in the sky.

'We'd better get moving.'

Wotan got to his feet and gave the bleached skull a sound kick. It rolled down the steep mountainside.

Freddi smiled. The two orphans had become brothers.

They moved off stiffly, feeling the sun's increasing warmth on their weary bones. The climb was gentler now. The peak was in sight.

The scene greeting them at the top was one they had scarce hoped to see. Looking over their shoulders they could see the deep blue of the Mediterranean. In front of them, steep cliffs fell into a glass sheet of turquoise. It seemed a different sea altogether. It was the Spanish coast.

They descended quickly avoiding the border village of Port Bou. At a pond with slimy, stagnant green water they were greeted tersely by a peasant. Wotan spoke a few words of Spanish with him, before the peasant turned and led them to safety.

XXVIII

On a peaceful Sunday in April Lili rowed out with her father to go fishing on the lake. The war was forgotten with each rhythmic stroke taking them further from land.

Despite the beauty of the day Lili's heart weighed as heavy as a stone in her chest. When she at last rested the oars, a single sigh left her lips. It was swallowed by the lake, and the lake returned it to the surface accompanied by a chorus of all the deceased souls of sailors awoken by its anguish.

Otto was troubled by what he saw.

'Are you suffering, my child?'

Lili looked down at the floor of the rowing boat and nodded wordlessly.

Her father struggled to find words of solace.

'I know what you are feeling. When I lost Leni, Helena…' he began.

In shock Lili looked up at her father.

Her eyes met his fleetingly. His lips suddenly parted as if he was about to say something. He averted his gaze. The sudden breaking of the taboo of her name was almost too much for him to bear.

Lili reached her hands behind her neck and undid the clasp of the silver chain. With a finger nail she prised open the oval locket. She hesitated.

'Papa, I'm so sorry...'

Her words were suffocated by unrestrained sobs of contrition. Her tears fell freely, sprinkling the wooden boards of the rowing boat.

She reached the opened locket to her father.

'Leni,' he said, 'my darling Leni.'

Otto was lost in contemplation of the long forgotten photograph.

'I didn't mean to take it ... I only wanted to know if it was true ... I panicked. Oh, I'm so sorry, Papa.'

He tore his eyes from the smiling face and looked up at Lili.

Her debt of guilt, once stored away, had increased a hundredfold over the years. Now the forlorn expression on her father's face made it beyond the currency of any words she could find.

Otto closed the locket and held it out for Lili.

'Take it, Lili,' he urged.

Lili shook her head. He took her hand and pressed the locket into it.

'I'm happy it was you who took it. Leni was your mother. You should have it. I've always had my memories. No one could ever deny me them. But you had nothing ... I'll always regret –'

'What was she like? Please tell me, Papa.'

It was a question she would have asked a thousand times.

'You remind me so much of her, Lili.'

He was smiling.

'She was beautiful, stubborn and wilful. She was only young when … I do know your pain, Lili. When she left me I felt as though I had been torn in two, and the good half had been stolen away. I walked and walked and walked. Through the meadows and forests; over hills and mountains. I retraced every step we had walked together. I thought that if I drove myself to exhaustion I would collapse into a deep sleep and forget. But she kept coming to me. Knowing I could not touch her face was unbearable. I wanted to throw myself from a precipice or simply drink myself to sleep on the mountain top and let the cold freeze me and my sorrow.'

'What stopped you?'

'Your mother. Anna. She nursed Leni at the end. When at last I lifted my eyes from my grief she was there for me. I was grateful to her.'

'Why did you never tell me – about Leni?'

'Anna made me swear I'd never mention her name. It was the one condition she insisted on. Later on I regretted agreeing to it, but by then –'

'And now?'

'She released me from my vow some time ago. She saw how much it was hurting me. But I still couldn't bring myself… I was a coward, Lili. Forgive me.'

'I do, Papa.'

'And don't be too hard on Anna. She's been a good mother to you.'

'I know, Papa.'

He paused, thinking of the words he wanted to say.

'I know your pain, Lili. But give it time. I was young. You are young. You've got the rest of your life ahead of you.'

He reached across the boat to touch her hand.

Lili held it tightly as she answered.

'The worst thing is not knowing; not knowing if he is dead or alive. And if he's dead, not knowing how … Such awful things are happening, Papa. If he has been taken to one of those unspeakable places…'

'You don't know that, my child.'

'Why should he survive when millions haven't? All over Europe trains are delivering thousands upon thousands to their deaths. There is no escape.'

Otto swallowed what he was about to say. His daughter was a grown woman. She had seen too much to tolerate any easy words of comfort.

'I just want to know,' Lili continued. 'If that has been his fate, I just want to know whether – in his last moments – he thought of me. Did he see my face and remember, remember some moment of joy we shared? If only that were so, I could find some consolation. But I can't know. I'll never –'

She choked on her words.

Otto looked on helplessly as his daughter burst into tears.

He remembered with painful longing how he used to carry her on his shoulders through the thick snow. He remembered the stories he would tell her against the dark and cold. What could he tell her now to banish the emptiness in his poor child's heart? What stories could have such power?

He plucked up his resolve.

'Lili, listen to me. I know I haven't been a good father…I know I've missed so much.'

'Papa…'

'When I went crazy after I lost Leni I couldn't see what was right in front of me. I couldn't see the affection your mother had for me. Perhaps it is the same for you.'

Lili dried her eyes. Her father's words were awakening her curiosity.

He stumbled on.

'I don't know. It's not for me to say but … Is there not someone, Lili? Someone who knows you well? Someone I know holds you in deep affection … I mean, someone strong enough to look after you, comfort you … and in time …. I know he's an older man…'

Lili's jaw dropped in astonishment. Surely he wasn't thinking of Rudolf Vischer?

'… but he's known you since you were so high. And you've got to know him. Your mother and I … we were too hasty. We were wrong … He's a decent man. I know that now. Surely you must have seen how he feels about you?'

Lili felt as though he'd slapped her hard across the cheek. She covered her face in her hands and sobbed uncontrollably.

They rowed back towards the shore bathed in afternoon sunshine. Pulling the oars as hard as she could through the water Lili wondered. How had her father been able to see what she had been so blind to?

After he secured the boat Lili hugged and kissed her surprised father.

*   *   *

That night the nightmare returned.

She knew where it was taking her. The Zeppelin hurtled at dizzying speed across rivers, lakes, deserts, mountains and oceans.

She burned and froze and burned once more.

Her head tossed about on her drenched pillow.

Then the crack of gunfire, explosions and fire. Children ran screaming from the fields clutching stomachs torn by lead.

In the end everything was consumed by flames.

Through the flames she saw faces.

Papa. Eva. Felix. Mama. Elsi. Friedel.

Freddi.

He was coming towards her. He was coming to save her.

He appeared out of the flames.

But it wasn't Freddi.

It was Max.

*   *   *

The villagers had got accustomed to the strange noises coming from the skies and the opposite shore. Young boys competed with each other to be the first to hear the grumbling of Flying Fortresses or recognise the silhouettes of fighter planes. After the bombings – or even during them, if they felt particularly brave – fishermen from all along the shore would race to the shoals of silver fish lying lifelessly on the surface of the lake providing an easy and plentiful catch, as though the Lord Jesus himself had just walked by.

One day even stranger sounds were heard from the other side of the lake. No one recognised them.

The villagers congregated in the street and speculated.

There was always one who knew.

Seeing a group of men arguing and gesticulating Vischer left his office, placing his peaked hat firmly on his head, and strode purposefully out to meet them.

'Good morning, gentlemen. Let me enlighten you. They're test flights. It's the miracle weapon. You'll see.'

His explanation was met with scepticism.

Rumours had circulated for weeks that the Germans were developing a weapon with enormous fire power which would turn the war back in their favour. Following defeat at Stalingrad and the retreat from the Eastern Front, Vischer had been walking around with a face like April weather. Now anyone he could collar was treated like a long-lost friend and subjected to long monologues on how the Red Army was going to be sent scuttling back with its tail between its legs.

One or two of the more mischievous villagers had taken to stringing the pompous policeman along.

'So what miracle weapon is that exactly, Herr Vischer?'

'I can't tell you that. It's secret. Absolutely top secret. Even the British spies haven't got a sniff of it.'

'Oh go on! We won't tell. What is it?'

And so the baiting continued.

Rudolf Vischer was about to get his comeuppance.

Spying from his office window he became aware of an excited huddle down at the lakeside. Fishermen had apparently hauled in something of great interest to children playing at the water's edge. Without hesitation he took his cap off its hook and strode out to see what all the fuss was about. When he arrived he found half the village gathered around.

'Allow me, please. Let me through. I'll deal with the matter.'

The small crowd eventually parted to let him through. Vischer was able to survey the scene properly for the first time.

His arrival was greeted by the occasional sarcastic comment from the fishermen who had brought the strange catch to land.

'Don't panic. Everything's under control.'

'The Sheriff's here!'

In front of him, beached on the stony shore among the reeds, Vischer saw two milk churns lying prostrate.

'What have we got here?' he asked himself out loud.

'They look like milk churns to me,' retorted one of the fishermen in open contempt for the policeman.

'Indeed, indeed.'

'Let's stand them up.'

'You can, Vischer. I'm not touching them. There might be a bomb inside.'

Vischer turned pale at the thought. But there was no turning back now. He had taken imperious control of the situation. He had to carry on the investigation.

'I think not,' he said uncertainly.

Without any help from the amused bystanders he strained and stood the two churns upright.

'They are unusually heavy,' he said, breathless from the effort.

'I wonder what's inside.'

'Milk, perhaps?'

There were more titters of laughter.

Vischer felt the need to reassert his diminishing authority.

'Stand well back, everyone. I shall open the containers to see what is inside. It is probably full of contraband or propaganda. I shall have to report and confiscate any contents. Please, move back.'

The mood of the crowd changed. The policeman's instructions were obeyed.

Vischer was feeling in charge of the situation again.

He went to open the lid of the first churn. However, he couldn't see how to do it. He looked hopefully around him. No one spoke, but one of the farmer's lads made a twisting motion with his hands.

Vischer followed the instruction and twisted the lid. He raised it slowly and held it away from his body in his left hand.

His head disappeared into the churn.

Several moments passed in hushed expectation as he struggled to make out what was in the churn.

His head reappeared.

His eyes were opened wide in horror.

His jaw dropped, and he reeled back as though he had been struck a fierce blow.

Vischer turned towards the astonished bystanders.

A thick stream of vomit shot out of his gaping mouth as he retched and retched.

The villagers stepped back in disgust at the puking policeman.

'What is it? What's in there?'

A hardened fisherman went up to the churn. He held his hand up to his mouth and nose as the stench rose from the container. He peered inside.

There he made out a pummelled head and severed arms and legs. He opened the other churn to discover a torso, in similar condition. Whoever it was had been beaten to death with an iron bar, carved up and buried in the lake with milk churns as coffins.

Still heaving uncontrollably Vischer staggered away from the scene.

The fisherman, who in decades spent on the lake had found any manner of decomposed bodies or body parts, the remains of hapless sailors or suicides fed on by eels and other creatures, twisted the lids back into place and called to his mates to help him carry the churns to Vischer's office.

Who was the man – for it turned out to be a man – in the churns?

All sorts of theories did the rounds.

A British agent, captured, interrogated and disposed of by the Gestapo? A German spy dealt with in like manner by the Swiss? A Jew? A Russian slave worker?

Or was he simply the victim of an 'ordinary' peacetime crime? A husband disposed of by his adulterous wife and her lover? A business man ambushed by vagrants, robbed and murdered in a manner most foul?

The authorities arrived within the hour from the county town to collect the churns. There was not much left to help them make any sort of identification.

Nothing was heard of Vischer after the incident.

Within two weeks he had gone.

No one saw him depart.

*   *   *

War resumed its quotidian activities.

Anti-aircraft canons carrying out exercises thudded dully across the lake. Shortly after, midday sirens pierced the still air. All along the opposite shoreline factories belched out black smoke from their chimneys. Canons fired further smudges into the sky. Soon a thick, deep lying blanket spread across the region concealing targets from enemy bombers. Only the highest spires and towers of the churches poked out of the impenetrable fog.

From the north-west came the familiar grumbling of heavy engines. It was getting louder and louder. Even with the naked eye it was possible to see squadron after squadron flying at a vertiginous height as they approached. Some held tight arrow-shaped formations; others were strewn randomly across the skies. The heavy bombers glinted like silver lances in the sunlight. Accompanying fighters darted around the almost cloudless sky. The armada was closing in on its target.

A long white banner slowly unfurled itself across the blue sky.

It was a sign for violence to begin.

Detonation followed detonation; explosion came after explosion. Houses shook. Window panes rattled. Pillars of smoke rose high into the air. In the midst of the grey pall, areas of conflagration could be identified. Angry flames consumed buildings and their inhabitants.

The squadrons continued to fly majestically through clouds of smoke. Out of nowhere came a vivid flash of colour as a bomber took a hit. Bursting into a riot of orange and yellow with a tail of black smoke it twisted in contortions before plunging into the lake.

The violence abated. The planes continued inland to attack more important targets.

Suddenly a Flying Fortress appeared against the sun. It was flying high in the sky. Anti-aircraft fire exploded all around it. Puffs of greyish white blotted the blue around the bomber. The plane appeared to be turning towards the southern shoreline and was crossing the lake. Salvoes of flak pursued it.

The heavy aircraft now seemed to be at no height at all. The groaning ceased. Its engines had cut out. It was moving towards a flotilla of fishing boats hugging the Swiss shore. Then it dipped in a steep curve towards the surface of the lake. It hit the lake with a sudden force which sent a fountain of water spurting high into the air. The plane disappeared from sight.

After a few moments the tail of the Flying Fortress reappeared above the surface. Having recovered from the shock of seeing the great beast hurtling towards them, some fishermen scurried towards the wreck in their boats. Where it entered the water they saw figures scrambling from the inside of the powerful machine and stumbling into two yellow rubber boats.

The first of the fishermen reached them.

The crew looked terrified. Their instruments had been knocked out, and they had lost all sense of where they were. One called out.

'Deutsch or Schweiz?'

The fisherman took out a red flag with a white cross and hung it over the side of the boat.

'Nicht Deutsche – Schwyzer!'

Wide smiles of white teeth beamed across the oil-smeared faces of the nine surviving crewmen. As they clambered into the fishing boats they looked back to see their aircraft sink and join the wreckage from previous millennia on the bottom of the lake.

XXIX

Since that afternoon on the lake, Lili had been pondering her father's words. They troubled and upset her. They comforted her. When she thought back she realised, yes! Max did care deeply for her.

There was more. She had seen it without recognising it for what it was – that look in his eyes.

She felt alone in the world, so alone. Her heart ached when thinking of Freddi's fate, yet for days and nights on end she could think of nothing else. At least for parts of the day she was occupied. At night, however, she tossed and turned and found no sleep. Dawn brought another day of anguish.

She had to see him. She had to find out how he really felt about her.

They had eaten supper together. It had been a desultory affair. Neither seemed inclined to talk. Occasionally one or other would make a half-hearted attempt to light a fire of conversation only for it to splutter and choke before going out.

The radio hummed in the background. Hiddigeigei slept on his usual chair; night-time hunting had lost its appeal.

They both knew the war was in its last throes. It had to be when cities across the lake were being razed to the ground. Max thought of the medieval town of his childhood with its pretty half-timbered houses and narrow winding streets. He thought of his neighbours, his school friends, and his family – what would become of them now they found themselves on the wrong side of the border?

His own relative safety no longer meant anything to him.

The evening dragged on. It was getting late. Lili was thinking of leaving, none the wiser.

They listened to the routine announcement on the German radio station regarding the situation in the skies. There were no enemy planes in the territory of the Reich.

It looked like they were in for an uneventful night.

'We shan't have to leave the lights on tonight, Max,' Lili said to break the awkward silence. There were so many unspoken thoughts between them.

Of late it had become usual on the Swiss side of the lake to leave lights on to help the Allied bombers find their way to their proper targets and avoid being bombed in error.

Two candles flickered on the dining room table. The dishes remained uncleared from hours before. The room was practically in darkness.

It was midnight.

Lili was on the point of saying good night.

'Listen! Isn't that the sound of aircraft in the distance? Can you hear it, Lili?'

They listened intently.

Hiddigeigei's ears twitched. He was getting old, and the noise of aircraft and bombs unsettled him.

Before long, all three of them were in no doubt that the distant drone signalled a bombing raid.

The air raid sirens howled as usual.

Those who had retired anticipating a peaceful night rose again from their beds. Lights twinkled all along the southern shoreline.

The best part of an hour passed.

Lili and Max stood at the study window and looked out at the familiar scene.

'Perhaps they'll just fly over on their way to other targets,' Lili said.

After all, that was what had happened during recent nights. Maybe they would simply see a few isolated fighter planes.

Across the lake spotlights pointed their long, luminous fingers into the starry night sky.

The calm lasted a brief moment longer.

The intensity of the drone had increased. There must have been hundreds of aircraft coming up the lake from the west, swarming in to form a concentrated host above Friedrichshafen.

'God help them,' sighed Max, his thoughts turning to those he once knew.

The German flak exploded in a powerful line of defensive fire. The sky flashed and flickered. Crowds of small clouds congregated. Despite the vehemence of the defence, the vanguard had penetrated the fire and smoke.

The sky above the German shoreline was decorated with a veil of red, yellow and orange bulbs of light. They hovered for minutes in the air. Slowly, very slowly, they made their way, gently twisting, towards the ground.

Lili couldn't help but think of the when she was a child and they rowed out with paper lanterns on to the lake. That was in times of peace, on the first day in August. From the water they would watch the fireworks light up the sky in celebration above their village.

The darkened region was gradually bathed in a fantastic light.

But the light was lighting the way for the destroyers.

Hell broke loose.

Infernal elements never before experienced by man or beast were unleashed.

Not even the most violent of storms over the lake could compare.

Not even the powerful wind which tore off roofs and uprooted trees.

Not even the scorching föhn which burnt the farmers' crops and orchards.

Not even the rushing waves rising and lashing the land in their fury.

Heaven, earth and water were thrown into utter turmoil.

The diabolical screech of the bombers reached a crescendo as they hurled down their bombs.

And even this far away the force of the violence made itself felt. Houses shook. Windows were blown out. Doors ripped off their hinges.

A false wind hissed, sucking everything in.

The earth shook out its own core.

Lili looked at Max.

'Max, I'm afraid,' she whispered.

Max seemed not to hear.

He had stopped feeling fear some time ago.

It had been replaced by numbness. What had he to fear anymore? Loss? Torture? Death? It would mean release from this vale of tears and suffering. Liberation from this never-ending cycle of desire and longing. Ambition, fame, power, wealth, love. Love was the worst! Everything ended in suffering.

There might be a few moments of agony – but after that? Nothing. Death had no sting. We were nothing before we came into this world; when we leave it we will be nothing. The rest was a fairy story to scare children.

Lili had moved closer to him.

The initial fury of destruction had passed, it seemed.

He took her in his arms.

Another wave was about to break. The same veil of globes illuminated the sky.

Max was fascinated by the colours of the lights reflected in Lili's eyes and on her cheeks. A rainstorm of bombs smashed into the ground once more. Everything shook and groaned, moaned and crashed.

The panes in the study windows rattled furiously.

Across the lake a black shroud of smoke rose from the shore. Its hem was embroidered by conflagration.

Max felt Lili press herself against him.

'Hold me tight, Max.'

He looked down and saw her face move nearer to his. Her lips, burning with the outside fires, came towards his.

Max was shaking.

No! Not like this!

He grabbed Lili by her shoulders and violently forced her away from him. Lili stumbled back in shock.

'Max! What are you doing? You're hurting me!'

In the candlelight he saw tears running down her cheeks.

His anger was extinguished. He immediately regretted treating her so harshly.

'Lili, listen to me,' he spoke tenderly to her, in the way he'd done when she was a child. 'You mustn't give up hope. It's Freddi you love – don't you think I know that? And he loves you. How can you abandon those feelings?'

Lili dropped her gaze in shame.

'But Max, it's hopeless. He's never coming back.'

'How do you know that? The war is ending. He might have survived – he's done it before. How do you think he got here in the first place? ... You're not the only one willing him to come through this.'

The intensity of his words startled Lili. For the first time she recognised the true strength of Max's feelings for Freddi.

'He may at this very moment have the thought of returning to you as his only hope, his only dream. Don't give up, Lili. Not until you've searched the four corners of the earth for him.'

She wiped away her tears; her resolve was rising up inside her.

'Lili, listen to me. There are survivors. Despite all that has happened. Some have even been snatched from certain death.'

Outside the worst of the violence had passed. In the darkened room calm was restored.

'One night, a few weeks ago, I couldn't sleep,' Max said, his voice soothing her fears. 'I got up and went for a walk. I wandered aimlessly through the empty streets and ended up at the railway station. It was deserted, of course. It was three in the morning. I sat down on a bench on the platform to think. Suddenly I was jolted out of my thoughts by a loud whistle. A train was approaching. In the middle of the night – at three in the morning! It was a long train, Lili. You wouldn't believe how long. It just kept coming and coming. I stood up and tried to peer into the illuminated carriages. It was rolling through slowly, so I could see in. ... It was crammed full of people. Who could be travelling at this time of night? I saw their clothes. I saw the faces of those leaning out of the windows breathing the air of freedom ... They were Jews, Lili. They'd been rescued from those awful places.'

'Where were they going? How had they escaped?'

'I asked myself the same questions. I had no idea at the time. A few days later, I bumped into an old acquaintance. He had connections with government circles. I told him about what I'd seen.'

'What did he say?'

'You'll find it hard to believe, Lili. It turns out they were all Hungarian Jews destined for the gas chambers.

A Swiss diplomat had haggled with the SS for their lives.'

'Haggled? What do you mean? He *bought* them?'

'Exactly. The Nazis are desperate. Their thousand-year Reich is on the point of collapse. Some haven't got the stomach anymore. They want an insurance policy for when the end comes.'

Max put his hand on Lili's shoulder. He waited for what he had told her to sink in.

'Lili … If he's survived till now, there's more than a good chance he'll make it through this hellish war.'

'I shan't give up, Max. I will keep looking for him.'

She embraced him tenderly. Max held her tight in his arms.

He was serene. It was over.

The last fires were extinguished in renunciation.

*　*　*

A gentle north-east breeze urged the cloud of smoke towards them, blotting out the stars in the sky. There was an all pervasive stench of burning, of soot and ash.

The last of the bombers withdrew.

On land fires raged for hours and hours.

Unexploded bombs wrought further violence in the aftermath. The crumbling church tower was all that could be seen above the sea of flames.

As day broke Max surveyed the inferno through his telescope. Still the fires burned.

The church collapsed.

Black smoke billowed into the sky.

The breeze carried ash into his garden. He went outside and picked up some fragments of burnt pages.

He tried to read the remnants of sentences blackened and turned to ash.

It was the end of civilization.

Late summer 1945

XXX

Maximilian Meyer studied the scene one more time. Two rowing boats had been half dragged up on to the land among the reeds on the shore. The rich brown earth underneath their green prows was dappled by the summer sunlight filtering through the canopy of the large trees which extended their boughs out towards the lake. In the distance the sails of a yacht broke the faint blue-grey of a tongue of land jutting into the lake.

He'd been working on the painting in his garden for several hours. The canvas testified to his endeavours. The scene had taken shape. Max critically surveyed the dark areas deep amongst the thick branches of the trees and the slightly lighter patches of shadow on the ground. Alizarin crimson and Prussian blue had provided the darkest shades. He'd mixed raw umber and cadmium red where some light had begun to filter through.

Max thought about those who had once sat in his garden. Some had entered that darkest realm of shadows for ever: Alfred with his scrapbook and cuttings. What fun he'd given Hiddigeigei! He'd taken the last road to freedom rather than suffer humiliation at the hands of his enemies.

Then there was Edmund – poor Edmund! He'd escaped the camps and prisons only to be struck down by the heavy bough of a tree when sheltering from a storm. And there was Stefan and his wife. Their journey into exile had taken them thousands of miles to Brazil. But they were never able to shake off their past. The news of events in their beloved homeland proved too much to bear. On the darkest night they took poison. If only they had waited till first light. The dawn brought news of the defeat of Hitler's vaunted Sixth Army at Stalingrad. The tide turned too late for them.

Max glanced at his palette. It was time to apply the last highlights to the composition. He loaded a small brush with a generous amount of Naples yellow and moved it towards the canvas. He flicked the boughs of the trees and the sides of the rowing boats with the same light touch as the sun.

He remembered those others who had survived: Harry, of course. He was a born survivor. The last he had heard, Harry was touting his wares at the Hollywood market.

Max chuckled to himself.

It's a crime to write about trees in times like these.

He wondered what Harry would have to say about him painting them.

Anyway, the dark times were over – for the moment.

And as far as he knew, George and Yvette were still performing their songs together in cabaret bars.

Looking back through the window of his study Max could see the vague outlines of boxes stacked on top of each other. His industrialist friend had been dropping hints about the house. Max knew it was time to move on. But wherever in the world he ended up, he wanted a reminder of this peaceful scene that had given him such delight for so many years.

Lili had been true to her resolve. With his help she left no stone unturned in her search for Freddi. Every other day he watched her set off early with a small rucksack. She walked purposefully to the station. There she took a local train eastwards along the lakeside. Large numbers of refugees, concentration camp survivors and prisoners-of-war had been flooding across at the border crossing of Sankt Margarethen. By now, however, the initial torrent had dried to a trickle.

Months had past. There was no news. Still she set off carrying her board with Freddi's photograph and her persistent request: Has anyone seen this man?

In the evening she walked back home past the house. He would call out to her.

'Lili, any news?'

She smiled as she shook her head.

'Tomorrow's another day,' she would say.

* * *

Max applied the finishing touches. He looked up from the canvas to the scene with the boats.

Beyond the subject of his composition something caught his attention. His eyesight had faded recently so he had to squeeze his eyes tight. On the path in the distance, coming around the tongue of land, he could make out two figures walking towards him.

He took little notice.

Max picked up a rag and started squeezing the excess paint from his brushes into it.

He looked up again.

The two figures had become clearer now. He could see that they were travellers. Both wore wide-brimmed hats and carried rucksacks. Plenty of people were still on the move, even though the war had ended months ago.

But there was something about the two wanderers which made him want to observe them more closely. They had stopped to discuss something. One seemed to be pointing towards the village; the other sank to the ground and opened his sack. He had decided to go no further. The one still standing gave him a quick wave and turned to continue along the path.

There was something familiar about the way he walked.

Max dropped his rag to the ground and threw his brushes carelessly into their box.

'It can't be!'

The stranger stopped for a moment and waved. He was waving at Max.

'No, surely it wasn't …' he muttered to himself.

Then he saw that it was.

It was Freddi.

'Didn't you recognise me, Max? I've been waving to you since we came around the corner.'

'Freddi! Good God! It is you – I didn't want to believe my eyes.'

Max embraced his long lost friend, transferring several shades of blue oil paint to Freddi's shirt in the process.

'You're still painting then?'

'Yes. As you can see, I'm using oils now. They're more permanent – perhaps. My God! Freddi! How did you get here?'

'That's a long story … Do you mind if I freshen up first?'

Max thought back to the times when Freddi returned from his escapades bursting to tell him all about what he had done. He seemed older and wearier now. He looked at him from head to toe. He was bedraggled, covered in dust. His clothes were tattered and his boots worn out. But it was the same Freddi.

'Of course … Of course!'

There was a moment's silence.

Freddi looked around the garden.

'Where's Hiddigeigei? I thought he'd be here to welcome me back.'

'Ah, Hiddigeigei. Alas, he's gone … The bombings were too much for him to bear. In any case, this is the age of warriors not philosophers. One day he left, and I've never seen him since.'

Freddi nodded in sympathy.

'But it isn't really Hiddigeigei you're looking for, is it?'

Freddi smiled.

'Where is she, Max?'

'Lili? Well …'

Max thought about telling Freddi how Lili had waited and waited for him to come back till eventually she couldn't wait any longer. How she'd grown into a very pretty woman and how sadness had added to her beauty. And that now she was married with two kids.

But then he looked into his young friend's eyes and thought better of it.

'She's gone to Sankt Margarethen, just along the lake. That's the crossing point for refugees from the east. That's where they are being registered. She's looking for you Freddi … Anyway, where have you come from?'

'You'll laugh, Max … Cuba.'

* * *

Freddi re-emerged from inside the house towelling his thick black hair. His companion through so many adventures was standing by the garden gate.

'Josef … Why are you hanging around out there? Come on in! Come and meet Max.'

Max turned around from his seat under the shade of the willow tree to see a Wagnerian apparition approach.

'Max … This is Josef, otherwise known as Wotan. I've told him all about you.'

They sat at the garden table and drank cool apple juice. They talked well into the afternoon.

Freddi stood up.

'Max. I'm going to find Lili. I mean … I want Lili to find me, if you understand.'

Max smiled.

'Are you coming, Wotan?'

Wotan snorted. 'I think I might be in the way. No, no. You go ahead. Anyway I want to look up a police officer in Sankt Gallen. He once showed me kindness many years ago.'

Max laughed. 'That wouldn't be Captain Reitlinger by any chance, would it?'

'Absolutely, do you know him?'

'Well, I've neither seen nor heard of him for a while. He's no longer a police captain; that much I can tell you.'

'Somehow that doesn't surprise me. Do you know where he is?'

'Oh yes. He's still in Sankt Gallen. I've got his last address somewhere. Lili looked him up once. He helped us when we were looking for you, Freddi, after you first went missing. His deeds have been forgotten, even though it's suddenly become fashionable to show humanity towards refugees.'

*   *   *

Lili had been standing for most of the day near the wooden bridge which funnelled the last surviving remnants of the catastrophe towards her.

It had been a quiet day.

She exchanged a few words with the border guards who knew her well by now. To those who passed through she showed her board with Freddi's photograph and the bold insistent lettering. It was her only question. She didn't even bother speaking the words any more. Refugees cast a glance and shook their heads as they passed by.

'Thank you anyway,' Lili called after them.

It was peaceful now. In the early days there had been chaos as hordes of refugees, displaced persons as the officials called them, came across the border. Lili recognised the haunted look in the eyes of camp survivors. On one occasion an emaciated, grey haired woman, held together by she knew not what, was standing by the officials' desk being registered. Suddenly a dog barked.

There was a deathly scream.

The woman fell to the ground. The best efforts of the guards failed to resuscitate her. Her body might have been liberated, but her soul had remained in whatever place of torture she had come from.

The sound of a barking dog came too soon for her.

* * *

Lili lay in the sunshine and smoked a cigarette.

It was late in the afternoon.

The heat of the day was easing.

Hardly any refugees had come through today. Another hour and she would go home.

She stood up feeling slightly dizzy from the heat. With a few brushes of her palms she swept the grass off her skirt.

Lili took up her position once more by the bridge.

'It's quiet today, Fräulein,' called over one of the border guards.

'At least it means less work for you,' Lili replied.

The guard laughed.

'Perhaps the young lady is looking in the wrong direction.'

Lili froze.

It wasn't the guard who had spoken the words.

The voice had come from behind her. She dared not move in case she was imagining things.

'Perhaps your search is over now…'

Lili turned slowly round.

How can we describe the joy of their long-yearned-for reunion?

They covered each other in kisses and tears.

Their names were spoken over and over again.

Words were few; many their embraces and caresses.

ACKNOWLEDGEMENTS

rhaptein (Grk) – to stitch or weave together into a tapestry

Homer was not there. He found his stories circulating around him in the collective memory, gathered those he wanted and wove them together into a magnificent tapestry of human fate.

This humble tale likewise draws on hundreds of stories, anecdotes and memories. They are far too numerous to acknowledge individually but the most important should not go unmentioned.

To my mother I owe the stories she told me of her childhood in the village by the lake; they were the inspiration for this novel. Details in Lili's Zeppelin dream sequences were provided by Eugen Bentele's memoir (*Ein Zeppelin-Machinist erzählt*). Lili's experiences in the internment camps of southern France, largely forgotten in historical accounts, are based on the diaries of a Swiss Red Cross nurse, Friedl Bohny-Reiter (*Vorhof der Vernichtung*), and Freddi's escape across the Pyrenees owes much to Lisa Fittko's *Mein Weg über die Pyrenäen*.

The inspiration for the football-loving police captain Paul Reitlinger is the real-life 'Swiss Schindler' Paul Grüninger. His is a story of individual bravery which deserves wider recognition. Stefan Keller's *Grüningers Fall* constructs his biography largely from the accounts of those several hundred Jews who owe their lives to him.

For her loving support, friendship and kind encouragement I will be forever grateful to Anne-Marie.

In recognition of my debt to all these voices, and many more, all proceeds from the sale of 'The House by the Lake' will go to help the work of the International Red Cross in saving refugees.

Mark Palmer

Front cover and map by Dennis Lascelles

Printed in Great
Britain
by Amazon